A VISITATION

OF SPIRITS

A VISITATION

OF SPIRITS

A NOVEL

RANDALL KENAN

Grove Press
New York

Originally published in the United States in 1989 by Vintage Books, a division of Random House, Inc.

Published simultaneously in Canada
Printed in Canada

This book was set in 13-pt. Centaur by Alpha Design & Composition of Pittsfield, NH

First Grove Atlantic paperback edition: May 2022

Library of Congress Cataloging-in-Publication data is available for this title.

ISBN 978-0-8021-5929-8
eISBN978-0-8021-5932-8

Grove Press
an imprint of Grove Atlantic
154 West 14th Street
New York, NY 10011

Distributed by Publishers Group West

groveatlantic.com

22 23 24 25   10 9 8 7 6 5 4 3 2 1

to the one who made a way out of no way

my mother,
Mrs. Mary Kenan Hall

and in memoriam

Maggie Williams Kenan
Leslie Norman Kenan
Roma Edward Kenan
Eric Robert Simmons

Quiet as it's kept, a first novel is not written on a mid-night candle and bread alone. This manuscript could not have been completed without the aid of: family—*Mae, Edythe, Brown, Candie, Nikki, George, Mathis, Eleanor, Cassandra, Jackie;* teachers—*Max Steele, Doris Betts, Daphne Athas, Louis Rubin, Lee Greene;* colleagues—*Ann Close, Bobbie Bristol, Karen Latuchie, Laurie Winer;* an editor—*Walter Bode;* an agent—*Eric Ashworth;* friends—*Randy, Patrick, Zollie, Gregory, Beth, Nell, Toby, Tom, Amy, Terrence, Robin, Alane, Joe, Nina . . .*

*And the inscrutable grace of the Host of Hosts
We thank you all.*

CONTENTS

"Are spirits' lives so short?" asked Scrooge.
"My life upon this globe is very brief," replied the
    Ghost. "It ends to-night."
"To-night!" cried Scrooge.
"To-night at midnight. Hark! The time is draw-
    ing near."

—CHARLES DICKENS
A Christmas Carol

To call up a demon you must learn its name. Men
dreamed that, once, but now it is real in another
way . . .

—WILLIAM GIBSON
Neuromancer

Introduction to
A Visitation of Spirits

It begins with a fall, the time of year, of Grace.

It begins with a spell, as it must, with Horace, young, gifted, and Black, calling on all a sixteen-year-old knows of the earth, all he can remember from church, and all the ancestors whisper in dreams, to aid him in his plight to *change*. Horace Thomas Cross in fictional Tims Creek, North Carolina, is determined to find the strength to up and fly away; away from all that won't understand him and that he himself does not understand.

Horace has made a self-discovery and needs to get out before anyone else uncovers it. And because *A Visitation of Spirits*, a story about an old family in the New World, ponders Grace and the mercurial absence of an omnipresent God, Horace's journey leads him through sudden storms, into woods dark and familiar, and at long last, face-to-face with himself.

I don't know if Mr. Randall Kenan meant to awaken me the way he did; startle me into self-awareness. I don't know if he came from a family described in the book as proud and matrilineal. I don't know if he meant for this book to be one that Black queer men of a certain age regard as "a first testament" to our lives in a wanning pandemic, a will to live, a recounting.

I don't know.

After his death in August of 2020, I sorted through my old email accounts to find our correspondences. He spoke to me like I was a nephew, he wished me well and hoped I would find peace. "Oh, take a vacation," one email laments. I don't know if he was saying it for me or him.

I only met him once, for tea, black for him and green for me, in a too-early cafe in midtown Manhattan. Our teatime was awkward, he allowed it to be, so that neither of us felt the tremendous pressure to be extraordinary as we often had to be in other spaces. As Cousin Ann recounts in *Visitation*, "But don't you know it yet, Horace? You the Chosen Nigger." But here, he knew, I needed, maybe we needed, to be ourselves, nothing more. He allowed deep pauses of nothing, for genuine questions to arise. He set the portrait I would come to replicate in my own work, the painting of two awkward men from the Southern United States who queerness had chosen and who, because it was the Blackest, truest thing to do, had chosen it back. We could love all the things that did not add up. We could love the quiet and the questions. We could embrace curiosity with a capital *C*.

"Curiosity" in this novel, Mr. Kenan assigns to Rev. James "Jimmy" Greene, the dutiful widowed pastor cousin/uncle to Horace. I don't have to explain a cousin/uncle, right? Maybe

I do. Your father's cousin is your cousin, yes? But said cousin is your mother's age; so, you give the respect you would of an uncle or aunt to that cousin. Right? Because . . . Because you do.

Horace, who as I said before, is right as we speak, as you read, if you turn these pages, trying desperately to change himself into something—anything else—with powers we dare not speak of; with answers he has braided together from the very book cousin/uncle Jimmy sites to counter his cousin/nephew's waxing, confusing desires. Even as Jimmy wants to make room for Horace's exploration, he is still a pastor and parishioner, mourning his inability to allow his own curiosity to dig him deeper into the murky and unknowable mire that is life. Maybe that's why his wife strayed? Maybe that's why his little cousin Horace is a . . . He can't even say it. "You know as well as I what the Bible says" is Jimmy's occupational answer to Horace's inquiry on same-sex love. For Horace, the clarity of damnation in that question still eludes his thirst for answers.

It would be something if this novel were a tome of thoughts and ideas from antiquity that save us from ourselves today. No lie, I wished it were, the twenty-year-old who first read this book sped through it and devoured it hoping its passages of longing and family misunderstandings—the quiet moments of surrender between the one you wished you could love and the one who loves you—all I hoped would be answered or explained away at the end of this book, pointing out the concise answer of "why?" But then how would Mr. Kenan get us to come back, keep us coming back? Keep us revisiting.

I have reread this book every two years (sometimes twice in a year) since 2001. I reread and I remember and sometimes I reflect. These hauntings, these revisits, are all fueled by beautiful questions Mr. Kenan gifted us and cast us not as scholars or simply readers but as the curious; it's the reason he talks directly to us and reminds us, through monologue of gentle inquiry, what Black life in the South was like prior to the cellphone. "But you've seen this, haven't you?"

It's as if he wants us to secretly nod to each other over these quandaries heavy in our heart or gather, huddle around this story's puzzle pieces together, finding and putting them next to each other, ultimately illuminating a work that feels foreign and all too familiar. Because there will be some, they come and they come, with questions like Horace, some will be curious like Jimmy, and even some will have questions like Aunt Ruth, the oldest living relative of Horace and Jimmy, though she makes sure they remember their kinship is through marriage, not by blood. Even she is wondering where the road turned. Some reads, you wish the characters would look around at all the gathered spirits and know that they are not alone in their questioning. We are not alone. Mr. Kenan makes sure we know it.

Indeed, he takes us through the things we forgot in order to remind us how deeply curious we are or were about each other but more importantly about ourselves. He gives us back our wonder. True graceful wonder. Wonder at a world that would deny love to a boy because he aimed it at another boy. Wonder for a town that could not keep the secret affair of a pastor's wife from diminishing his following. Wonder for an elderly woman, mad at the world, bent on heavenly reward, finding grace and joy at a child's game like Pac-Man. That wonder will have you back reading, feeding the fire of questions that continue to consume you, burnishing your spirit with each revisit, each time more curious with a capital *C.*

—Tarell Alvin McCraney
December 2021

A VISITATION

OF SPIRITS

White Sorcery

The Lord is in his Holy Temple; let all the earth keep silent before him. I was glad when they said unto me, Let us go into the House of the Lord . . .

"Lord, Lord, Lord," she said.

The first time she slipped on the grass and fell that morning, he rushed to her, but she shooed him away and clambered, slowly, to her feet. But then, after a few precious steps, she fell again.

"Lord, Lord, Lord."

This time she just sat there on the frost-covered lawn, between her house and Jimmy's car, her head hung down, her eyes closed.

"You okay, Aunt Ruth? You want some help?"

Jimmy stood less than two feet from his great-aunt, but he hesitated. When he walked up to her and stooped over to pick her up, she opened her eyes and shot him a look that sent slivers of ice through his veins.

"I'm fine! Leave me be! I can get up on my own. Just leave me a spell."

Reluctantly, Jimmy stepped back and watched her jam her cane into the earth as though she were driving a stake, and, after getting up onto her knees, put one foot on the ground and stop.

"Helpher, boy."

From the car Zeke called to Jimmy. He leaned out the window from the front seat of the blue Oldsmobile and watched the old woman with impatience. Like her, he was wearing Sunday-go-to-meeting best; his fedora, perhaps as old as he, sat in his lap.

"I don't need no help, Ezekiel Cross!"

"You do, Ruth. Let this boy help you."

"I been standing up on my own for ninety-two years and I—"

"Yeah, but look like you ain't doing too good a job right now."

Her cane slipped again and down she went with an umph and a sigh like grey.

This time she offered no resistance when Jimmy gently lifted her to her feet and dusted off her clothes. She stood still at first, her brow covered with sweat, though the air was frigid. Taking her first step like a calf trying out new legs, slowly, more and more confidently, she walked to the car.

"Just old," she finally mumbled to herself. "Just old."

"You need any help getting in, Aunt Ruth?"

Ignoring Jimmy, she slid her cane onto the floor of the back-seat first, and holding onto the door frame as though a mighty wind might come along and snatch her away, she eased into the car, head first. Sitting, she pulled her legs in with great effort. Once in, puffing and wheezing and wiping away the sweat on her forehead, she impatiently motioned for Jimmy to close the door.

Without saying a word, Jimmy got into the car, closed the door, and started down the dirt road.

"Cold today, ain't it?" Zeke yawned.

"Yes, but the weatherman says it should warm up some. Said it's going to rain too."

Ruth grunted. She stared out over the empty fields as the car drove past, her hands folded like heavy rags in her lap.

A flock of black birds with red-tipped wings covered a field to the left. When the car passed they rose, as one, squawking and chirping, into the air, a sheer black cloth caught up in the wind, the tips of their wings crimson flashes. The black cloud sailed up and over the road, over the car, into the wood on the other side, fitting onto the tree limbs like black Christmas ornaments.

"Ain't gone rain. It's gone snow."

"You think it will, Aunt Ruth?"

"Ruth," Zeke glanced back at her and clicked his mouth. "You know it ain't gone snow in no December."

Ruth made her own clicking sound. "'Think.' Think? Boy, in all my ninety-some years, I spect I can tell when it's gone snow or no. You see a sky like it is, and then on top of that see a swarm of them red-tipped blackbirds on the ground like that—You just wait and see. Besides. I feels it in my bones." She turned and looked out the window.

"Lord, Ruth, you make it sound like you know everything once you pass ninety."

"Well, you just get to ninety and see for yourself."

"I ain't got but six years."

In a short while they passed a few cars lined up on the road, near the entrance to a driveway. Yet, more cars were in the driveway and in the yard of the white, A-framed house. People were milling all about the yard.

Smoke rose off from the side of the house. Men congregated out near the barn; women stood around under the shed a few yards from the house.

Zeke perked up. "Hog killing. Did you all know Bud Stokes was going to have a hog killing today?"

"No."

"Of course," Ruth said, scoldingly. "How can you live right here and not know somebody was having a hog killing? Nosey as you is?"

"You all want to stop?" Jimmy looked at his watch.

"No." Ruth looked the other way. "Seen enough hog killings to last me another ninety-two years. Sides. I wants to get this here trip over and done with. Don't like no long trip in no car, no how."

"You, Uncle Zeke?"

Zeke looked out at the busy yard with the yearning of a sailor for the sea. "You heard her, boy. Drive on."

Soon the car turned off the dirt road onto the highway and drove on.

ADVENT
(or The Beginning of the End)

You've been to a hog killing before, haven't you? They don't happen as often as they once did. People simply don't raise hogs like they used to.

Once, in this very North Carolina town, practically everyone with a piece of land kept a hog or two, at least. And come the cold months of December and January folk would begin to butcher and salt and smoke and pickle. In those days a hog was a mighty good thing to have, to see you through the winter. But you know all this, don't you?

Remember how excited all the children would be on hog-killing day? Running about, gnawing at cracklings. A tan-and-black mongrel would be snarling and barking and tugging with a German shepherd over some bloody piece of meat. People would be rushing about, here and yon. The men would crowd about the hogpen, the women would stand around long tables under a shed, and somewhere in the yard huge iron cauldrons full of water would boil and boil, stoked with oak and pine timber. The air would be thick with smoke and the smell of sage and pepper and cooked meats and blood. You can even smell it now, I'm sure.

Do you recall the two or three women who stand out in the middle of the field—a field not planted in the winter rye grass that has just begun to peek from the stiff earth? They stand about the hole the men dug the day before, a hole as deep and as wide as a grave. The women stand there at its edge: one holds a huge intestine that looks more like a monstrous, hairless cat-erpillar. She squeezes the thing from top to bottom, time after time, forcing all the foul matter down and out, into the hole; and when the bulk is through the second woman pours steaming hot water dipped from a bucket into one end of the fleshy sac as the other woman holds it steady. She sloshes the gut gently back and forth, back and forth like a balloon full of water, until she finally slings the nasty grey water into the reeking hole in the ground. All the while they talk, their faces placid, their fingers deft, their aprons splattered with fecal matter, the hole sending steam up into the air like a huge cooking pot, reeking, stinking.

Surely someone told you of the huge vat of water over the fire, the blue-red flames licking the sides. Here they will dunk the fat corpses, to scald the skin and hair. Four men, two on either end of two chains, will roll, heave-ho, the thing over into the vat and then round and round and round in the boiling water, until you can reach down and yank out hair by the handfuls. They will roll the creature out and scrape it clean of hair and skin, and it will be pinkish white like the bellies of dead fish. They will bind and skewer its hind feet with a thick wooden peg, drag it over by the old smokehouse, and then hoist it up onto a pole braced high, higher than a man.

Then someone will take a great silver knife and make a thin true line down the belly of the beast, from the rectum to the top of its throat. He will make a deep incision at the top and with a wet and ripping sound like the bursting of a watermelon, the creature will be split clear in two, its delicate organs spilling down like vomit, the fine, shiny sacs waiting there to be cut loose, one by one. The blood left in the hog will drip from its snout, in slow, long drips, dripping, staining the brown winter grass a deep maroon. But I'm certain you've witnessed all this, of course . . .

At the same time, beneath the shed, the women would be busy, with knives, with grinders, with spoons and forks; the greasy tables littered with salts and peppers and spices, hunks of meat, bloody and in pans to be made into sausages, pans of cooked liver to be made into liver pudding. Remember the odor of cooking meats and spices, so thick, so heady? Remember the women talking? Their jabber is constant and unchecked, rising and falling, recollection and gossip, observation and complaint, in and out, out and in, round and round, the rhythm, the chant, a chaotic symphony.

I need not tell you of the hog pen? It will be a fenced-off place with a shelter jutting off from the barn. The hogs will all be closed off in their stalls. And the men will stand around the fence, talking, gossiping, bragging, complaining in the crisp air, their breath rising, converging in a cloud about their heads, and vanishing.

Some older man will give a young boy a gun, perhaps, and instruct him not to be afraid, to take his time, to aim straight. The men will all look at one another and the boy with a sense of mutual pride, as the man goes over to the gate and with some effort moves the three slats that close off the hogpen. Then with a beanpole he beats all the hogs back except for the largest, and he will proceed to corral it into the outside area, saying: Gee there, Hog! Whoa! Get, now, get! The hog, a rusty, rough-hided, brown hog, shambles out into the yard and trips over a plank, letting out an all-too-human, fat sigh as its belly hits the ground. The man pops it on the behind with the beanpole and it clambers quickly to its feet with a grunt, a snort, a squeal. It circles the fence, eyeing the standing men with something less than suspicion.

Then the hog will stop and uncannily eye the boy who holds the gun, unmoving and solid; you might say it resembles a rhinoceros or an elephant about to charge. It lets out another snort, steam jetting into the cold air. But it remains still. Its eyes are tiny and mean, but bewildered just the same. The boy will, carefully, take his aim slowly, slowly, taking his time. He squeezes. The gun fires. The hog jumps, snorts: you will see a red dot appear on the broad plain between the eyes, hear the bang of the gun. The hog rears up on its hind legs like a horse, bucking, tossing its head, but only once, twice. It seems to land miraculously on its front legs, but only for a split second. It topples, hitting the ground with a thud, and lets out a sound that you might call a death rattle—all in a matter of seconds. Its eyes fix intensely on nothing. Its breathing comes labored; the dot in its forehead runs red. The man pulls out a long, silver knife, rushes to the expiring mound, catches the flesh under the thing's great head, and, with a very steady hand, makes a deep and long incision in its throat, slicing the artery there. The thick, deep-red blood, steaming in the cold December air, gushes, bathing his hands and shoes. The hog shivers: trembles: quakes: its legs spasm and thrust in the air like a sleeping dog's until, in a few minutes, it ceases to twitch, lying in a pool of red.

But you've seen this, haven't you? When you were younger? Perhaps . . .

Of course it's a way of life that has evaporated. You'd be hard-pressed to find a hogpen these days, let alone a hog. No, folk nowadays go to the A&P for their sausages, to the Winn Dixie for their liver pudding, to the Food Lion for their cured ham. Nobody seems to eat pickled pig's feet anymore and chitlins are . . .

But the ghosts of those times are stubborn; and though the hog stalls are empty, a herd can be heard, trampling the grasses and flowers and fancy bushes, trampling the foreign trees of the new families, living in their new homes. A ghostly herd waiting to be butchered.

. . . What to become?

At first Horace was sure he would turn himself into a rabbit. But then, no. Though they were swift as pebbles skipping across a pond, they were vulnerable, liable to be snatched up in a fox's jaws or a hawk's talons. Squirrels fell too easily into traps. And though mice and wood rats had a magical smallness, in the end they were much smaller than he wished to be. Snakes' heads were too easily crushed, and he didn't like the idea of his entire body slithering across all those twigs and feces and spit. Dogs lacked the physical grace he needed. More than anything else, he wanted to have grace. If he was going to the trouble of transforming himself, he might as well get exactly that. Butterflies were too frail, victims to wind. Cats had a physical freedom he loved to watch, the svelte, smooth, sliding motion of the great cats of Africa, but he could not see transforming himself into anything that would not fit the swampy woodlands of South-eastern North Carolina. He had to stay here.

No, truth to tell, what he wanted more than anything, he now realized, was to fly. A bird. He had known before, but he felt the need to sit down and ponder the possibilities. A ritual of choice, to make it real. A bird.

With that thought he rose, his stomach churning with excitement. A bird. Now to select the type. The species. The genus. He knew the very book to use in the school library; he knew the shelf, and could see the book there in its exact placement, now, slightly askew between a volume on bird-feeders no one ever moved and a treatise on egg collecting; he could see the exact angle at which it would be resting. Hadn't the librarian, Mrs. Stokes, always teased him that he knew the library better than she ever would? And wasn't she right?

He was sitting on the wall at the far end of the school campus, on the other side of the football field, beyond the gymnasium, beyond the main school building. He had wanted to be alone, to think undistracted. But now he was buoyed by the realization that he knew how he would spend the rest of his appointed time on this earth. Not as a tortured human, but as a bird free to swoop and dive, to dip and swerve over the cornfields and tobacco patches he had slaved in for what already seemed decades to his sixteen years. No longer would he be bound by human laws and human rules that he had constantly tripped over and frowned at. Now was his chance, for he had stumbled upon a passage by an ancient mystic, a monk, a man of God, and had found his salvation. It was so simple he wondered why no one had discovered it before. Yet how would anyone know? Suddenly, poor old Jeremiah or poor old Julia disappears. Everybody's distraught; everybody worries. They search. They wait. Finally, the missing person is declared dead. And the silly folk go on about their business and don't realize that old Julia turned herself into an eel and went to the bottom of the deep blue sea to see what she could see. There are no moral laws that say: You must remain human. And he would not.

His morning break was over. The other students were hustling back to third period. But he decided to skip. What did it matter? In a few days he would be transformed into a creature of the air. He could soar by his physics class and listen to Mrs. Hedgeson deliver her monotone lecture about electrons; he could perch on the ledge and watch the biology students dissect pickled frogs; hear the Spanish class tripping over their tongues; glide over the school band as they practiced their awkward maneuvers on the football field, squawking their gleaming instruments. All unfettered, unbound and free.

As he walked down the hall he suddenly realized he had no hall pass and that the vice-principal might walk by and demand it. But no. He was Horace Thomas Cross, the Great Black Hope, as his friend John Anthony had called him. The Straight-A Kid. Or once, at least. Where most students would be pulled aside and severely reprimanded, he could walk unquestioned. In his mind he could see his Cousin Ann smiling her cinnamon smile and hear her say in her small, raspy voice: But don't you know it yet, Horace? You the Chosen Nigger.

The library was empty except for old Mrs. Stokes, who stood by the card catalogue and smiled at him, nodding knowingly. If she only realized—her grey hair would turn white. He walked straight to the exact aisle, the exact shelf, selected the exact book, and took it to a table in the back of the library, even though he was the only other person in that large room. He sat by a window overlooking the long, sloping lawn, spring green, that dipped into the pine-filled woods.

It was a huge book. White cloth with elegant gold lettering: *Encyclopedia of North American Birds*, a book he had known since elementary school, with its crisp photographs and neat diagrams and its definitions upon definitions upon definitions. Because it was a reference book he couldn't check it out, so for long hours he would sit and read about migratory paths, the use of tail feathers, the gestation periods of eggs . . .

As he opened the book he felt the blood rush to his head, and the first color plates cranked up his imagination like a locomotive: gulls, cranes, owls, storks, turkeys, eagles. He flipped through the book, faster and faster. Which bird? Sparrow, wren, jay. No, *larger.* Mallard, grouse, pheasant. *Larger.* Goose, swan, cormorant. *Larger.* Egret, heron, condor. Pages flipped; his heart beat faster; his mind grew fuzzy with possibilities. Raven, rook, blackbird. Crow . . .

He slammed the book shut, realizing that he had been riffling through the pages like a madman. Mrs. Stokes looked up quickly, startled, then gave him that brief, knowing smile.

He closed his eyes and thought of the only way he could make his decision. He thought about the land: the soybean fields surrounding his grandfather's house, the woods that surrounded the fields, the tall, massive long-leaf pines. He thought of the miles and miles of highways, asphalt poured over mule trails that etched themselves into the North Carolina landscape, onto the beach, the sandy white, the sea, a murky, churning, the foam, spray, white, the smell of fish and rotting wood. He thought of winters, the floor of the woods a carpet of dry leaves, brown-and-black patchwork carpet. He thought of the sky, not a blue picture-book sky with a few thin clouds, but a storm sky, black and mean, full of wind and hate, God's wrath, thunder, pelting rain. He thought of houses, new and old, brick and wood, high and low, roofs mildewed and black, chimneys, lightning rods, TV antennas. He was trying to think like a bird, *the* bird, the only bird he could become. And when he saw a rabbit, dashing, darting through a field of brown rye grass, and when he saw talons sink into the soft brown fur, he knew.

But he had known before, had realized when he stumbled across the pact the old monk had made with the demon in the book, that if he were to transform himself, irrevocably, uncon-ditionally, he would choose a red-tailed hawk. He opened the book to the hawk family—pausing at the eagle, but knowing that was too corny, too noticeable, not indigenous to North Carolina—and flipped to the picture of his future self. He could not help but smile. The creature sat perched on a fence post, its wings brought up about its neck, its eyes murderous. Many times he had admired the strong flight of the bird, the way it would circle the field like a buzzard, but not like a buzzard, since the rat or the rabbit or the coon it was after was not dead—yet. Talons would clutch the thrashing critter tighter than a vise, its little heart would beat in sixteenth-notes, excited even more by the flapping wings that beat the air like hammers and blocked the sun like Armageddon. Then the piercing of the neck, the rush of hot, sticky blood. The taste of red flesh. He felt a touch of empathy for the small mammal, its tail caught in the violent twitching of death thralls, but he was still thrilled.

He turned and looked to the woods and sighed, the sigh of an old man, of resigned resolve and inevitable conclusion. A sigh too old for a sixteen-year-old boy. He rose and replaced the book. The bell rang, signaling the end of third period. He thought of never walking down this aisle and past that shelf again; he would read none of these volumes again. He allowed himself to swell up. Not with sadness, but with pride. He had found the escape route, of which they were all ignorant. Mrs. Stokes once again gave her knowing nod. He winked at her and did not look back.

He sat through the rest of his classes, taking no notes, not listening, more as a matter of form, a fare-thee-well. No one bothered him. He had noticed that for the last few weeks people had been staying away from him, whispering behind his back that he was acting strange. But it was no matter. Soon it would all be over.

He rode the bus home in peace. Track practice was over. There were only two weeks left before summer vacation, but he would have skipped practice anyway. He sat back and watched the other students in their horseplay and shenanigans, the girls lost in their gossip, the boys bragging and arm-wrestling, playing cards. From the window he watched the land, the land over which he would soon rise. Soon and very soon.

Looking out the window, he felt a brief wave of doubt flicker within. Had he gone mad? Somehow slipped beyond the veil of right reasoning and gone off into some deep, unsettled land of fantasy? The very thought made him cringe. Of course he was not crazy, he told himself; his was a very rational mind, acquainted with science and mathematics. But he was also a believer in an unseen world full of archangels and prophets and folk rising from the dead, a world preached to him from the cradle on, and a world he was powerless not to believe in as firmly as he believed in gravity and the times table. The two contradicting worlds were not contradictions in his mind. At the moment it was not the world of digits and decimal points he required, but the world of messiahs and miracles. It was faith, not facts he needed; magic, not math; salvation, not science. Belief would save him, not only belief, but belief in belief. Like Daniel, like Isaac, like the woman at the well. I am sane, he thought, smoothing over any kinks in his reasoning and clutching fear by the neck. He had no alternative, he kept saying to himself. No other way out.

When he got home, he went straight to his room and closed the door. His grandfather was out, but he didn't want to risk tipping his hand. His room, the entire house, smelled of hard pine and the lingering smell of paint and floor varnish, of cypress window frames and heavily oiled oak furniture and dust trapped in the curtains, the farmhouse dust from the dirt road and the fields—but more than anything there was the ever-present smell of pine. Heart pine, the old folks called it. The hardest there is. Better than oak. A seventy-one-year-old smell he had smelled all his life, through the many coats of antique white paint, through the well-coated floors, through the dust. In his mind it was the smell of prayer, the smell of childbirth, the smell of laughter, the smell of tears, dancing, sweat, the smell of work, sex, death.

On the white walls of his room hung his many friends. Over the bed was the Sorcerer—the Conjurer, the Supreme Magician. His eyes were a mysterious blue, piercing and all-knowing. Over his eyes hung a great shock of black hair, showing his virility; the hair at his temples was snowy white, showing his wisdom. His great red cape was caught in a wind, making it billow as dramatically as a thunderclap. His stance—you could tell he was commencing to cast a spell because his hands were surrounded by an electric blue glow—resembled a pouncing tiger's. His body was well muscled and lean, covered in skin-tight blue leggings and a blue tunic with an Egyptian ankh on its chest. A huge amulet was suspended from a chain about his neck, a half-open eye peering through.

On the other walls hung a huge green monster-man so muscled he appeared to be a green lump, with huge bare feet, clad only in tattered purple pants, giving an animal leer; a woman whirling a golden lasso, wearing a brassiere shaped like an eagle and zooming through the air atop an airplane made of glass; a Viking with long yellow hair and bulging muscles, swinging a hammer as large as he, his icy blue eyes flashing a solemn warning; a man dressed in a midnight-blue cowl with pointy ears like a cat and a midnight-blue cape to match, which billowed even more than the sorcerer's, the emblem of a bat planted across his chest. There were posters of little creatures with hair on their feet as thick as rugs, who possessed round bellies and smoked huge pipes. There were designs for starships, and diagrams of battlestars, star maps and star charts, a list of names of demons and pictures of gryphons and krakens and gorgons . . .

Papers were scattered about the room; on the bed, on the floor, on the desk and the dresser and the nightstand. And the books. Books piled high, opened and marked. Old books, new books. Colorful and drab. Books half-read standing on their parted pages, the spines pointing toward the ceiling. Boy, his grandfather would say, cross and vexed, Can't you keep your room no neater than this? What you gone do when they puts you in the army? They don't have no such foolishness there. But the A's and A-pluses on his report card would quiet his grandfather's commands—Clean up that room, boy—to mere grumbles, mild reproaches, disapproving shakes of his head.

The school library allowed Horace, or any other student, to check out only three books at a time. So he also belonged to both the county library in Crosstown and the local library in Sutton. Then there were the book clubs: the Book-of-the-Month Club; the History Book Club; the Science Fiction Book Club . . . He borrowed books from his teachers, from his friends. When he went to larger cities—Wilmington, Kinston, Goldsboro—he would buy even more books, usually paperbacks. Most of them he had read, some more than once; in others, mostly the nonfiction, he read the parts that interested him most, from ancient Chinese history to shipbuilding to biographies of famous businessmen and great scientists. But that had been before; now he concentrated on the occult.

Littered about the room were books with titles like *Black Magic/White Magic*; *The Arcane Art*; *Witches, Voodoo*; *Essays on the Dark Arts*; *Third World Religions*; *A History of Magic*; *Magicians of the Bible*;

Gray's Index to the Bizarre and the Unusual; Demon Lore. It was in one of these volumes that he found the key, and he had spent weeks checking and double-checking, cross-referencing, correlating, compiling his facts and perfecting the perfect spell. To him this room was not a high-school lad's bedroom in an old farmhouse on a dirt road in the backwoods, but the secluded and mysterious lair of an apprentice sorcerer about to step into the realm of a true mystic. The walls were not wood; they were ancient and chipped stone. The books were not paperbacks and library loans; they were parched scrolls and musty tomes.

Simplicity. The simplicity alone swept him away. The very notion that the entire ordeal was no ordeal at all—not for those who read and thought and were unafraid. He looked at the list before him. On the surface it looked like a grocery list, but as you read it the oddity struck. What kind of cake could be baked from cat's urine and the whole head of a hummingbird? The list was long and complicated, each ingredient demanding its own special care and sometimes an ingenious method of collection. It had taken well over a month to compile this list. How do you capture the stale breath of a hag threescore and ten? Where could he possibly find the ground tooth of a leviathan? But after painfully checking and rechecking with similar recipes and rites, he was sure it was okay to substitute nail clippings for the breath. And a shark's tooth instead of a real sea monster's. He was confident the substitutions would work, except for one: the most powerful ingredient was the body of a babe, no older than three years. He could not decide if the "babe" had to be human or whether it could be any species of infant. The worry had caused him many a sleepless night and many dark dreams of sneaking into a house after midnight and stealthily snatching an infant who would look dolefully into his eyes, innocent and quiet, sucking its thumb in sweet contentment. In the dream he would sing to the child, singing: *Hush, little baby, don't you cry*, as he smothered it to its white death beneath a goose-stuffed pillow and when he raised the pillow in the dim starlight the silent child would still be staring at him, this time the eyes a little puzzled, unfocused, slobber rolling fresh from its still-smiling, slightly parted lips. He would wake from these dreams with a moan at the back of his throat, chill sweat beading his forehead, the fear of the wrath of the one true God beating in his breast, frantic to escape. But it would be madness to commit such a horrible sin to obtain his freedom. For was not this dipping, this dunking, this drowning in magic an attempt to escape from that sin he would surely commit if he remained human?

So, confident that his spells would work, he collected the sackcloth bag containing all the powerful talismans of his liberation and left the room, walking down the heart-of-pine floor and out the back door. In the backyard, beyond the lawn, was an apple orchard, begun with saplings his grandfather's mother had planted even before the house was built. Most of the yard had been a chicken pen, with bare dirt from their scratching. But when his grandmother died his grandfather decided to get shed of the chickens and let the grass grow over the earth. Here he now cut the grass once a week, beginning in May going almost into October, grass that grew greener and tougher with each summer rain.

The apple trees bore pale-green fruit no larger than his thumb this time of the year. By August they would be a little smaller than his fist and red like roses' red. They were what people called horse apples, sour and small, only good for making tart apple pies and cobblers. Come July he would pluck one off every now and again, remembering how as a little boy he would be so sternly reprimanded: Boy, them green apples will give you a stomachache. Make you sick as a dog. But he would eat them anyway. And miraculously he never got those green-apple bellyaches. He did so love that tart and sour taste that drew his mouth up the way a lemon would, the texture of the white flesh on the inside, even the crisp crunch it made when you bit into it. While thinking this a wave of sadness washed over him, for he realized birds can't really bite into an apple, they peck. And only chickens peck at barnyard apples. But he would feast on squirrel and rabbit—he would lose green apples for a real chance at eternal life.

Twilight was falling. The days were beginning to lengthen, so he had time to prepare; he knew his grandfather would be away until very late. The day before he had set up the pyre. A slab of metal to hold the ingredients. A few pieces of old pine, dripping strong with turpentine. Oak and hickory. A little tar, because one spell called for pitch. Then he spread the sack over the pyre and checked his grim ingredients against the list. The plastic bag that held the body of the kitten he had killed was thick with moisture, the animal's hair matted, black, and lank. Then with a strike-anywhere match he set it all afire. It was slow to blaze, but after a while—he had stuck some straw between also—its flames licked and belched and farted and sparked in a way that aroused him. The black smoke from the tar wisped up through the apple trees and danced high.

He began to chant some archaic words, most of whose meaning he had no notion of, but which he suspected had to be powerful, words he had spliced together from different rites and rituals from similar conjurings and acts of high sorcery. The words sounded German and French and Latin and Greek, and because he had no true knowledge of any other language than his high-school Spanish, he created a special accent for this chant, which he fancied a cross between High German and French. And in the middle of his chant the smell of the burning cat struck him full in the face—a green, vile smell of guts and hair and dried urine and feces. But he continued, as he choked on the noxious fumes, to recite in his elegant accent.

When he had finished chanting the chant, thrice—an act that would make the ashes holy and protect him from the demon he would summon—he committed the paper with the chant and the paper with the list to the fire and went behind an apple tree and retched in violent spasms that brought tears to his eyes. Weakly he walked to the water spigot by the pump house that sat on top of the very well where once his great-grandmother had hauled up water in a wooden pail. The water was still well-sweet and well-bitter and tasted thick with iron. First he washed his mouth out and then he drank deeply of the sweet and bitter water, finally washing his face in its coolness. He sat on the back stoop, watching the fire die down and down. The sky, which had been high and blue earlier, streaked with thin white clouds, was now collecting clouds the color of tar smoke. His stomach began to knot for fear of what the gathering clouds could mean or should mean to a true mystic.

About an hour later, when the fire was no more than coals crackling with heat, he went to bank the smoldering ashes so they would be ready for the hour of his transfiguration. He went into the house, into his room, and began to tidy up, the neatest it had ever been. Books stacked in straight piles, papers filed away, clothes folded and put in a drawer. He did not worry about the library loans, for it would all be part of his disappearance. Now he was excited and restless. He considered leaving his grandfather a note: Granddaddy, I have been transformed. I will see you in the rapture. But no, his grandfather would think it a queer and peculiar joke. It would confound and confuse him and then, when his grandson did indeed actually disappear without a trace, it would leave him thinking strange and bizarre thoughts, because he would have no knowledge of the dazzling, wondrous truth.

He went back out to the pile of ashes, now all white and less hot. He stoked them yet higher and went back inside to complete the last leg of his conjuring. His grandfather had returned while he had been outside and asked why he had not touched the food his aunts had left. Horace complained of not being hungry and went into his neat room and lay down in the darkness, knowing he would not fall asleep. He set his alarm clock for fifteen minutes to twelve. Then, suddenly appearing in the doorway, his grandfather asked: What you been burning, boy? Smells like you been burning tires or something. He told his grandfather: Just some old planks that kept getting in my way when I cut grass. His grandfather stood silently for a while, peering into the black, silhouetted by the light from the kitchen. Rather than ask, as Horace was sure he would, if he was feeling sick, the old man turned and went back into the kitchen. Horace heard the sounds of his grandfather washing his one dish: the waterpipes clunking; the water splashing; a plate being set in the dish rack to dry; the refrigerator door opening and closing. He heard the light go out—for his eyes were closed—and the sound of the metal chain chinking like a pendulum against the hollow light bulb; then he and the house were locked in one dark velvet quiet. He listened to his grandfather shuffle out to the porch where he sat in his rocking chair and rocked, the planks of the wooden porch beneath groaning in a slow rhythm. Had the doctor not made his grandfather give up chewing tobacco, he knew he would have heard the splat of juice, flawlessly aimed, hit the azalea bush.

Crickets and frogs and cicadas chirped the beating of a thousand tiny hearts. A turtledove cooed in the woods in the distance, and he did not think of birds and soaring and freedom as he had earlier, but of his humanity, his flesh, his blood, his soon-to-be-gone, soon-to-be-changed life. He considered the deep quiet called death and how different it was from this blue solitude, here, now, on his bed surrounded by thinly made sound and soft black.

After an hour or so his grandfather stopped rocking, stood, and walked into the house. The screen door banged behind him loudly. Well, his grandfather said, good night. After a pause his grandfather asked if he was all right. Quickly, too quickly, Horace said yes, in a voice that was almost puzzled. His grandfather said nothing more, shuffling softly to his room, turning on no light. Horace heard the old man remove his clothes and get into his pajamas—he was sure they were the light-blue pajamas he wore in summer, the ones his aunts ironed with too much starch—and ease into bed. Then the light came on and he heard the rustle of paper, the onionskin pages of a book. He knew it was the Bible his grandfather kept on his nightstand, for that was the only book his grandfather ever read, save the *Lady's Birthday Almanac* (which was really a magazine). Not long after the book went back on the nightstand, the light went out, and his grandfather sighed a long sigh, almost a sound of frustration. Once again there were only the other sounds, the natural, small music of the night.

He would not look at the clock—though, in truth, he had stolen a glance earlier to see if it was working. It was. So he just lay immobile, thinking of white ashes. At one point his grandfather rose to go to the bathroom. Sounds of the house, settling, sounds he once thought—and sometimes still thought—to be ghosts drifted in and out. But soon it was time, and five minutes before the alarm was to go off he rose, retrieved the candle from his drawer, and walked quietly out the front door.

The candle was a regular white affair, but he had placed it under the pulpit that past Sunday before the services and had snuck it out afterward, so he was confident it had been sufficiently blessed. Once outside he struck a match and lit the candle. Its light was weak, but intense enough to blind his dark-adjusted eyes. A breeze played with the flame and finally blew it out. He stuffed it into his pocket and went on about his task.

Though the moon was not full—the rituals did not call for a full moon—there was a good-sized crescent peeking through the thick clouds to light his activity. The ashes were now only warm; there was but a faint glow in the very middle. With a trowel he stirred the center of the pile, and after he had a substantial heap of what he was sure was the mixture of powder he wanted, he carried a shovelful over to what was roughly the center of the apple orchard and began to design a pattern on the ground. It was a complicated and jagged pattern, a combination of the European Circle of Power and an American Indian figure he thought to be Hopi. After eleven trips with the trowel he was sure the design was complete. The breezes were strong, but his intensity was such that he barely noticed. Finally, he sat in the center of the design—careful not to step on the ashes—and once again he lit the candle, blocking the wind with his body.

It was after twelve, he was sure. The time when demons walked the earth most freely. He tried to clear his mind of all except for the name of the High Demon confronted by the good monk, in the story, who forced the demon to do his bidding—the great and fierce demon who would ordinarily crush this puny child. But he was ready, armed not with the armor of righteousness and the shield of truth, but with the arcane knowledge that he firmly believed was the more powerful. It had chained the demon once and he would be damned if he did not chain the demon again.

The breeze turned to gusts, which he took for a sign that his mojo was working. Some of the ashes blew in his face, but he was concentrating, concentrating, concentrating on the name of the name. Kneeling, he began to repeat the dread name aloud, his chest pounding as if his heart would jump out and run away. When the clouds covered what moon there was, he took it for His sinister presence. As he continued to chant the name of the demon, his eyes wide with fright, he wondered in part of his mind what the demon would look like. Tall, perhaps taller than the apple trees, the pine trees even. Red and fierce, with huge yellow teeth and foul breath. But no, this was a great demon, a member of Satan's High Court, the Inner Cabal. Maybe it would take the form of a centaur, of a gigantic fiery bird; mayhap it would come as a snake or a wooly beast. Or even in the form of a man, a devil like the one Reverend Hezekiah preached about, not with horns and a pitchfork, but in a white suit, with a handsome face and white teeth, smiling, as the devil is known to do.

He chanted. The name became a mantra, losing all meaning; it was a beautiful name with nice vowels and a foreign sound. He repeated and repeated and repeated. The intense fear that had crouched in his stomach started to fade, and for the first time he really allowed himself to think how silly this all was; how foolish and juvenile and desperate and impossible and insane; how there was no monk who saved a village by chaining a demon and releasing him only after he did his bidding; how there were, in fact, no such things as demons who walked the earth after midnight, or at any other time for that matter; how if there were such things as demons he hadn't the slightest notion of how to force them to transform him, or even how to plead with them; how all those people who disappeared either really ran away or just died—the way he would.

Then, at first like a gentle kiss, here, there, light but unmistakable. Rain. Soon it was falling in a downpour. Water and water. The candle had long ago been doused. Now he sat with the water soaking him, streaming into his eyes and his mouth. A joke, he realized, this had been an elaborate joke he had played on himself. He was sixteen years of age and out in a rainstorm in the wee hours of the morning, calling on ancient demons to save him from—from what?—from himself? He noticed he was crying; hot tears stung his eyes. He shivered and slumped, and finally sprawled on the wet earth, cold not with the freezing cold of winter, but with a surface chill, like swimming in the ocean after dark in July.

He was not aware of the rain stopping or of the cloud drifting away from the crescent moon. He just lay there, wet and shivering; even the sobs had gone, leaving him with an empty feeling of exhaustion and confusion. His was the sudden feeling of falling down a well, knowing no one will come to the rescue for days. The dread of a horrible, inevitable, known future.

A voice. Where? In his head? In his mind? In his soul? It was the voice of a chorus, a host like the host that welcomed Jesus to the earth on that starry night in Bethlehem, and at the same time the voice of a wizened old man racked with pain, and the very voice of pain and anguish and sorrow itself, and the voice of lust and hate and war-torn plains with wind whistling and whispering through trees, the voice of wisdom, old and all-knowing, and the voice of foolishness, ignorance, and childish bliss. But a voice. One voice.

The voice said: Come.

The sky, now a classic spring sky after a quick rainstorm, seemed higher, wider, cleaner. The frogs, now happy and wet, sang joyous and raucous songs. He smiled and reached into the mud, into the soggy sod where the ashes had melted, and in one motion smeared his face with them, as though to reacquaint himself with the sensation of touch. Again he smiled, his face as vacant as his soul. The voice said rise, and he rose, stripping buck naked, as the voice told him, tearing off his clothing as though he were afire, wallowing like a hog where the ashes were, with innocent abandon. The voice told him to go in to the house and get his grandfather's old rifle. He did, and turned and waited for the voice in his head, staring over the starlit fields toward the woods. The voice said merely, Walk. He did, his body mottled in clotted wood ash and mud, his skin cool but not cold, listening, listening for the voice that now seemed his only salvation. Salvation? Was that it, now? Beyond hope, beyond faith? Just to survive in some way. To live.

Did he see the low swooping owl or the scurrying wood rat as it dashed into a gulley just by his bare foot? His mind was on spiritual things. For it was just as preachers had been preaching it all the years of his life, warning: there are wretched, wicked spirits that possess us and force us to commit unnatural acts. It was clear to him now: he had been possessed of just such a wicked spirit, and the rain was a sign to prove that he could not be purged. Why fight any longer? said his brain.

So he listened to the voice, the voice that was old and young, and mean and good. He put all his faith in that voice. The voice said march, so he marched, surrounded by hobgoblins and sprites and evil faeries and wargs—aberrations like himself, fierce and untamed, who frolicked about him with hellish glee at his acceptance of his doomed, delicious fate, and he was happy, O so happy, as he cradled the gun in his hand like a cool phallus, happy for the first time in so, so many months, for he knew the voice would take care of him and teach him and save him, and there was feeling, full and ribald and dangerous, and he reveled in the sensation and whatever felt good, and he marched leading his devilish crew, listening for the commands of the one voice, the only voice, which said, Go, and he went, surrounded by fiends who quaffed strong ales as they marched along through the fields, who danced about on the tree limbs and on the surfaces of streams all by the light of the crescent moon and fornicated and let blood from one another in bouts more violent than cockfights, smearing excrement on one another, jerking and touching and biting, shouting profanity and blasphemies, all with cheers and loud laughter, and he smiled and joined in for this was his salvation, the way to final peace, and as he marched along aware of the gun that he held tight in his hand, glad to be free, if free was a word to describe what he felt, he began to wonder—though it was much, much too late—as he pranced along alone down the road, somewhere in the small bit of his mind yet sane, he pondered: Perhaps I should have used, instead of a kitten, a babe.

Black Necromancy

Whosoever will, let him come . . .

James Malachai Greene
Confessions

One of my professors at seminary was a man named Schnider. Philip Schnider. We called him Rabbi. He got a kick out of it too, he being one of the rarest of birds, a Christian Jew. At the time it struck me as one of the most fascinating combinations in the world.

Sometimes I would ask him why and how—but mostly why—he had become a Christian. He would answer with great honesty, the way a man about to unfold a great tale does: "Why, Jimmy, it's simple."

He was a short man, not fat—but as they say around home, well fed—bespectacled, and with a great mop of unruly black hair. At times he reminded me of pictures I had seen of Einstein. His voice was somewhat gravelly, yet he used it in a way that got your attention and held it—perfect for a lecturer. "My father was a physicist," he would say. "He worked on the Manhattan Project, I think, or something like that. I was really too young

35

to grasp it. Anyhow, he left my mother when I was about four. Yeah. Or rather I should say my mother sent him away."

He would put out his cigarette, sigh, and look to the side, at nothing in particular. "You know," he would say finally, "people need a certain amount of somebody else. And if you're not getting it from one place, you get it from another. That's what my mother did. She was that kind of person. Not selfish, you understand, but she knew what she had to do to get what she wanted, and boy, did she go after it."

That was really about as far along as he would get into an explanation of why he had renounced—if renounced he had—his traditional faith and taken up the Cross. His eyes would almost glaze over, not with tears, but with memories. All of which made me uncomfortable. He would smile a sort of resigned and detached smile, the way a person smiles after remembering a funny situation with a long-dead friend. I would be afraid to break the silence.

Were any other of his family members Christian?

No.

His wife?

Not married.

At this point I would give up for fear of seeming too ignorant. But it didn't bother him in the least. It was just unimportant to him to discuss the whys and whens of his entrance into Christendom. Which struck me as odd, even though he made it clear to me, over time, that his conversion was a very personal thing to him. He was a scholar, not an evangelist; a theologian, not a proselytizer . . . except where I was concerned.

I was teaching in Cary then, living in Durham with Anne, and taking classes toward my theology degree in the summers. I was attending Southeastern Seminary, which is in Old Wake Forest just outside Raleigh. At first I thought it was sexual, this seemingly intense interest he had in me, which made me hesitant. It was anything but sexual. He made the suggestion we have lunch one day in late July. I thought it was about my last paper having something to do with Kierkegaard. He taught hermeneutics mainly, what most people there considered the *hard* course. But he also gave lectures in the philosophy of religion and early church history. He had written only one book, an interpretation of a very obscure movement in theology that occurred in eighteenth-century Spain. I checked it out from the library but never finished it. I found it far too specialized and dull. Particularly dull. As a lecturer he was an amazement, but he was far from a great writer.

We would sit outside at a group of picnic tables on the common beneath a pair of old sycamores . . . for some reason grass on the seminary campus always looked greener than grass usually does. Perhaps it's holy. We both would bring our lunch.

"You," he would say, picking pear from his teeth, "you, Greene, will make a great theologian. You know why?" He spoke in that special New York way that I find equally belligerent and charming, as brusque as it is disarming.

Before I could answer, he would say, "Cause you have a particular brand of curiosity. Curiosity with a capital C. Understand what I'm saying? This is a gift, now. Don't get me wrong. There are plenty of guys here who've got curiosity. But they don't have it with a capital C. Understand? They're bright, sure.

Some maybe brighter than you—though you're no dummy by a long shot. Still, they don't have what Teilhard de Chardin or Niebuhr or Bonhöffer had. You know? They don't have desire. A *real* desire. Few people nowadays do."

He would finish the last of his pear. "I know I don't." Then he would haul out his handkerchief and begin to wipe his face and hands.

"They don't want to *know God*, you know what I mean, in that Old Testament way. Like some of the prophets or David or Joseph." He would pause, looking at me a little embarrassed. "I bet you realize this stuff yourself?"

It was a question, a question for which I had no answer. I wanted to ask what made him think this? . . . my questions in class? . . . my papers? . . . my face?

But he would continue: "Now I'm not talking this grassroots, fundamentalist crap either—which is okay by me compared to these conformist, suburban, going-through-the-motions, fair-Sunday Christ-claimers—but please don't get me wrong—it's something individual, what I'm talking about, and it's something pure, and it's something powerful, and in some people—and I've seen it happen too—it can even be something dangerous. You see, it's a gift, like any gift. Know what I mean?"

No, I thought, I have no idea what you mean. For this was no straightforward, textbook theology. I could not simply apply Hegelian logic. And I was not prepared for a mystical, mumbo-jumbo assault so like the superstitious Call for which I had been groomed—not from this representative of the "rational" theological establishment. It took me by surprise. I would smile, graciously, as good Southern colored boys who want to grow up to be preachers do, while he lit another cigarette. He was a chain smoker, or the closest thing in my experience at that point to a chain smoker.

"What I'm saying is that you've got to get out of here. Southeastern is fine for a year. Maybe. But really. Why don't you try to get into Union or Princeton or even Duke, for chrissakes . . ."

But then he would say, No. I should "get the fuck" out of the South (though he was not a minister, it still made me uncomfortable to hear "cuss words" float from the mouth of a respected theologian, mixed in with any subject from Jesus to Jezebel). New York. Boston. Chicago. San Francisco. Philadelphia. Washington. (Though he confessed Washington was not *northern* enough for his tastes.) Go North, young man. Go North.

This, on the other hand, I understood. It was neither mystical nor superstitious. My brother, Franklin, who had just completed Howard Law and had been taken on as a junior associate in Washington, and my sister, Isador, who was working on her doctorate in architecture at Berkeley, had both been singing the same old song to me. Leave North Carolina. Get out. As if it were on fire. As if, like Sodom or Gomorrah, the Almighty would at any moment rain down fire to punish the wicked for all the evil done on Southern soil.

But with me it was just the opposite. And I summed it up in one simple question: "If we all 'get out,' who will stay?"

Of course Franklin blamed it all on Anne. Saying that what had kept me here in "Klan country" was not my high-minded clerical desire to keep God's will and shepherd his flock among the tobacco patches and hogpens, but one high-minded, high-yalla, rich, militant-talking Northern girl with sweet poontang, who had descended from her mighty chariot and declared for herself the South, the big bad, bloody South, to be her mission field, and had sweet-talked, brainwashed, and pussy-whipped me into believing that this was my place as well, down in the trenches preaching the Gospel while she handed out sandwiches, bandages, and ammunition, convincing me—in Franklin's characteristically salty words—that some Goddamned thing could actually be done.

There are times I think that Franklin might not be far off the mark.

At Anne's funeral Franklin attempted to apologize, not verbally, but the way brothers do. He never pretended to like Anne. She knew it and didn't have to pretend that it didn't bother her. In fact I believe it was only the circumstances that made them adversaries, for they went about it with a certain relish, as if it were a game and they merely playing roles: the harsh, direct older brother looking out for what he sees as his weak younger brother's better interests; and the equally direct, strong, and gritty sister-in-law who is firm in her convictions, and will be all politic and smiling with her brother-in-law but will brook no interference in her marriage. At times I thought they would have made a spectacular couple with the energy they had . . . maybe even better than Anne and me. But he made it clear after the funeral what he was thinking: Now that she has left you here, there is nothing holding you back. Now you can leave.

More and more I wonder if he was right and if my "mission" is just fear on my part. Anne had true courage. She left a comfortable life in upstate New York, family and friends, for the hot backwoods of the Southeast, to make sure that pregnant mothers with umpteen children, living in trailers with no running water, had milk and heat in the winter, and to make sure that men and women stooped with age had enough food and a way to the doctor, and even a doctor to go to.

Anne was not a romantic; I am.

So was Horace. But he had something more, that damned curiosity . . . with a capital C.

I keep dreaming about him, about that morning. Keep thinking there was something I could have done. Said. If not that morning then before, long before . . . but that's just me being a romantic.

These mornings, my mornings, usually begin with thoughts like these. Images, bright and clear, markers of my past and present; or images, dark and murky, symbols of indecision and doubt. I usually rise at five—not that I wake easily. I just like it, the morning. Just before dawn. I look out the window to the dim woods, and it's almost sacred, especially those mornings you catch a thin mist rolling down under the trees.

But I don't appreciate the scenery until I have bumped around a bit, drunk a glass of orange juice, taken a long shower, dressed and made a cup of coffee. Then I sit on the porch and wait for the sun. All the while pondering my dreams of Anne. And Horace. And of my grandmother. It's as if I were a mathematician contemplating the equation of eternal life. Why? How?

Our house. We bought it when it was on the verge of collapse. It sat here, on the edge of the wood, only four hundred yards from where I grew up, abandoned for seven years. The Crum family had been its only owners. Mr. Josiah Crum himself built it (he had married one of the Greene sisters, Virginia, in about 1910 with the customary help from the community). All seven sons had left home by the mid-fifties. Josiah died in '66. The sons put Aunt Virginia in a rest home in 1970. She lingered there for three years. No one even visited the house until we bought it from the sons in '75.

The money we spent restoring it could have easily built a new house. But Anne had fallen in love with it. The way it sat back from the road, down a little trail that cut through a soybean field, perched there between the field and the woods. She liked the way the porches circled the house, and the ancient long-leaf pine that sat in the front yard. She put so much of herself into the rebuilding, painting, sanding; making little window-boxes and picking out furniture and curtains, all with such loving attention. It really surprised me the way she made the transition from urban radical to backwoods hausfrau. Now when I think about it everything fit a little too perfectly, as if she had had some preplanned scenario worked out in her head, her personal myth, down to her death, about the number of places, the sorts of places she would live in, and to the exact nature of her life from the gifts she gave on Christmas to the color of the bathroom. It was not cosmetic. She genuinely loved the power she had over her life. Her social work continued, fitting in easily between trips to the garden shop and the hardware store and the post office. She was fine, to the last hour. Fulfilled. She almost glowed at times, she was so full of purpose. Life was so smooth, so damn near idyllic, that it unnerved me.

"Oh, you just preach and teach and make love to me," she would say. "God's in his heaven, a cake's in the oven, and Mrs.

Williams is waiting for me to take her to the Social Security office." She would kiss me lightly and glide from the room.

I have gotten good at telling time from the light these days, so I know when it's time for me to go in from the porch. I pour another cup of coffee and go into the study. The clock will read six-thirty. At first I will be disquieted by the house, the smell and look, from the crocheted pillow slips to the bluish shade of the rug in the parlor to the knives and forks in the kitchen. It's all Anne. Three years later. All Anne. As if she would bound into the room full of business and mischief, a piece of bread in her mouth, a pen stuck in her hair, a list in her hand. Then I think I should rearrange the house, get new furniture, paint the room another color . . . or just move. At this point I usually stop thinking.

I will turn my mind to Sunday's sermon. There was a time when I would prepare Sunday's sermon on Saturday night. I have a feeling the congregation wouldn't notice very much—I've certainly done it enough to be good at wiping up a pretty good Saturday-night special. But I would notice. It's as if I'm trying to write the sermon I want to hear, not the perfect sermon, but the perfect sermon for me.

So I pore over the Bible, reading, taking notes, making tentative outlines. Banishing from my mind any thoughts of the present, of the recent past, of the uncertain future. Thinking only of God and his laws.

Most mornings on the way to the office I stop by Aunt Ruth's house and check on her. She is usually up, sitting on her porch. The conversation is quick, short.

I'm usually in the office by seven-thirty, before the teachers, though Mrs. Just is already there, the telltale clack of her type-writer echoing in the empty school halls.

The teachers begin to arrive. The children arrive. The day officially begins. I do my usual morning patrols, which frequently involve reprimands and warnings. Teachers visit me to talk about topics ranging from discipline in the classroom, to benefits, to leave time. I read over quarterly school reports, weekly school reports, biweekly school reports, make corrections, have them retyped. I meet with a county supervisor, an assistant superintendent, a member of the Board of Education. Speak on the phone to the president of the PTA, explaining why the school board doesn't want to add another night of student performances. Meet with the band director to investigate parents' complaints about teachers and the quality of the instruments. Listen to the complaints of the cafeteria manager over the lateness of supplies, the teachers who think they are privileged to take free seconds, and the spacing time between classes in the lunch schedule. Give the janitor, Mr. Thomas, a list of must-be-done-this-weeks from broken windows to stopped-up commodes to broken light fixtures; meet with the basketball and football coach about the new season and his proposed lineups and discuss the equipment requests; write letters to parents whose children are doing poorly; write letters of recommendation for old students . . .

When the last teacher has driven off, when Mrs. Just has put the cover on her typewriter and departed, when the janitor has stuck his head in the office door ("Have a good one, Mr. Greene"), I am bent over my desk scribbling yet another letter. Finally hunger drives me to push away from the desk and see that the old school is secure before I head home.

It is usually this time of day that I reflect on the ironies of my position, on being the first black principal of this school, the first black principal of an integrated school in the county. So it merely heightens my sense of irony that the old school looks like an old plantation, a huge Georgian vision of red brick complete with white columns holding up the long roof of the verandah, the long symmetrical facade with high rectangular windows trimmed in white, the great front lawn that rolls down toward the highway, majestically, the rows of conical cypress trees lining the lane right up to the high and heavy double doors at the entrance. It is only about sixty years old, this prisonlike place of learning, though it seems in many ways much, much older—the cobwebs and cracked plaster, the way the structure sags here and there. Yet I am its master, I think, as I walk around to check the doors and see that no windows are left open.

But my feeling of triumph tends to leave me as I walk around to the back of the school and behold the vast meadow that serves as playground and sports field, on which the baseball diamond is a small thing. I will see woods at the end of the field and be saddened . . . not always thinking of the exact reason why; not always staring, merely knowing that if I look it will be there. The woods, the place, is enough. Sometimes I think those woods are cold and incomprehensible. Wild things happen there. When I look there I see futility and waste. As if the very air had become fetid and rank. Sometimes I just stare.

Depressed, I turn to go, listening for the sound of children who are already many miles away in their many homes, telling their parents of their adventures at school today, chewing on chicken and peas.

> *Place:* The Schoolyard behind the Tims Creek Elemen-
> tary School.
> *Time:* 7:05 A.M. April 30, 1984.

The sun is just above the trees in the east. The sunlight sparkles in morning dew on the grass. JIMMY *stands at the rear of a large red-brick structure trimmed in white. He stands at the edge of a long meadow. Across the grass,* HORACE *walks near the woods. He is dressed in a large navy-blue woolen coat. He wears nothing else, no pants, no shoes or shirt. The coat is not buttoned.* HORACE *is carrying a gun. He motions for* JIMMY *to come to him.* JIMMY *is hesitant at first, but walks slowly toward* HORACE. HORACE *advances toward* JIMMY. HORACE *has a strange, almost clownlike smile on his face.*

JIMMY (*baffled*): Horace? What . . . What are you doing here? What are you wearing? What are you doing with Uncle Zeke's gun? Do you realize you can catch TB walking around here practically naked? Have you lost your mind?

HORACE: (*leveling the gun at* JIMMY): I think he has . . . lost his mind—to me, that is.

JIMMY (*angrily*): What is on your face? Horace, is this some kind of game?

HORACE (*smiling*): Fraid not, Preacher-boy.

JIMMY: Horace, I don't—

HORACE: Bulletin, Chief: A: Name's not Horace. B: I don't care what you think.

JIMMY (*hesitant at first, then sarcastic*): Oh, you don't, huh? What is your name then . . . sir?

HORACE: Wouldn't you like to know?

JIMMY (*pausing awhile with a look of disbelief*): Horace, I'm really not in the mood for this. You're reaching the end of my patience. Do you want to explain this—

HORACE: No. I do not want to explain anything to you, mate.

JIMMY: Horace! Damn it—

HORACE: Ah-ah-ah. Horace ain't home.

(*They stand this way for minutes,* JIMMY *narrowing his eyes as if to think of some reason behind this strange sight. He finally shakes his head, shrugs, and turns away.*)

JIMMY: Okay, Horace. Have it your way. If you want to play Indians or whatever, go ahead; if you want to you can keep up this charade of not knowing anything and being rude, fine; but I—

(HORACE *runs around in front of* JIMMY. HORACE *points the gun in Jimmy's face.*)

HORACE: I don't think so, Preacher-boy. (*Pause.*) Come into the woods with me.

JIMMY (*whispers through his teeth*): Are you crazy?

HORACE: (*smiling*): I'm beyond crazy, Love. You might say insane is not a strong enough word for what I am.

(HORACE *motions toward the woods with the gun.* JIMMY *pushes the gun aside in fury and starts to walk away.* HORACE *rams the gun into Jimmys belly.* JIMMY *keels over and falls to his knees in the grass.*)

JIMMY (*catching his breath*): I am going to kill you.

HORACE: Promises, promises. Get up.

JIMMY: Horace, why are you doing this? The joke is over. Okay.

HORACE (*testy*); Get up, Preacher-boy. Get up.

(HORACE *pulls* JIMMY *up by the lapels of his jacket.*)

Listen, Love. First, my name ain't Horace. Okay? He ain't coming back. Second, I'm used to getting my way. So when I say, Walk, I do mean . . . Walk.

(JIMMY *and* HORACE *stare at one another at length. Slowly* JIMMY *becomes visibly nervous, realizing that* HORACE *is serious.* HORACE *steps back and motions to the woods again.* JIMMY *goes after some hesitation.*)

JIMMY: If you're not Horace, then who are you?

HORACE (*laughing*): Well, my name ain't Legion, cause I ain't many. But I suspect you get the picture, Preacher-boy.

(JIMMY *suddenly swings around to face* HORACE. *His look is once again full of anger and disbelief.*)

JIMMY: Oh, come on, Horace. If you expect me to fall for this possessed bullshit, you've got another think coming. I don't know what you've got up your sleeve, young man, but blaming it on the devil is not going to get you out of the hot water you're already in.

(HORACE *raises the gun. A calm, unperturbed look is on his face. He cocks the gun, the end of the barrel no more than two inches from Jimmys head.*)

HORACE: Now, you can go on preaching, Preacher-boy. Or you can do like I say. Cause if you get on my nerves, I'll just blow your fucking brains out. Just that simple. You read me, Parson?

(*Jimmys eyes grow wide in horror. He swallows.*)

JIMMY: I'm supposed to believe my cousin has been possessed? By a demon?

HORACE: Yeah. Something like that.

I don't prepare elaborate meals for myself. Many is the night that I have eaten from a can. On the nights that I have no church business, no deacon board meetings, no prayer meetings, no auxiliary meetings or trustee board meetings, I try to read. I still enjoy Augustine and Erasmus. Maybe Freud, or Jung, or Foucault. Black history: Franklin, Quarles, Fanon. Occasionally fiction. But invariably I wind up asleep after about ninety minutes, only to awaken without fail around eleven o'clock to watch the late news. Then it's back to bed, which in many ways seems the object of leaving bed in the first place.

December 8, 1985
9:30 am

Above them a winter sky, white-grey and desolate, stretched like the hand of God, high and wide, while inside the mechanical hum and rush of the car heater blew out the smell of new cars, plastic, metal, rubber. Ezekiel Cross sat in the car peering out at the landscape rushing by. His hands were cold, and he rubbed them and placed them before the vents and blew on them, but they were still cold. Lord, won't these hands ever warm up? Look like every cold day come is like a plague on this body, joints don't act right, back hurt like the devil and just can't seem to warm up to save my life.

The road to Fayetteville was pretty simple. You take Highway 50, north, all the way into Warsaw, and then you switch to Highway 24, which will take you into Clinton, which will take you straight into Fayetteville. Once you get into Fayetteville, he remembered, you take one left (onto a street whose name he couldn't remember, if he ever knew), and that would take you straight to the Veterans Hospital where Asa Cross, his cousin, lay on his bed of affliction. Seems cancer come to take us all. I remember the day won't no such word—least to my knowledge —of no cancer. Folk just died. He recollected that within the last year six people had died in the small community of Tims Creek. And five of them went with cancer. All of them his age or younger. There was Emma Frazier—she was seventy-eight. I believe she was—let me see, I believe she was born in 1906, yeah, that would be right, cause she was six years younger than me. And there was Carl Jones, and he won't but fifty-nine, and there was—

"I guess I'd better stop for gas, now. Cause Sam Pickett says it's cheaper here than anywhere else between here and Fayetteville."

Jimmy turned the car off the highway into the filling station to the right with a high Sunoco sign that should have turned round and round, but did not. Come to think of it, I ain't seen none of them gas signs turn in a long time. Wonder if it's to conserve energy or what?

"You all want anything?" Jimmy turned to Zeke and Ruth, looking with his phony, I'm-the-preacher-now look that his grandmother Jonnie Mae had taught him.

"Nooooo!" said Ruth, who sang it more than said it, looking out the window, impatiently shifting her weight. Zeke could tell they were in for one storm with that hussy today.

"No a thank you, Jim," he said in his sunniest manner to counter his sister-in-law's sour melancholy. His hands still ached from the cold, and he winced as a spasm clamped down on them.

Jimmy got out of the car and began to pump in unleaded gas. From within the car Zeke could hear the whuz and clip of the pump and the sputter and slosh of the petroleum. A grey pickup truck pulled up behind the Oldsmobile. Some white man Zeke didn't recognize sat in the driver's seat. Zeke craned his neck to see its city plates in the rearview mirror but failed to catch a glimpse. Ruth made another clicking, impatient sound.

"What you looking for?" she asked.

"Just trying to see who that is."

"Why come you got to know every Tom, Dick, and Peter come along?"

"Ruth, you feeling all right today?"

"Yes, I'm all right. Why come you ask me if I'm all right? Don't I look all right? Are *you* all right? Good God, I—"

"Ruth! Ruth, I'm sorry, I was just asking. I didn't mean no harm."

She tisked again, shifting her weight in her hen-sitting-on-an-egg fashion. He could see her face from the mirror, tight and knotted; evil—what makes that woman so dang evil? I reckon I'd a took to drink too if I was Jethro. Man can't stand but so much ill temper. Commence to cutting out after a while . . . a pain shot through his hand again.

After paying for the gas in the station, Jimmy got back in the car and they were on their way. They would drive through a score of little towns and hamlets today, villages and communities with names like Hankensville, Turkey, Bull Rush, Vander, Roseboro. Mostly they would pass through fields, stretching on either side of them for miles, or forests, high timberwoods, composed mostly of pine trees. The idea set him to thinking about roads. Remembering. Was a time when there wont no paved highways—just little two-rut trails and footpaths. Now, of course, there was that wood-plank road twixt Fayetteville and Wilmington, but shoot, it'd behoove a man to go on and take a train than drive a mule and cart all them seventy-so miles. But now folks drive cars. Take them for granted. Hop in a car to go here. Hop in a car to go there. Don't ever stop to think: how did folks get about before the au-to-mo-bile? I remember the first car I ever seen. A old Model A Ford, old man Geoffrey Hodder got it, onliest man in the county with as much money as that old devil Ben Henry. He come over Tims Creek that day with that thing aspitting and afiring, making more fuss than a snakebit horse. And come stopping at old Henry's General Store. All the colored folks and the white folks come out to inspect it. All of them but old man Henry, he just sat there in the store, looking out the window—but trying to act like he won't paying none of it no mind. Envious as hell. And I don't think I ever seen anything to beat what happened—come to show why the white man got so much dang money—cause I declare if Geoffrey Hodder didn't start taking folk to ride, the white and the black, for a penny apiece—a penny was a fair piece of money in them days—and he'd drive them down the road a piece—three or four head at a time. And people just went hog wild, it was like a little fair. Folks were there anyway from doing their trading—I reckon it was on a Saturday cause there wouldn't a been so many people there—but then again people use to work on Saturday back then just like they works any other day—and here come still more folk and the folk there ain't leaving. But old Henry, vexed as he was over the whole situation, about being showed up and all cause he wont the first with an automobile, made out like a bandit too, cause people were buying, buying everything, including that old tart lemonade he sold, and I couldn't stand the mess, reckon other folks hated it too, but it was about the onliest thing you could get cool besides water and there wont no pump nearby—it must of been in the summertime, just before tobacco-cropping time, cause I remember that Aunt Sally had come with Aunt Viola who was visiting from Wilmington and had first got in town and had stopped to see me cause I was loading wagons for old man Henry before Papa's tobacco was ripe for picking.

Yep, I do remember it clear, cause there was a fight too. That Cyrus Johns and old Cicero Edmunds was both crazy over that little Amy Williams gal, who was too young, in the first place, for two grown men like that, but her family was so poor that her mama was trying to push her off to get married to the first thing that shook his tail her way. But that girl didn't have a bit more sense about no courting than a sagebush, and both them men could strike a figure when they pleased to. Cyrus was taller than Cicero, but Cicero was a big man, and strong as a mule; course, Cyrus won't no weakling as I remember. And old Cicero decided he was going to pay for Amy's ride and was gone sit with her on the backseat to boot, but he didn't think to ask old Cyrus what he thought about the arrangement—not that he would a thought much of it anyhow. Lord, I can see them boys now (both of them dead now—Amy, too—all three of them married different people, even though they tell me, and I don't know whether I believe it or no, that she went on and had a child for each of them boys after she got married since her husband wont as headstrong as them two) dust was flying everywhichaway, blood dripping around, clothes ripping and floating in the air—that girl was just a screaming and jumping up and down and hollering: Stop that, now! Oh, stop! Please, stop! Oh, somebody stop them, please! But nobody was fool enough to step into that tussle, so what folks done, well, the menfolks at least—well, no, as I remember the womenfolks was just as bad—commenced to place a little wager here and there as to who was gone come out on top. And it did go on for a spell, interrupting old Geoffrey's riding business considerable. Oh, but it was entertaining. Both them boys, big and strong as oxes, would have fought till the sun went down, but what stopped it was old Miss Lystra Edmunds, Cicero's mamma, who was just as big and as black and as strong as Cicero, and she took a beanpole—reckon she come up to the store in the middle of it in all that confusion and dust and yelling and screaming and betting and seen her boy fighting—so she grabbed that bean-pole and took to whopping that boy upside the head for all she was worth—and let me tell you she was one ferocious black woman—hitting him with the pole in one hand and gathering up her skirt in the other, chasing him and keeping up with him, just a beating and a whopping that head up, and asking him over and over: Do you love the Lord Jesus? Do you love the Lord Jesus? Uh-huh? Well, you better, cause I aim to send you to him this very day . . .

". . . Radio?"

   "Huh? . . . What's that you say, Jim?"

   "I said, 'Do you mind if I turn on the radio?'"

   "Shoot, boy, this is your car. You can play what you please."

   "Do you mind, Aunt Ruth?"

Under his breath Zeke said, "Lord, what you ask her for?"

"What did you say, Ezekiel Cross?"

"Nothing, Ruth. I ain't say a word."

"Humph. No. No, boy. I don't care what you do," she said sharply, staring out the window. "Just don't play it too loud, that's all. Can't stand no loud fuss in my ears. Don't see what you all likes so darn—"

"Well I won't turn it on then, Aunt—"

"No, no, go on and turn it on, boy. I'm just saying don't play it too loud, that's all. That is all in this world."

Dismayed, Jimmy turned the switch. A high-pitched guitar riff exploded from the speakers like a rocket. A dry, maniacal voice shouted something atonal and arhythmical over it all as though he, or she, or it was atop that rocket on its way to Venus. It all made Zeke jump.

"Now, Jim—" Ruth started.

"Sorry, Aunt Ruth." He quickly turned the volume down and switched the station. A silky smooth Dionne Warwick crooned: *Walk on by. Walk on by, foolish pride. That's all that I have left so . . .*

His hands once again gave a sharp ache, even though they were slightly warmer. Arthritis or the rheumatism, don't know what the difference is, myself. It's all pain. When folk say they want to live forever they don't stop to think about how this old body gives out after a while. This body been going for nigh on eighty-four years. Been going for eighty-four years. Eighty . . .

To him the music on the radio was sweet. He did love pretty music, but there wont nothing no better than a good church song. He thought of his father and how he loved to sing. That was always the way he thought of Papa, singing. Papa had one of them deep bass voices. I reckon we was both disappointed that my voice didn't come out to be deep like his. He loved to lead a chant, whether it was prayer meeting, funeral, church service, in the fields—

> *What have I to dread,*
> *What have I to fear,*
> *Leaning on the everlasting arms?*
> *I have blessed peace*
> *With my Lord so near,*
> *Leaning on the everlasting arms.*

Old man Thomas Cross was the second chairman of the deacon board of First Baptist of Tims Creek, and his father, Ezra, who got so much land from the old Cross family, so the saying goes, in the 1870s, once slavery was over, was the first—he even donated the land the church stands on. (Folks like to say how we got our land cause we belonged to the Cross family who was given almost half North Carolina in the eighteenth century. But truth is most of that land, which actually was a considerable piece, wont nothing to a man who owns thousands and thousands of acres of land, so much land he ain't seen a fifth of it his ownself—course we lost almost three-thirds of that in the thirties. So what we got today, we built up out of sheer hard work. Ain't nobody give us nothing.) But Grandpap couldn't have been more than thirteen or so around Emancipation cause he use to tell us a tale about how he was a boy running around in the quarters the time Lincoln come down to Crosstown to meet with Geoffrey Cross who had been a

senator from North Carolina before the Civil War. How he—
and I suspect he added right much to the tale whether it was
true or no—peeped through a window of the big house and
saw Lincoln and old Geoffrey puffing cigars and playing poker.
But Grandpap was a good taleteller. He could put together the
best lie I ever heard come out of a man's mouth, and not crack
smile the first. He'd talk about sailing to Africa and Europe
and all overseas, just as pretty, talking about them mountains
and hills, so green, coconut trees against the shore and giraffe
heads poking up over them, and wild cannibals with clothes
made out of human hair, about sailing down the Mississippi,
fighting wild Indians, about the time he went up to Canada
tracking bear and had to kill one with a fishing knife . . . and
we sitting there, with our mouths gaped open, believing every
word of it, knowing at the same time full well that Grandpap
hadn't been no further south than Wilmington, not further west
than Fayetteville, and no further north than Raleigh—and that
when he was sixty at least . . .

The Dionne Warwick tune faded into a James Taylor song:
Just yesterday morning they let me know you were gone . . . The guitar's sound registered something familiar inside him, the gentle
strum, the relaxed rhythm. He hummed just to hum, a hum
sounding nothing like the melody, really, not trying to match
it at all. When he became head deacon after Papa died, he considered that to be one of his main duties, to lead the congregation in song. But his father's songs were different from his: He
felt his songs to be more of fried fish, cornbread and . . . a bit
of corn liquor. Papa's songs felt like harvest in October, sweat
in August, a little sorrow, a little mild, well-tempered joy. For

a while he let it worry him, and he'd sit up late in the evening studying on it. Not that his singing wont hard like his papa's, but because, in the end, he didn't grow up to be more like him, just like him, and that was a hard thing for him to settle square with himself, for in a strange way he was glad.

Thomas Cross was a solemn man. His eyes—Zeke could still see them—were like a wild animal's. Seemed like he could pull more stuff through his eyes than most folk do. He didn't look at you, he looked inside you, saw everything, and it was casual for him. But you came away with the feeling that you had no secrets from this man, cause he done looked into the very place where you locked your stinkingest secrets, and the bad thing was, you never knew if he approved of what he saw, despised it, loved it . . . you just never knew with that man. Never. And he could scare me to death. You'd be doing something—chopping wood, mending a fence, slopping hogs—and turn around and he'd be there, sitting and peering right into your mind, reading your thoughts, I'd swear, like the devil or something . . . Once or twice I remember I let out a holler, he scared me so. But he was like that. Quiet as a Indian. Didn't talk much, always sneaking . . . well, really, there won't no sneak to it, it's just that he moved so quick and fast; you turn, he'd be there; you blink, he'd be gone. Horace would sometimes ask me about Papa and I couldn't fix on nothing to say about him, except he was a big, strong, hardworking, Christian man, who walked in the way of righteousness, but now I reckon I'd tell him about them eyes of his and the way he moved and the way I wanted to be just like him . . . then. Yes, indeed. I would imitate him—his way of standing, his walk, his talk, trying to make my voice deep and booming. Wonder if he ever noticed.

The music on the radio faded away and an announcer, a white man, talking loud and silly about a new motion picture they were giving away free tickets to the next one-hundred-and-fiftieth caller, replaced it. Annoyed, Zeke stopped listening and watched the houses rolling by: old houses of wood badly in need of painting, new houses of earthen brick and bright white trimming and roofs like gingerbread, houses of gleaming white siding, houses of treated reddish wood, square houses, oblong houses, houses with two stories, houses on hills, houses in valleys, pretty houses, ugly houses . . . I wonder if Papa noticed me when we were building that house of ours. I couldn't have been more than fourteen—a little younger than Horace was—when we built that house. Me, Papa, and Jonnie Mae—Lord, she won't but about eleven or twelve—stayed in a tent for over a week. I was trying to be like him even more than ever, at least I was more aware of it then than I ever was. Miss Edna was in Burgaw with the other two children. And everybody round Tims Creek made it their business to come and help us put up the house, the foundation—ole Fred Wilson helped Papa put that down, and Uncle Louis and Uncle Frank, Papa's brothers and William Chasten, and a whole lot of folks—and then the chimney. People was more willing to help then than they are now. I spect if somebody had to put up a house that way now, he'd be there by hisself. Old Herman Williams got us the timber done cheap. And the window frames, pure cedar—probably can't get cedar window frames these days without paying an arm and a leg—come special from way over Thomasville way. Papa wanted them special, said they'd last longer than anything else in the house, maybe even the chimney.

It didn't take long, neither. Almost all the menfolk knew something about carpentry. So it went up quick. And me and Papa and Jonnie Mae moved in from the tent when the frame was up. It's a strange thing to sleep in the midst of poles and boards and no walls nor roof over your head. It's like a joke or waking up in a dream, and soon as you open your eyes there go Papa measuring here, walking over there. Then there was the roof-raising; and after that there wont much else. Papa took care of most of the little things, but in a house there's a lot of them. And seems he spent the rest of his life trying to finish what he started.

"... that girl of Ida Mae's?"

"No, ma'am, I haven't. What's the matter with her?" Jimmy glanced at Ruth through the rearview mirror.

"I don't know," she said. "Henrietta was telling me on the phone this morning. Said it was the same thing that ailed her before. I bet she's pregnant again. The hussy. Already had one youngin and she ain't even out of school. She ought to get sick."

"Now, Aunt Ruth," Jimmy said. The tone of his voice indicated that he could not, would not say more, cautioning, pleading for her to leave the subject alone. Zeke did not like Ruth's disposition, but what he disliked more was Jimmy's way of behaving like a child toward Ruth. Now that was one thing I got from Papa: how not to cower to nobody. My boy, Sam, he learned that too well, but that grandboy, Horace ... Lord, he was like this here Jimmy. Quiet. Polite. There ain't nothing wrong with quiet. Papa was quiet. Or polite, cause Papa was as

good a gentleman as the rest of them. But there was a difference
—there he was, again, measuring things by his father. Had he
not come to terms with the fact he was not Thomas Cross and
that it was all right—all right—to be Ezekiel Cross?

Now Horace's daddy—yeah, Sammy was completely different. Sammy was smart, but he was sly with his smartness, just
as cunning as a cat. It wont books he was always studying. No,
what he was after had two legs and a nice behind and a nice
squeezebox. The boy loved him some pussy more than any man
I know; and in my day I have felt my oats all I pleased and ain't
shamed to admit it . . . but I did turn away, thank the Lord
Jesus. But ole Sammy. Sammy. Sammy. Sammy. Sammy. I do
miss that boy. Miss his smart mouth. He could always make
me laugh. Paw, you ever wonder why a black man born to be
poor? Boy, get away from me with your foolishness. Cause if he
was rich he'd have to be white, cause the white man would kill
him off. Sammy, big like his grandaddy, Sammy, the color of
his mama, brown like pine needles, brown, Sammy, laughing in
the tobacco patch like he got Rockefeller's money—Papa, ain't
you heard, you don't need to pray no more? Boy, you better get
back to work. No, Paw, this here is hell; ain't nothing left to
worry over; cause you ain't gone die—can you figure anything
more hell than a tobacco patch in August? Sammy drinking his
liquor, Sammy fussing with his mamma, Sammy chasing after
women, Sammy coming in at three o'clock in the morning.

Boy, I can't have you laying up in this house, doing all such
wickedness like you do . . .

Wickedness?

Wickedness! If you plan to stay here, you gone tighten up.

Leave me alone, old man.

Boy, don't talk disrespectful to me. This is my house.

Paw, I'm tired. Let me rest.

No, I ain't gone have it. There are rules to this house. If you live here, you live by them.

I'm grown, old man.

Then get your own house.

Goddamn it. I will.

Don't take the Lord's name in vain in this house.

Oh, well, excuse me, Mr. Deacon. I'm sorry I took your precious massa's name for granted. But it looks to me you the one been taken for granted. You old fool.

You make me sad, boy. You make me right sad.

Oh, yeah. Well, you just wait. You just wait.

". . . Zeke?"

"Huh? What's that you say, Jimmy?"

"I was asking if you knew what floor Asa was on?"

"No, I don't. All I know is intensive care. That gal told me, but I done forgot." Zeke grunted. They were now outside Clinton, where Highway 50 became a four-lane highway, with overpasses and wide intersections, with stoplights and huge green signs with all this information about where to get on here and where to get off there. It was all too confusing for him. Too much sort and figure. It made him feel old. Clinton done grown up too much for me. It always was one of the bigger towns in the area—on account of that lumberyard, I reckon—but t'won't near as big as Wilmington or even Kinston. Then after they built that meat-packing plant, and then that big Du Pont plant, next thing you know there's all kinds of plants and warehouses, shopping centers (they were passing one at that moment, a new one with a fat, squat Belk's Department store perched in the center), a community college . . . shoot. Things change. That's for sure. Grandpap use to say, if a man can't get use to change, he can't get use to living. So I wonder what that means for me? I keep picturing the grave. My being in it. I know heaven is my home, praise God, but I keep having this dream over and over, this same dream. I wonder if there's anything to it. The Good Book do say: Their young men shall see visions and their old men shall dream dreams. But this dream . . .

The temperature of the car was just right, now. His head sank into his chest . . . . . . *a funeral* . . . big funeral, the church so full of people, people I ain't seen in years, people I ain't seen since I was a boy, people who was old men when I was born, people who died before I was born and who exist only in my mind, the church is First Baptist, but not the new one with the new carpet and fine cushioned pews and right white walls and a piano, the old one with bare wood floors and no ceiling, just rafters up over us, dusty and cobwebby like a barn, Jesus was born in a barn, and people dressed fine but old timey, in bright colors, greens and reds and oranges and blues, no blacks, no veils, nobody's crying but nobody's smiling neither, everybody's just quiet, quiet, and I believe I hear water, gurgling, gurgling, but I don't see nothing, maybe it's Jordan? I see a coffin, it's new and pretty, a brassy copper-brown color, shiny, with silver rails, shiny, and the cushions and cloth and pillows and veils are a mellow light brown that match the coffin nice, I see me, there, in the coffin, my face is drawn and dark and old, I look black as coal, I'm chalky about the face, my lips are too drawn, too tight, my eyes seem to bulge behind those lids, my cheekbones they stick out too much, too much, like an Indian's, I'm in the coffin looking out, out, flowers all about, bright fluffy mums and lilacs, lavender and roses, red and yellow, and lilies, white, but they don't smell, all I smell is a smell like incense, and I suspect it's frankincense and myrrh, but I never smelt frankincense nor myrrh, but I know, I know it's frankincense and myrrh, I know it, and I'm looking out at all the people, all the people looking in, Reverend Barden is there and Reverend Hensen who was before him and Reverend Thomas who was before him, and Reverend Fitzhugh who was before him and Jimmy who is now, and there is Ruth and her old husband Jethro and my sister Jonnie Mae and her husband William and their children Rachel and Rose and Rebecca and Ruthester and Lester, but they ain't crying none and there's Sammy and Horace and Retha, Aretha? Retha, no, and we're all outside now, the water is gurgling, trickle, trickle, still don't see it, this ain't the right cemetery, too many trees to be the Cross-Davis place, and I still smell the frankincense and myrrh, and hear that trickle, trickle, trickle in my ears, and Jimmy and Hezekiah Barden come to preach but they saying different things, Jimmy is preaching a wedding, if any man should see why these two should not be united let him speak now or forever hold his peace, and Reverend Barden is preaching a Christmas service, and they were in the same country shepherds abiding in the fields, keeping watch over their flock by night, and lo, the angel of the Lord came upon them, and the glory of the Lord shone round about them, and they were sore afraid, and the angel said unto them, fear not, for behold I bring you good tidings of great joy, and a rat, a great big red-eyed hungry-looking thing, moves at my feet, and I try to holler, but nobody hears me, or nobody pays attention, and the choir stops, and Retha walks up to the coffin and crushes a yellow mum in my face, and I can't feel one petal, not one, but I can feel the rat crawling up, up my leg, Retha, oh, Retha, stop them, honey, please get me out of here, Lord, Lord, please, and she steps back, she ain't smiling, she ain't crying, Sammy and Horace come to close the lid, stop, boys, stop, let me out of here, now, I ain't playing, can't you see that rat? You're both dead anyway, you're dead Sammy, and you're dead Horace, and you're dead, too, Retha, don't let me be dead too, not yet, not with these two preachers who don't know what's what, they look at me, but they don't hear me, they lower the lid, dead men burying a live man, the lid coming down, please Lord, don't, click. Nothing but water and gurgling and that damn rat crawling up, up

"You ain't sleep there, are you, fellow?"

Zeke's eyes burned from being closed. He had to clear his throat, which was dry like ash. "No . . . no, just checking the backs of my eyelids."

"They all right?"

"Same as I left them the last time."

Finally he was warm, and the comfortable buzz and hum and whirl of the car had made him doze, his mind left thick and cottony.

On either side of the car rose high timber, tall pines surrounded by thick underbrush. They drove across a bridge over a swamp that was low and murky, huge water oaks, their gnarled and wicked roots perching at the shore. The road wound and meandered through the forests, causing the car to dip and rock. This made Zeke's drowsiness harder to fight, but he sat up, shaking his head, determined not to succumb to sleep.

Retha. The image from the dream left him with a bittersweet feeling. A feeling that had been rising and rising in him over the years. Had their relationship been what he had thought it had been? Or was it what he imagined? What he had created in his mind? Was it an illusion to satisfy himself? One day a few years after her death, he began to be slowly gripped by the fear that she had never been truly happy in their marriage. He had married her when she was sixteen, he eighteen. She had been pregnant, not with Sammy, but with another boy, Thomas, who died five years later. Then there was a girl, who lived only a year. She was called Edna. And after Sammy there had been one stillborn boy, and no more. Everybody knew that Zeke wanted children, and Zeke did too. And yes, there were children by other women—well, shoot . . . a twenty-two-year-old boy . . . well, he got needs, well, maybe they ain't needs, but they are mighty powerful wants. And I declare if you wants something enough in your mind it becomes a need. I ain't ashamed (Oh yes, I am ashamed) to admit that I snuck behind her back and carried on like I done—yes, and I did enjoy it, too . . . that little Pickett gal could make a man happy. Time was I wished I'd a married her instead—no, no, no, old man, now that ain't right. Just ain't right.

I probably made two children outside my union with Retha, one with that Pickett girl—and Retha knew about it, that I'm sure of—and the other by Clara Davis, but that was it. I was young, Lord I was. No more than twenty-five then. So young. Didn't have the sense God give me. And Lord, you know I have begged forgiveness for my philandering, and did right by them boys when I was needed. After Sammy was born I ain't as much as looked at another woman but Retha . . . and that's another lie, too. But yet and still, I did, I do love Retha. Retha taught me, brought me back. She and Papa. But Papa, he didn't take to Retha at the first.

Boy, what you want with that spindly-leg, low-butt gal for? She can't bear you no children worth nothing. Them women over the creek . . .

But I got to, Papa.

Why?

Well . . .

You reckon you gone make her any more honest by marrying her, boy? Is that it? You ain't the first to waste your seed. And won't be the last. Just bring the boy here when he's born and me and Miss Edna'll raise him right.

And what about old man Davis? You think he and his shotgun gone take kindly to that arrangement?

Well . . .

And besides, Papa. I think . . . well, I believe I loves her.

Think? Believe? You *think* you in love with that little low-tail gal and cause you *believe* you's in love you gone up and get married?

Yes, sir—

Well—

I do.

Uh-huh. And she gone have your youngin, is she?

Yes.

Well . . . you bring him here, like I said, when he's born anyway, cause I don't believe no gal from over the creek know how to raise no youngin. And you too much of a damn fool to raise anybody right. And let me tell you one thing, boy: Love ain't what it takes to make a marriage. It takes something else.

What's that?

You'll find it when you need it.

Papa?

What?

Why you think it's gone be a boy?

Cause I said so, that's why. You damn fool.

But Retha was a good, hardworking woman. She could cook better than Miss Edna when she set her mind to it. Only time Papa ever said a kind word to her was after he ate one of her Sunday meals—that breaded fried chicken what she dipped in a special batter she called it, with all kinds of spices, the crust was better than the flesh; and skillet bread, just a fluffy and light, good with some fresh-caught, hot-fried catfish. She could make plain food, hog mawls and turnip greens and field peas, taste like something you ain't never had in this world. Peach cobblers, sweet-potato pie. Her buttermilk biscuits on a cold winter morning, I can smell them now, right light, with cane syrup and crisp bacon, oh, she could fry it just right so it wont burnt, but was still crunchy. Miss Edna couldn't never cook no bacon that way.

But it scared me how that woman worked. I guess that's why I began to worry so about her. Why did she work herself so? In the house she'd clean, sweeping floors, scrubbing the floors, dusting, cleaning the windows, making the kitchen shine, and when we finally got a bathroom, making that shine, too. Cooking, cooking. For two head, for three head. Work. And in the fields, tying tobacco, helping to set it out, grading the cured tobacco. Corn. Helping to break it and put it up. Cucumbers. The hogs, helping to slop them, keep them up, kill them, and then smoke them. Raising chickens, killing chickens, cleaning and cutting up chickens. Keeping a garden, collards, string beans, tomatoes, beets, mustard greens, sweet corn, squash, butter beans. Then the canning and the pickling, and when we got a freezer it was freezing. Work. Seems that was all she knew. I know I expected her to work, to be beside me . . . a man with a farm needs a helpmeet. He don't need, can't use, a woman that won't work. So I'm grateful. But . . . I just can't put my finger on it. Maybe it was her face. Was it bitter? No, she won't no bitter woman. There won't no scorn nowhere about her. Was she sad? Could a been. But the thing is she never said a word. Oh, we'd talk about folk, about the work, but did she ever say how she felt? Did she ever once break down and say she loved me? That she hated me? Did I?

But she loved that boy, Horace—how old was he when she died? Ten? Eleven? The day Sammy brought him there to the house until the day she died, that was her joy. I knew she was happy. It had been so long since she had a child to touch, to hold, to feed and diaper. Doing the little things like putting powder on him, teaching him to talk, watching him do his first steps. When he got old enough, helping him with his writing and his reading. He was so smart. Oh, was she pleased: her grandbaby. Teachers stopping by the house to tell her how smart her little grandson was; oh, she was happy over him.

I spect her dying had some effect on that youngin. Maybe I'm just saying that, thinking it to take the blame away from where it ought to be. No, the boy was fine all through grade school. A little quiet, a mite shy, damned bookish. But he was all right. Didn't give me no trouble. And them girls of Jonnie Mae's helped so much—he was ungrateful, that's what the matter was. Life had been too easy for him. I made Sammy work. And I worked right there with him. Two men together. So I had a idea what was going on in his head. But Horace. Oh, he'd put in a few days of tobacco in summer—I had stopped farming by the time he was old enough and all our land leased out— he worked some, but I see now it wont enough. When he said he wanted to run on the track team, I was so happy he finally wanted to do something other than read in a book, I said go right ahead. But he started to change. Now, in grade school it was all right to have his little white friends, cause they wont friends. They was schoolmates. The way it ought to been. But when he went over to South York High School and commenced to "hanging out" with them white boys, his "group" he called it . . . just messed his mind up. Piercing his ear. I couldn't tell him he couldn't do stuff outside class. That wouldn't a been right either. He was foreign to me. Trying to be like them white folks is what it was. And then that summer I let him work at that theater. Lord . . . he'd have been better off in the fields. It was just like Sammy all over again. Coming home late. Coming home drunk.

Boy, where you been? Do you know what time it is? I been sitting up here all night, worrying. Waiting and waiting and waiting.

Yes, sir. It's three o'clock.

Boy, this is my house and if you think you too grown to abide by my rules, then I spect you better get up and go.

I'm sorry, sir. There . . . there was a party . . . it was opening night.

Don't mumble to me, boy. You been drinking.

Sir?

I said have you been drinking?—Of course you have. Look at you. Just look at you.

I said . . . I said I'm sorry. It won't happen again.

I know it won't.

There had once been hundreds, perhaps thousands of them, up and down the East Coast, Zeke had read. Also, he had read, this was the last one standing. He remembered hearing his grandpappy telling tales of the slave markets, how the folks were treated when placed on the block. He reckoned there was no way he could imagine the humiliation.

The Fayetteville slave market stood in the center of traffic, in what Zeke figured to be the center of town, or near its center anyway. Red brick. Fancy arches. Flowers. He could not count the times he had actually been to Fayetteville, nor the times he had seen the . . . monument? . . . but he had always been disappointed. Surely a slave market should have been a vast, oppressive thing, to his mind, to represent what it represented. But no. Look at it. A sorry excuse for a one-room house. And he had heard that the city council wanted to tear it down, said it just stood there dredging up old hurts, but there was a lot of ruckus over the fact that it was one of two or three left. Some people felt it was necessary to preserve it. As a warning. Or at least a reminder. He didn't know what to think.

The car moved along in the traffic like a barge on a busy river, a multitude of different-colored cars—reds, blues, whites, blacks—flowed past them, honking their horns, jerking and going. Jimmy made only one turn, bore right at a fork and pretty soon after reaching town, they were there.

Memorial Hospital was a great brick block that sat, not atop a hill, but more in a valley, down. Across the road from the entrance rose a cemetery with bleached white markers sitting like white birds awaiting a good wind to take them away. The lawn of the hospital, now green in winter rye, sloped downward in a great, green wave. The parking lot, binding the green on either side, a wide maze of asphalt and yellow streaks, was bordered by rows of cedar trees shaped like cones. Too perfect to seem real. Jimmy wound around the lot until they found a free space and parked. Cold air, yet warmer than earlier that day, rushed in when the door was opened, striking them across their faces, their necks, their hands. Zeke wondered when his joints would begin to hurt again.

"Well, Miss Ruth, looks like we're here."

April 30, 1984
1:15 am

The yellow-white orbs focused ferociously as the dragon took off in a full gallop toward Horace. He could hear it groaning and growling as it hurled itself forward, and he could make out the thin line that was its mouth, set firmly in steely concentration.

The demon said, Kill it.

The horde on either side of the road screeched and yelled for him to slay the beast. So he walked into the middle of the black asphalt road and leveled his gun, aiming between the headlights of the speeding chicken truck.

He stood his ground, finger on the trigger, as a gnome cried out, Kill it! Kill it! But for some reason he was frozen, transfixed on that place in the road. As the headlights became brighter, illuminating him in full, there was the sound of screeching tires and the truck lurched to the left, hitting the soft shoulder of the road, arcing back onto the highway after some pitching and yawing, the chickens in the back not roused one bit by the sharp swerve. Perhaps the driver, his eyes maybe blood-shot from driving twenty hours straight, his pendulous belly full of coffee and doughnuts and two eggs over easy and toast, had dozed for a mere second, just a second, only to wake to a wraith standing in the middle of this country road; and perhaps now he rubbed his eyes and face, considering what he had beheld, or thought he had beheld. His first thought: a naked black boy with a gun. A thought he would quickly discard after realizing how improbable and ridiculous the idea was, then he would touch on the idea of a ghost, which would make him smile nervously, then he would realize it was nothing more than a deer, and convince himself that the coffee and the doughnuts and the eggs and the twenty hours straight driving had made him envision a colored boy where there was only a deer, and he would maybe turn up his Willie Nelson tape, and refocus on the white stripe on the asphalt hurtling by him, dizzyingly, and forget about the incident entirely.

Why didn't you kill it? the demon asked.

Horace shrugged, his head down.

I said, Why didn't you kill it?

Horace turned to look at a Masai warrior before him, his eyes glowing a neon orange, his teeth a luminous white against skin the very color of the night air.

Why? it asked.

I couldn't.

The warrior whacked him in the stomach hard with his spear shaft. Horace doubled up in pain, as the ache radiated in a circular fashion throughout his body. He hung there doubled over until he heard the voice say, Walk, Goddamn it. Walk. And he did.

Noises emanated from the hollows down by the side of the road: the fluttering of wings, the soft padding of hooves on pine needles, the clicking of claws into oak bark. But he was not as aware of those natural sounds as he was of the preternatural sounds of the multitude in his mind. There, to his left, upon an old sycamore tree was a crucifixion, a man with wings full and white and glorious like an egret's and with the graceful lean body of an athlete, spread-eagled against the massive trunk. He had been scalped, the raw flesh hanging in tatters along his head, his eyes wide and dead in a fixed and distant gaze, the blood streaking and streaming down the lean body, splattered all over the once-magnificent wings. About the base of the tree a gang of reptilian creatures were busy lighting a fire beneath him, and they sang a song without words.

Horace asked, Why?

The demon chuckled. Why not? Then he said, Walk along. Walk along.

Down the road, where the highway bent and the huge billboard advertised the piers down by the sea, only twenty-five miles yet, Horace could see the few buildings that huddled together and called themselves the town of Tims Creek.

Continue, said the voice.

Down the lane he walked. To his left, off to the distance, was the sound of yapping hounds. The huge cornfield that stretched down to the edge of the town shimmered in the starlight as the breeze tossed the wet-green leaves of the young cornstalks, ever so gently, like a calm sea.

Stop, said the demon. Do you know where you are?

Horace nodded.

Where?

At my church.

Ah-hah.

Why—Horace started to speak but the demon said, Shssh.

First Baptist Church of Tims Creek rose before him in the clear night like a dark vision, moonshadows speckling the white steeples, its red brick appearing murky in the wee morning light. The limbs of the giant oak tree that grew just to the left of the edifice swayed in the slight breeze. Beneath Horace's bare feet he could feel the freshly cut grass, tickling, and he smelled its sweet scent and began to miss the idea of grass. As he approached the front door, two tall whitewashed gates, he heard music from inside and the stained glass windows began to glow.

At the door he stopped. Open it, said the demon.

But . . . how?

From behind him stepped a munchkin, no more than three-feet-five, its face painted white like a clown's, its nose ridiculously red. It had a mocking expression on its face. Pointing first at Horace's gun and then toward the door, it mimed for Horace to jam the gun in between the two doors and then pop it open. Its eyes grew wide as if to say, Presto! It looked at Horace, rolled its eyes while dusting off its gloved hands, and walked away, into the darkness. The singing inside continued.

Do it, said the voice.

The doors gave with a loud, wood-cracking bust and swung open with a gothic creak. The demon laughed. Horace stepped into the vestibule and was greeted by the familiar musty scent of dust and pews and hymnals and cobwebs. To his left hung the rope for the church bell, and he remembered as a child the glee he felt each Sunday morning after Sunday school when his grandfather let him ring it to announce service.

Ring the bell.

Ring the bell? But it's late.

I don't give a shit, said the demon. Ring it.

As Horace approached the cord it began to sway ever so slightly, then to undulate in a serpentine fashion, and the end rose up, the knot opening to reveal long yellow fangs. Horace jumped back and gasped.

The voice chuckled. You're such a fucking pussy. Ring the Goddamned bell!

When Horace grasped the rope he felt no animation there, just the old familiar touch of frayed cord that had hung from this roof, this church, this bell, for over fifty years.

He tugged and heard the telltale rumble from the belfry, the creak and groan of seemingly ancient wheels, gears, hitched poles, and he couldn't imagine what else—who had ever seen up there? The bell sounded, true and clear. He tugged again. And again. It rocked of its own weight, the tone pealing and rippling high above him, the great wrought ornament rocking, rocking, making such a ruckus, making the whole church quake, making Horace think, as it always did, that it might fall at any minute.

Stop. Stop. Enough.

Horace released the rope that swung back and forth, slower and slower as the clanging overhead diminished, its echo reverberating in his head, and he suddenly remembered that people in the community, those who were not lost in dreams of labor or lust or long-lost loves, might have been awakened and perhaps wondered, Who's that ringing that bell at this hour of the night?

Go in.

Horace pushed through the doors to the sanctuary and walked inside. The sanctuary of Tims Creek was grafted to Horace's memory as strongly as his home or the look of his face in the mirror, but he just could not remember the walls gleaming quite so white, or the carpet that led down the aisle to the pulpit being quite so red, or the oak pews for the congregation to be polished with quite that glossy a finish—and the pews were full, all of them, crammed with more people than Horace had memory of ever seeing. They were singing:

> *Lead me, guide me*
> *along the way*
> *Lord if you lead me,*
> *I will not stray*
> *Lord let me walk*
> *each day with thee*
> *Lead me, O Lord*
> *Lead me.*

The choir in the rear of the church, beneath a gigantic stained-glass window, swayed in rhythm with the music, singing with gusto, clad in their red gowns. Carefully he walked a few steps into the church, but none noticed him or the ragtag crew of assorted ghouls that rushed in after him. He looked for his grandfather and saw him in his navy suit and tie, sitting there in his place among the other deacons in the Amen Corner, singing.

He was overcome by the memory of his grandfather. His hands were large and dark, callused from long days in the field and at the barn. He remembered the smell of his Old English aftershave and the faint hint of the strong black coffee he drank each morning. His moans and grunts, which had seemed almost aloof, royal acknowledgments. He was a righteous man, Horace had been told from an early age, a man who walked and talked and slept with God on his lips, at his side, in his breast. His grandfather, in his childhood, was the grave man talking to people in the living room, people who had come to discuss their problems, their burdens, their cares. Horace would watch them as they came in, heavy laden with their grief. Perhaps they would glance down at him, pat him on his head, give him candy—which his grandfather would take from him later—and return to their gloom and enter his room of confession, repentance, and rebirth. But most people left as somber as they had entered, which led Horace to wonder about his grandfather, though in his mind there was no other way.

As he grew older he came to understand who his grandfather was and what it meant to be chairman of the deacon board. Because of him people in the community were slightly more congenial toward Horace, slightly more respectful, slightly more deferential than they were to every other little snot-nosed boy running around with his shirt tail hanging out. As it was explained to him, his grandfather was the center, the source of the church's memory, the link to the terrible past they all had to remember. His father and his father's father before him were church leaders, and it had fallen upon him to lead, to guide, to counsel his people, their people. A chief, a great elder. His place was higher than the pastor's, and to Horace this seemed so very close to God that he realized, one day, that his grandfather was something of a David. He was grandson of a shaman.

*Lead me, guide me
along the way*

Across from the deacons and trustees of the church sat the women, the deaconesses, the elderly sisters, the mothers of the church. Sober and potent they sat there, fans in their hands, their bodies keeping time with the music in a joyful way. There sat his grandmother in a blue dress, and next to her sat Horace, a boy of no more than five, sitting erect in his brown suit, suppressing a yawn.

He remembered his grandmother's hands to be small and firm, also callused from hard work, but still soft in a womanly way. Tender. People called her Retha. Aretha Davis Cross. A mother of the church. His mother. Hers were the hands that were his beginnings: *In the beginning were hands, and hands were the beginning; all things that were made were made by hands, and without hands was not anything made that was made.* In her hands was life; and the life was in her hands. Her hands reached through the darkness. Her hands lifted and supported. Undid and did up. Comforted. Scolded. Fed. Clothed. Bathed. Her hands did the teaching, the sending, the receiving, the mending, the straightening, the strengthening. Her hands spoke and listened, smiled and encouraged. She died when he was ten.

She's dead, said Horace. Most of these people are. I . . .

We all are, boy, said the demon.

But how can these people be here? I mean . . . are they ghosts?

Are you really as dumb as you look? asked the demon. You know, for all your damned learning you don't know a mother-fucking thing, do you? Ghosts? Yeah, you might call them ghosts. Ghosts of the past. The presence of the present. The very stuff of which the future is made. This is the effluvium of souls that surround men daily. All you have to do is take the scales off your eyes and look and see. You are seeing. I have removed the scales from your eyes.

Why?

"Why? Why?" mocked the spirit. Look, damn it, and see "Why."

> *Lord if you lead me*
> *I will not stray*

The congregation sat in their finery, their pastel pinks and greens and reds and blues absorbing and reflecting the early-morning light against the pristine white walls of the sanctuary. Expressions on their faces ran the gamut of all the feelings Horace had felt while sitting in those pews: boredom; anticipation of meals to come, the sermon, a ball game, seeing a friend after a long spell; tiredness; worry; restfulness; contentment. They were fat and thin, light and dark, tall and short, farmers, schoolteachers, plumbers, bus drivers, butchers, carpenters, salesmen, mechanics, barbers, nurses, mothers, fathers, aunts, uncles, cousins, lovers, friends. Here was community, not a word but a being. Horace felt it as though for the first time. Here, amid these singing, fanning, breathing beings were his folk, his kin. Did he know them? Had they known him? It was from them he was running. Why?

His aunts sat together very near the front of the church, just behind the mourners' bench, over near the church mothers, near his Great-Aunt Jonnie Mae, who though stolid, stolidly sang the song:

> *Lord let me walk*
> *each day with thee*

She, as frightening as his grandfather, had been the one to quiz him about his schooling each week; she, who knit him multicolored sweaters and socks and toboggans and scarves, who made his favorite pecan pies when he made A-pluses, and who would verbally chastise him when he made less than a B on any of his tests, all of which he had to report to her; she lectured him about his family's struggles all these years and his responsibility to that family; she, large, dark, quiet, but who laughed, when she laughed, in a hearty, heartfelt tone; she, who gave him a dollar to rake her yard in the fall and who took him with her to pick blueberries and who told him tales of his great-grandfather's adventures after slavery and how he came to Tims Creek; she who died last year, the mother of his aunts.

Rachel. Rebecca. Ruthester. His Aunt Rachel was his favorite. Her skin was cinnamon and ginger. She had a rebellious spirit, uncensored and harsh. Whatever came to her mind, she said; whatever she felt, she expressed. She was the youngest. Aunt Rebecca was dark, the color of coffee without cream. She was the oldest and the most like her mother. Aunt Ruthester was a color between the two, a teak, a honey color. She was the emotional one, prone to cry and rail, easily swayed, kind and soft. They sat together, there before Horace, dressed in tailored tweed jackets, lushly printed dresses, bright hats, gloves. They rocked with the music.

Looking at them, here, with their mother, his grandmother, his grandfather just across the way, surrounded by the rhythms and beats of his childhood, he remembered the day his grandmother died. It had been during school, when he was in the fourth grade. His Aunt Rachel came to take him from class. They walked down the high hallway to the cafeteria where his other two aunts sat, huddled in that high empty space. She held his hand. Their footsteps echoed, her womanly heels clicking, his small feet scuffling and imprecise.

Ruthester was sobbing, raggedly breathing, staring out at the tall windows streaked with spring rain. "Lord, she's gone. She's gone." She sat rocking like a child alone.

Rebecca and Rachel exchanged a glance. Rebecca, whose eyes were damp, was not crying. She rolled her eyes and looked away. Rachel sighed and moved to her weeping sister, patting her back and speaking in low, comforting tones. Rebecca motioned to Horace with her finger. She hoisted him up on her lap and raised her head to speak, looking down at him. She wore half-rimmed silver glasses that hung below her neck, resting on her bosom.

"Your grandmother passed away this morning." Rebecca's voice was calm as night.

"Does that mean she's dead?"

"Yes, Horace, it does."

"Is she in heaven?"

"Oh, yes. I believe she is."

Ruthester let out a wretched sigh and blew her nose. Rachel looked at Rebecca, annoyed.

"I'm all right. I'm fine, really," Ruthester said as she turned away from her sister. She stood and walked out of the room.

Rebecca did not hug him, only clutched each shoulder, squeezing him firmly, and got up following her sister. It was Rachel who took him in her arms and whispered: It's all right, Tiger.

From that moment they had stepped into the void left by the death of Retha Cross. They cooked, they cleaned and cared for the two womenless men. Becoming, in a sense, Horace's mother.

Now Horace stood naked and mottled in their midst, ashamed and cold, but the voice told him to walk up to the altar. He did.

The minister rose. A dark-hued, bald-headed man, he was slight of build, yet in his black suit he seemed to emit an aura, not of holiness, but of wisdom, wry and canny.

That's Reverend Barden, Horace said. He was the last preacher we had before Jimmy.

No shit? mocked the voice. I thought it was Malcolm X.

As Barden flipped through the large Bible on the lectern, Horace stepped closer. He remembered the Right Reverend Hezekiah Barden with warmth—there had always been something overwhelmingly honest and sincere about that stalwart, though he was as firm and as direct as any hellfire-and-brimstone preacher. And he made no bones about being one.

Barden began: "Lead me, guide me . . . Along the way . . . Lord . . . if you lead me . . . I will not stray. Notice, brothers and sisters, what the songwriter said: 'I *will* not . . . stray.'"

Barden turned to the choir. "That was a good selection, children. Yes, indeed."

Together the congregation moaned, Uh-huh.

"Lead me. Guide me." Barden took his handkerchief out of his breast pocket with a gingerly gesture, but did not wipe his face, smoothing the handkerchief out instead atop the huge book. "Now some people don't want to be led. They don't want to be preached to. They think they got too much sense. You all know it's true."

There came muffled chuckles from the congregation.

"And then you got folks who know they's doing wrong, but you see, they won't go on and admit it and turn from wrong-doing and to right. Oh, yes. Well, brothers and sisters, I can't turn my head."

Oh, no, said the congregation.

"Now some of us have the notion that we can carry on just like we please to. That if—how is it they say it: 'If it feels good, do it.' Now I'm talking about fleshly things. You say, 'What you mean, Brother Barden?' You know what I mean. My Jesus. Now I'm gone step on some toes this morning, but that's what my job is, now ain't it?"

. . . Oh yeah . . .

"That's right. Now hear what Paul says in Romans Chapter One:

"'They are without excuse: Because that, when they knew God, they glorified him not as God, neither were thankful; but became vain in their imaginations, and their foolish heart was darkened.

"'Professing themselves to be wise, they became fools,

"'And changed the glory of the uncorruptible God into an image made like to corruptible man, and to birds, and four-footed beasts, and creeping things.

"'Wherefore God also gave them up to uncleanness through the lusts of their own hearts, to dishonor their own bodies between themselves:

"'Who changed the truth of God into a lie, and worshipped and served the creature more than the Creator, who is blessed for ever. Amen.

"'For this cause God gave them up unto vile affections: for even their women did change the natural use into that which is against nature:

"'And likewise also the men, leaving the natural use of the woman, burned in their lust one toward another; men with men working that which is unseemly, and receiving in themselves that recompense of their error which was meet.

"'And even as they did not like to retain God in their knowledge, God gave them over to a reprobate mind, to do those things which are not convenient . . .'"

Reverend Barden paused and picked up his pocket handkerchief, slowly unfolding it, looking down at it carefully as if composing his thoughts. He wiped his forehead, which was wet with sweat, paused for a moment, then refolded the handkerchief and placed it gently down. He brought his hands together prayerfully, but narrowed his eyes with a vengeance.

"Now the other week," he began, "I saw something on the TV that upset me right much. It was one of them talk shows, you know, where you got the host and him talking with this one today and that one tomorrow and so forth. You all see them, you see them every day. Well, this particular morning, I switched on my TV set and you know what I found?"

. . . No, Lord . . .

"Well, this host fellow was talking to about six people, up on that little stage of his (they was all white, you know), two women, four men. And their topic was . . ." Reverend Barden stopped and leaned forward, his shoulder first, as though he were about to part with something in confidence. ". . . Live-in Lovers." The expression on his face read, Can you believe it?

"And you know they wont talking about men and women living and loving together as our Lord prescripted it here." He pointed a firm finger at the Bible. "Not in holy matrimony. Of course not. They was talking about men and women, men and men, women and women—help me, Jesus—living together in sin. Like it wont nothing. Normal. Tolerable. Righteous. Lord, yes, it was on TV in between 'Little House on the Prairie' and 'The Waltons' so your children, my children could have been up watching this filth, as if it were as natural as a horse foaling or a chicken molting. But, dearly beloved . . . it ain't. It just ain't. You heard what the book said.

"Now you can say, 'Well, Brother Barden, you ain't *liberated*. You ain't up with the *times*.' And verily I say unto you . . ." He thumped the Bible. "This is my liberation, this is my salvation, my rock and my shield, my place to go when I get weary, what picks me up when I fall down, and sets my feet on solid ground. *Liberated? Behind the times?* Brothers and sisters, there is no time but now, and now I am telling you: It's unclean. You heard what Paul wrote to the Romans: Unclean."

. . . Unclean . . .

"That's right. Unclean. That's what it is. Unclean. And you knows it." Reverend Barden picked up his handkerchief, wiping his face as he said, more calmly now, "I know some folks here today don't want to hear what I got to say. Think I'm doing what you might call stepping on some toes—"

Someone in the corner, Horace believed it was old Miss Christopher, said, Step, Rev. Go on and step.

"But I can't look at evil and turn my back. It saddens me. Oh, yes it does. To see people, especially people who were once on the path to righteousness, slip into these here ways. And you know what it is, don't you? You know what causes it?"

What's that, Reverend? asked Zeke.

"Why, a weak spirit. Ain't nothing more. Can't say the folks don't know, cause they do. But it's like the writer said another time: The spirit is willing—O my Jesus, help me this morning— but the flesh is weak. Ain't nothing else but weak-willed people. What else is gone cause this mess, children?"

. . . Go head, Reverend, and preach, now . . .

"It's the devil working. Like it says in James: 'Let no man say when he is tempted, I am tempted of God: for God cannot be tempted with evil, neither tempteth he any man: But every man is tempted, when he is drawn away of his own lust, and enticed. Then when lust hath conceived, it bringeth forth sin: and sin, when it is finished, bringeth forth death.'"

. . . My Jesus . . .

"You got to do like the songwriter said when he wrote:
'*Yield not to temptation*
For yielding is sin'
And he'll do it. That's his job. See, the devil ain't like us. *No*, he ain't lazy. He don't lay up in the bed to all hours of the morning *thinking* about what he's got to do. He's doing. He's working. He's always busy. And what's he busy doing? Tempting. After your soul . . . Now you all help me preach this morning . . ."

. . . Go on ahead. Tell it . . .

"See, the soul is a valuable thing. And it's our responsibility to keep it up, like a house. You got to repair it, clean it, redecorate it every now and again. You got to lock the door when you go to bed or you might find somebody there when you wake up that you didn't leave there when you went to sleep. You all ain't listening this morning . . ."

. . . Go ahead now . . .

"See, that's what he does, Satan and his demons, they come around to taint the soul, to make it unfit, O yes he does, he come, come on in and he whispers, whispers, O yes in your ear, and he tells you—ha-ha—to do wrong. When you lets your guard down—oh, just a little bit—he's waiting right there, O yes, to come in and set you on the way to hell, to the fire and brimstone prepared for him and his angels—my Lord! He'll come for you in middle of the night . . ."

. . . Yeah . . .

"He'll come for you when things get weary . . ."

. . . Yeah . . .

"He'll come for you when you can't find your way . . ."

. . . Yeah . . .

"He'll come for you when things get kind of hard and you don't know which way to turn . . ."

. . . O yeah . . .

"He'll come for you when you on your knees crying . . ."

. . . Yes . . .

"He will come. O yes. He'll come pretty. Yes he will.

"He don't come with a frown and a leer. No, he comes with a smile. O my Jesus, see, the last thing the devil wants to do is scare you away. He wants to seduce you. And you weak . . ."

. . . Weak, Lord . . .

". . . and troubled . . ."

. . . Troubled . . .

". . . and you don't know your way . . ."

. . . My Lord! . . .

"That's why, beloved, we have to pray and keep watch over our souls and fear not. We have to pray that the Lord our God will deliver us from evil. Neither the terror that flies by day, nor the terror that walks by night shall overtake us. Be vigilant. Be steadfast. Be true."

As the pastor closed his eyes and let his voice ring out in prayer, the voice whispered, Such a bore. Kill him.

What?

Kill him, now.

But I can't.

You can't? Or you won't?

No.

Boy, what do you think this is? A bad dream?

A screech, bloodcurdling and maintained, something like a baby's crying, a woman being violated, and an ambulance siren, pierced Horace's ears; then a yellow-face harpie, complete with shot-through-with-electricity hair and red eyes, walked up to him, her song of indignation searing through his head. With a swipe of her clawed hand she slashed Horace's face, knocking him down. His face stung and he felt the blood trickling warmly.

You are worthless, the demon said to Horace.

Through the blood, tears, and sweat Horace heard feet padding on the carpet next to him, he heard the rustling of cloth and looked up to see a tall figure clad in dull black, hooded and carrying a gleaming silver scimitar.

The voice in Horace's head seemed to giggle, and the figure began toward the pulpit. Horace heard no sound, not the sound of the old women in the Amen Corner fanning, not the sound of a child—himself?—shifting his weight, not the sound of the piano player's foot slipping or the cars passing by on the highway. All he heard was the sound of those damned and accused black feet pounding, like the beat of his heart, stepping, stepping, walking toward the pulpit. He looked, but he had to cover his ears—yet the sound did not dull. The figure carrying the scimitar, its robes flowing beautifully, magnificently, walked up to the pulpit and stood next to the praying minister. Reverend Barden's lips were moving. Horace could not hear, but he knew the pastor was praying, that his supplication was for all God's children, to deliver them from sin. Horace did not have to hear, he knew that everyone within the sound of Reverend Barden's voice heard, but he did not have to hear to know he was excluded.

The figure raised the shining sword and without pause brought it to bear on the thin, wizened neck that held the praying head of the old man, lopping it off with such elegance that Horace first registered admiration rather than terror; and as the head rolled through the air, rolling like a football, the mouth still working, crafting holy words to its Lord, rolling toward Horace, there came a deep rumble, louder, louder. The head hit the carpet with a dull thud before Horace, the eyes staring, and Horace heard one word from those brown lips: Unclean.

Horace looked up to the hooded figure standing in the pulpit and saw himself grinning, clad in black.

The baptismal pool of First Baptist is beneath the pulpit. Horace knew this. As a child sitting in services, his mind often drifted to the fact that beneath the rampaging minister were gallons of water. Now the slats of wood that made the floor of the pulpit began to shake and clatter, the water was bubbling, bubbling as if something wanted exit. Then, with uncanny suddenness, the water leapt up—yes, he thought as he witnessed it, it is as if it were alive—like a wave, sending splintered wood, chairs, lamps, Bibles, plants, tatters of carpet, and hymnals in a moist conflagration, wet fire, into the air. The dark-clad figure was gone. But the water began to rain down on Horace standing before the altar, and the articles and planks battered him, and he began to lose his breath, not able to stand, and he fought and tried to run, and was knocked down, but could not escape the water, and could not find air, and thought, Am I to die like this, and when he had finally given up, disoriented, withdrawn, thinking, Death, come, there was suddenly . . . silence.

Afraid to open his eyes, his ears opened first, and he heard:

> *Take me to the water*
> *Take me to the water*
> *Take me to the water*
> *To be baptized*

He knew where he was now, among those who spawned him. He opened his eyes, finding that his wounds were no more, and wondered where the ubiquitous voice had gone.

> *I know I got religion*
> *I know I got religion*

He could see it from where he stood. The baptismal pool, the floor of the pulpit—not disintegrated—but propped up like the mouth of an alligator, on poles. To Horace it appeared a deep concrete crater, the color of storm clouds. In the middle of the pool stood the Reverend Hezekiah Barden, his head resting securely on his shoulders, a solemn, reassuring expression on his face. He now wore a special white robe that billowed in slow motion beneath the water; Horace could hear the water trickle down from the faucet that had run all the night before to fill the pool for this morning. The old women and the old men sang:

Take me to the water
Take me to the water
Take me to the water
To be baptized

Haunting. Ancient. The chant conjured in him feelings of funerals, yet not the sadness. It moved him in a solemn way; their voices blended, merged, focused . . . on him? The song seemed to reach out from their combined souls and tug him, pull him forward. But he was scared as he stood at the edge—it was too steep, surely he would fall, crack his skull on the cold concrete and turn the purifying water to scarlet.

The parson held out his hand. It was both a sweet gesture and a command. Horace saw the hand, wan and lean and brown. He stepped toward it. He stepped down. Down. Down. He stopped and turned to look at his grandfather, who sat with his eyes closed singing:

Take me to the water
Take me to the water
Take me to the water
To be baptized

As he descended into the pool his teeth chattered, so cold was the water. Or was it his nerves? The water eddied and swirled about him as he waded forward.

Barden placed his thin hand on Horace's head and raised his other toward the roof, as if he were about to cast a spell, saying: "Then cometh Jesus from Galilee to Jordan unto John, to be baptized of him. But John forbad him, saying, I have need to be baptized of thee, and comest thou to me? And Jesus answering said unto him, Suffer it to be so now: for thus it becometh us to fulfill all righteousness. Then he suffered him."

Somebody cried, Lord, Lord, Lord.

The minister's voice grew louder, almost a holler, and he threw back his head as though preaching to heaven:

"I baptize you, my brother, in the name of the Father, the Son, and the Holy Ghost."

The Reverend put his hand over Horace's mouth and nose and, with the other hand behind his head, dunked him backwards. There was a gurgling and a surging in Horace's ears and his heart thumped with panic. He considered: What did indeed transpire underneath? His eyes closed? Submerged? How did the water cleave that old wicked person away and recharge his body with a new, righteous and saved person? Did the bubbles that escaped from his trembling mouth contain that evil, former self?

When he emerged he was gasping, and he lost his footing and went under again, thrashing. He came back up suddenly, spitting water. Reverend Barden clutched him firmly and led him to the steps, which were still cold, and he stepped out, his jeans heavy, his shirt sticking to him. His Aunt Rachel stood there with a huge white towel and enveloped him as in what seemed a new womb, as he heard his grandfather's hearty voice belt into a new, faster hymn.

At the Cross, at the Cross
Where I first saw the Light
And the burdens of my heart rolled away, rolled away.

It was there by sight,
I received my faith,
And now I am happy all the day, all the day.

He looked at his grandfather and, briefly, their eyes met. His grandfather smiled.

How he wished he could be his grandfather at that moment, and at that moment he was overwhelmed with a sadness both red and blue, and at that moment he realized he could never be like his grandfather, never be his grandfather, and, most painfully, that he did not really want to be his grandfather after all, and at that moment he faltered and stumbled only to find, not his aunt's arms, but the floor, and that the lights were out and that he was naked, kneeling in the pulpit, clutching his grandfather's gun, sobbing. The music was now still; he heard only the occasional gust of wind, which made a quiet noise against the eaves. The moonlight diffused through the high windows in the back of the church, casting grotesque shadows in midnight shades, twisted and profane, across the pews and the altar and Horace himself.

Horace sat in the throne of a chair in the pulpit, feeling his soft ballocks resting gently on the velvet upholstery, the gun at his feet. As he wiped his eyes he began to think about the demon again. Where had it gone? He listened, listening for the voice, listening, listening for church mice scuttering across the piano, listening for the creaks and groans of the church as it shifted on its foundation, listened for the silence to be disturbed.

At first he didn't want to notice in the shadows the menagerie of forms and limblike appearances, he did not want to see them begin to shift in a swirling interchange of patterns and patterns, he did not want to see the shapes they assumed and lost, and reassumed and changed into. Then the voices started, first from this corner, then from that, from overhead, then from below.

Wicked. Wicked.

Abomination.

Man lover!

Child molester!

Sissy!

Greyboy!

Old men, little girls, widows and workers, he saw no faces, knew no names, but the voices, the voices . . .

Unclean bastard!

Be ashamed of yourself!

Filthy knob polisher!

And they grew louder and the shadows changed patterns more swiftly.

Cocksucker.

Oreo.

He grabbed the gun and stood and ran to the front door, through the shadows, past the voices. His heart once again reminded him of his mortality, as he begged, Stop. Stop. Oh, please. Stop. The voices grew louder, harsher.

Homo-suck-shual!

Ashamed. Be ashamed.

Faggot!

Son of a—

He burst through the front doors and they were there, all of them, laughing and hooting and pointing. The voices from the church had ceased and were replaced by the magical, malevolent chorus of unholy elves and imps and griffins and werewolves and pale-faced phantoms, and strangely he was relieved.

The voice began again, this time with a hearty guffaw that rose, Horace was sure, from the very depths themselves. Don't you see? it said. Don't you see now? It's better this way. Better. It had to be this way. There is no other way. You belong.

Horace sighed. There were no more tears. No more chances. No more.

Tims Creek Elementary School, in its plantationlike grandeur, made Horace wonder about hell. As he and his felons roamed its grounds he thought, Will life there be as harsh as the lives of slaves? Will there be hierarchies and exclusives and differences to battle over? Injustice and greed? Or would the temperature be the major worry?

They moved through the trees at the edge of the building, walking toward it beneath the low-hanging water oak branches. From here he could see the high windows where Mrs. Crum taught him fourth grade. Weekly Readers. Filmstrips. Math problems. Jigsaw puzzles. Spelling tests. The library. Here was the world he had come to love, his mission field, his church away from church. The real world. Here he had been introduced to words, sentences, and books. Books. He relished books, books on religion, history, science. Books that vivisected frogs and insects, birds and elephants. Books that revealed Hinduism and Islam, Judaism and Buddhism. Books that replayed bloody battles in Gettysburg and Peking, Paris and Cairo. At home there were no answers, only questions, only faith, hope, and believing. Here, amid the books and tools of modern information, there were answers, concrete and inviolate.

He found himself seduced by this new world, awed by all the many things it held—there were homes, houses, palaces, small and vast, grand and dismal, dotting this great blue planet in countries (Russia, Ethiopia, Japan, Greece, England, Argentina) peopled by races of men and women who worshipped odd and different gods in strange and unusual places—so unlike Tims Creek and First Baptist and the Crosses, so astonishingly, refreshingly, captivatingly different. It all called to him, the numbers, the governments, the history, the religions, speaking to him of another, another, another . . . though he could never quite picture that other, the thing that called him so severely. Yet he labored and longed for it; as if his very life depended on knowing it; as if, somehow, he had to change his life.

Now, walking toward the old school, seeing it half-cloaked in moonshadow and moonbeams, Horace wondered if even then he had dreamed of transforming himself, through knowledge. But into what? And why?

Even television had played a role in his mysterious search. It was the magical blue box, soon to become the yardstick against which he measured the world. He came to love it and watch it when he was not reading; and, though he read a lot, no one stopped him from sitting so many hours before that incredible glowing machine. Perhaps his aunts did realize its mesmerizing allure, its dazzling power over small minds. He could remember, faintly, their protests.

But I'm telling you, it's no good for him, Ruthester. I was reading the other day in—

It would be different if Horace didn't read so much but—

There are some good shows on TV. He'll be all right. If—

Yet their protestations never resulted in much. They too succumbed to the power of the speaking box, and Horace continued to watch. Here all was right with the world. Or so it seemed. In fact it was closer to right, for the world on the screen looked more the way it should. Its doctrines were easy. The bland, humorous shows contained no racial controversy, no strife, no pain. The only horror was the occasional vampire movie. Poverty involved no malnutrition; injustice was sure to be righted. It all was right, and in the end good.

But he knew better. The evils of the world had been put before him, solidly and plainly. He had heard the menfolk around the barber shop and in the fields talk about the white man; he had heard his aunts and the womenfolk hiss and revile the name of whites; he had heard his grandfather lecture and spin yarns about how black folk had been mistreated at the hands of the white man. He had heard. He was hearing. But did he understand?

It sat there murkily in his mind, this information, the look on their faces as the menfolk spoke, the tension, the veins popping out on their foreheads, the clenched hands. Along with them he hated the majority for the injustices done, and he hated the injustices and the things denied him as a result. But he never really personalized their anger, remaining more curious than mad, more intrigued than bitter.

Not that he had no encounters with racism on his own. From the first day at school there had been name calling, foul and disdainful attitudes, humorless pranks, unflattering innuendo, and out-and-out fights between blacks and whites. Regularly he was taken aside and instructed in how to deal with "those people." His aunts were of a single mind, and though they now taught white children, they regarded them with a strong and bitter wariness, especially his Aunt Rachel: Now they can call you names—and they will. But you just ignore it. You know you're somebody. Most of them don't have a pot to piss in. But if one hits you, I want you to haul off and smack the shit out of him. Do you hear me? We can't have any of that. If they ever get the notion you're a punching bag, you'll be one for the rest of your life. You've got to learn how to stand up for yourself and defend yourself. You more than most.

He had known they were right. Yet he could never envision himself having to smack the shit out of somebody.

Come around front, ordered the voice.

Horace and his crew marched around, walking under a tall nightlamp that illuminated the front of the school, but Horace did not think about anyone seeing him from the road, or the fact that he was naked. They walked up onto the long verandah, and Horace saw a light on in the principal's office. He tiptoed over and peered in, thinking, What is Jimmy doing in the office so late?

But Jimmy was not at his desk. A middle-aged white man sat there instead, and as Horace looked over by the door he was surprised to see himself sitting on the bench across the room, no more than ten, next to a young white boy with straw-colored hair and crooked teeth. Willy Smith, Horace remembered. Both boys had busted lips bright with fresh blood. Mr. Stubbs, then the principal, sat at his desk scribbling something with a hand that darted across the page, his face fixed in consternation. He was a round, red-faced man who was easily flustered; his eyeglasses seemed constantly to be slipping askew and he seemed constantly to be pushing them back on straight.

Willy had accused Horace of taking his Fantastic Four comic book, a special anniversary issue. But Horace had purchased the book the weekend before at a Wilmington drugstore. The boy pushed him and called him a liar and a thief, and they wound up in Mr. Stubbs's office.

Suddenly the door was flung open, and his aunts rushed in. Peering in, Horace noticed how well dressed they were, made up in earth tones, their hair straightened with not a hair out of place, their posture impeccable. He could almost smell their perfume from where he stood.

Mr. Stubbs flinched, turning red as a beet. He stood up and automatically went on the defense.

"Now, Mrs. Edgar, Mrs. Johnson, Mrs. McShane, your cousin was caught fighting, *fighting*, with—"

"Why?" Rachel was blunt, her eyes like a dangerous animal's, mere slits. "Did you even ask him *why*?"

"Well, I—"

"And did you ask the people around them?" Rebecca was looking down at him, her face calm, yet threatening. "Who was the teacher in charge? Why did she *let* this happen?"

"I believe it was Mrs.—"

"Horace is a Cross." Ruthester pointed her finger at Mr. Stubbs, who recoiled involuntarily, as though poked with a needle. "He is not a fighting child. I'm certain he would not be fighting if not provoked."

"Ladies, there—"

"And where is that teacher? Who did you say it was?"

"Mrs.—"

"Where is the little brat? Did you ask him?"

"Ladies, really, I—"

"I want to see Horace. Now. Where is he? He could be hurt!"

"Yes. Now."

"That's right. Now."

"Ladies!" Mr. Stubbs was now the color of strawberry soda. Sweat covered his forehead, and he gulped to calm himself before pointing behind them to the bench and saying, "They're both right here."

"Oooooohh!" Ruthester rushed to Horace, snatching some tissue from the principal's desk, and, falling to her knees before him, dabbed at his swollen lip. "Are you all right, baby?"

"Yes, ma'am," he said demurely.

Horace remembered now, looking through the window on this peculiar scene, how he had felt at once rescued and sorry for Willy. He sat there on that hard wooden judge's bench, no longer the mean and hateful accuser, but a mere boy with a busted lip, alone and with no lion aunts to rush to his aid. And because he had felt this ambivalence, Horace had sensed he was wrong, inside, for not feeling the way he should. There was still anger, but there was an odd sense of unfairness, unequalness, and all in his favor.

Bewildered and outdone, Mr. Stubbs relegated Horace into the capable, as he termed it, hands of his aunts for "stern and complete reproachment" for fighting. Promising, with all the trustworthiness at the disposal of a white Southern gentleman in the face of three regal black Furies, that he would personally call Mrs. Smith and make sure little Willy received "equal and just" punishment. Which Horace thought meant nothing would happen to either of them.

Later his aunts congratulated him for standing up for himself —and regardless of what "that man" said, if he must fight, he must fight and damn the consequences, for not to fight would hold graver, more shameful consequences than any punishment the principal could ever dole out. There was an armor one wore to beat the consequences, invisible, but powerful and evident; an armor he heard in the edge of his grandfather's voice, in the stoop of his great-aunt's walk, in the glint of their eyes when they encountered white people. Integrity. Dignity. Pride. At the time these words had not been available to him. But he felt it, saw it, in their carriage, heard it in their speech. Not to have this quality would be, must be, like being lost. It became clear to him that he had to achieve this mysterious state, to learn this shielding knowledge, and thus avoid the consequences.

The images in the office faded as mist dissipating on a mirror, and Horace turned to continue walking around the building. A car zoomed by on the highway, but being seen did not cross his mind, now distracted by the hellhounds who were fighting just at the steps of the school or the blue horses galloping to and fro in the schoolyard.

As he came around to the side of the building, he looked down the lawn by the way and was taken by anxiety. Fourth, fifth, sixth, seventh, eighth grades, all here in this building. Those years were like the struggle of some little clay figure to take form, of some small ugly creature to grow feathers and wings and gain majesty. Only four years. But such struggle in so short a time, such contortions and envies and imbalance. Teachers. Cafeteria food. Spankings. Chocolate milk and Lorna Doone cookies. The notion of high school was as far away and impossible as the idea of death or marriage or anything outside the realm of Tom Swift and the Flintstones. To Horace, now, the innocence was not so attractive, the ignorance repellent, the pains horrible. To be a child.

Yet there had been bright times, more than bright, joyous. Green, yellow, and orange-red days of field trips and sack races and science experiments and practical jokes and books, always books. John Anthony had been his best friend since kindergarten. A copper-skinned, spindly boy in elementary school, John Anthony had loved books too, in the beginning. They spoke of robots and rocket ships and monsters. They had designed a space ship and made plans to build a base on Europa, the moon of Jupiter. They had laid out plans for a city at the bottom of the Atlantic Ocean in the middle of its deepest trench. Together they formed a society of young scientists called the Young Wizards' Club, with only two members, Horace and John Anthony, and fought over who would be president. Many recesses were spent speculating and fantasizing about becoming adventurous globe-trotting geologist-biologist-chemist-Egyptologists rushing here and there to save the planet from evil men. But as the years went by their conversations began to include less lofty, more immediate goals.

John Anthony got a girlfriend first—Gina Pierce, a long-legged, loose sort of tart at whom all the boys winked and who was brazen enough to wink back. At age eleven John Anthony knew everything there was to know about women, and women and men, and sex. Horace had pieced together a working knowledge of procreation that was both clinical and solemn. Though there was something mysterious and secret surrounding the whole affair, the mechanics were clear to him. But there had to be something more, something dank and sweet and forbidding, and even powerful. It had been John Anthony, with his precocious knowledge and experience—mostly secondhand from his older brother Perry's uncensored and X-rated tales—who filled in much of the void of Horace's precise, yet woefully lacking, knowledge of sex. First it was a matter of widening his vocabulary to include words such as—

Fucking.

What? Funking?

No, fool, "fucking." You know what that is, don't you?

They would be high on the monkey bars, away from the rest of the class. John Anthony would be reclining very mannishly, his elbows stuck between two bars.

No . . . I ain't never heard of that one.

Horace, Horace, Horace. Do you have to talk so countrified? All three of your aunts teachers and you saying "ain't"?

What should I say then, Mr. Perfect-Talking?

You should have said, "I *haven't* never heard of that one."

Well, what is it anyway?

What?

Funking.

Fucking!

Okay, fucking. What is it?

You know, silly. When a man and a woman do it.

"It"? What's "it"? Do you mean sexual intercourse?

Jesus! Listen at him: "sexual intercourse." Using them big fancy words and don't even know what the hell you're talking about.

I do too. It's when a man inserts his penis into a lady's vagena and ejaculates spermazoa into her utertum and it grows up to be a fletus and then it get to be a baby. See?

Well, I don't know about all that. All I know—and I know cause Perry told me—is that a man takes his dick and puts it in a woman's pussy and they fuck. See?

A dic—what?

A dick, fool. Ain't you never heard it call that before?

Wha-what is it?

This fool.

Shoot. And a pussy is . . .

Yeah.

Oh . . . and fucking is . . .

Yeah.

Oh. But why do folks do it?

Now ain't you the dumb bunny. Perry says folks do it cause it's the best feeling in the world.

Yeah?

That's what he says.

Shoot.

But that had been elementary school, long before he discovered a far more complex truth about men and women. He thought of John Anthony now, the high-school letterman in three sports, surrounded by girls and the aura of bullish manhood, no longer the nearsighted little boy who dreamed of building space ships to Uranus. Now they would go weeks and months without seeing one another. When they did they would only exchange Hellos, How you doings, Let's do something soons. Horace taking chemistry, trig, advanced English, and music theory; John Anthony taking auto mechanics, advanced P.E., drafting, and bricklaying.

Horace became obsessed with having a girl friend. He had had a feeling that if a girl saw something in him, perhaps the reflections of a man to be, perhaps irresistible cuteness, or perhaps just the fact that somebody nice liked him, somebody outside his family and church members, then he would be whole. He set out, while in the sixth grade, to catch a girl friend, more like a hunter after a deer than a cavalier after a maiden.

He had absolutely no luck. Girls avoided him like a polecat. He smiled, talked pretty, wrote love notes, even gave a present or two, but the girls, like fickle fish, would not bite. Of course he was not the only fellow left without a Sallie, but he was baffled. Why not him? Did he not look okay? Did he smell bad? Have bad breath? Were his clothes not up to par? He had even asked his Aunt Rachel in a concealed way: Is there anything the matter with me? To which she responded with so many accolades about his cuteness and his cleverness and his charm that he really believed only a quarter of what she said, but realized that a quarter of it was probably true.

Then one day he happened upon it, not the truth, but a reason of sorts. It came from Emma Dobson, who, though not a perfect angel, fit all the criteria for a girl friend, pretty enough, charming enough. He had become so anxious at that point that she took to running whenever he came near, confessing to him that day when he cornered her behind the cafeteria that he was just plain "weird."

And when he asked what "weird" was supposed to mean, she replied: "Well . . . I don't know. All you do is read books and stuff. You don't play ball like the other guys. You're just kind of . . . I don't know . . . kind of like Gideon—I mean, you ain't a sissy or nothing—and you're kind of cute, really, but, but . . . shoot, Horace. I just can't be your girl friend! I don't want a boyfriend everybody calls *weird!* Now let me go!"

It was true, he had reflected. He wasn't like the other guys. He wasn't all that interested in playing touch football and soccer and baseball and basketball. It all just bored him. He wasn't a fat child, nor was he lean and muscled like John Anthony who played everything, and was always captain, always the high scorer, always hailed and cheered by the girls—a twinge of envy would touch Horace lightly. Yet John Anthony was his buddy, but Gideon . . . to have been compared to Gideon was the insult of insults.

Gideon Stone was without a doubt the prettiest boy in Horace's class. And everyone used that term for him. Pretty. Gideon had, as the old men say, sugar in his blood. But unlike decent folk, he was not reticent about it; in fact he paraded it about.

He cultivated a dainty, feminine air, delicate and girllike. His hands formed flowery gestures in midair, and he had something of a mincing walk. People snickered. And though Horace disdained Gideon's "ways," as everyone called them, the true reason Horace despised Gideon was because Gideon was known as the smartest in the class.

Not only smarter, but Gideon was as mean as hell. Most folk said he came by it honest. He was the youngest son of Lucius Stone, Tims Creek's only bootlegger. A thin, tall man, Lucius had asthma, was usually weak as a kitten, and stayed drunk on his own corn whiskey more often than he ought. But his sons—there were seven: Henry, John, Michael, Peter, David, Nathaniel, and Gideon (or Bo-Peep, Bob-Cat, Shotgun, Bago, Hot Rod, Boy-boy, and Gideon)—took after his wife, Viola, who was a Honeyblue, and Honeyblues are known for being large-boned, evil people remembered for their sloth and their strength, but never their industry. Viola was the force behind Lucius, making sure he got the whiskey down on time and taking care of the money. Gideon was their godsend, and Gideon knew it, developing an arrogance that he wielded like a weapon against all outsiders. In his father's eyes he could do no wrong, and rarely did.

Folk in the community who did not purchase Lucius Stone's elixir turned their noses up when a Stone walked by. And many who bought it did too. Women especially shunned Viola, saying no more than Good day, and even that grudgingly. The Stones were labeled shameful backsliders, as Ezekiel Cross would say at the dinner table. Them folks done forgot, if they ever knew, the way of the Lord. Gideon had, or at least Horace pictured it thus, selected Horace to bear the contempt he felt for the community's throwing of the stone.

Sitting there on the stoop, Horace suddenly spied a group of boys rushing in front of the steps before him.

There were five of them, Horace, Rufus, Willie John, John Anthony, and Gideon. Horace knew he was looking at them as they had been in the seventh grade, twelve and thirteen years old. Gideon stood apart from them, a look of sheer anger on his face.

"So tell us, Gid." John Anthony nudged Horace. "What's it feel like to kiss a man?"

"I don't know." Calmly, Gideon kicked at the dirt. "Your daddy ain't much of a man." The guys looked at John Anthony saying, Oooooh, expecting a reaction from him.

He balled up his fist. "Don't talk about my old man, faggot."

Rufus ran around behind Gideon. "Hey, Gid. Want to mess around? Huh? Come on."

"What with? . . . You? I don't play with little animals like you farmboys." Again, there were assorted ooohs and aaahs.

"Hey, Giiideeeooon!" Willie John stepped out, mimicking Gideon's effeminate walk and speech, his wrist limp, his back arched, one hand on his hip. "Can you give me a tip on my makeup?"

"Willie John, honey. There ain't no help for a face like that."

The boys all guffawed, pointing at Willie John, who frowned and backed away from Gideon.

Before the laughter had died down, like a snake going in for the kill, Gideon's voice darted out: "So Horace? Aren't you going to join in on the queer-baiting?" Gideon looked both amused and bored, and he poked around in the gravel beneath his feet. "Ain't you got something better than your running buddies here to come at me with? Come on. Don't make me wait."

"Oooooh, Horace. He wants you. He's begging for it. Go get it, Horace. Make him call you, Daddy." The boys hooted even louder than before. Willie John pushed Horace toward Gideon.

Confused, Horace flicked his shoulder angrily at Willie John and stood there staring at Gideon.

"Scared, Horace?"

"Shut up, you sissy."

"Oh, come on, you can do better than that."

"Do you know what I think about you, Gideon?" Horace forced an expression of disgust. "Do you?"

"I'm sure you have pleasant dreams." Gideon cracked a smile. There came the obligatory ooooh from the guys.

"I think you're disgusting, Gideon Stone. I think you're low and . . . and . . . unclean. An abomination!"

"Oh, Horace. You talk so pretty." Gideon winked at him.

"Damn you, Gideon."

"I'm sure you have other things on your mind." With that Gideon blew Horace a kiss and turned to walk away.

"Faggot." Horace almost whispered the condemnation, but it sizzled in the air.

Gideon turned around and looked at Horace. He paid no attention to the snickering boys who stood about Horace; he just fixed Horace with a gaze whose intensity frightened him. Now, looking at the phantoms, Horace realized how it had seemed to be more than an angry glare. It was more of a curse. A prophecy.

Gideon turned, without a word, unnerving all the boys, and walked away, and the phantoms all were gone.

Horace sat a spell, naked on the steps, feeling the night breeze caress his bare haunches. So that is what the fear looks like? He thought about the first time he had realized his grave fault, but seeing himself there, then, made him know he was aware, even then, of his true mind. And mortified of considering what it meant. In fact he was sure that at the time—when he was twelve? thirteen?—he had no idea what the consequences were. But he sensed them.

By the eighth grade he had discovered how to sin with his hands. He knew he was doomed to hellfire and damnation, for try as he might, he could not stop. He would go for days, weeks, without touching himself, only to succumb in delicious fury, and afterwards feel the guilt of a murderer. The image of God he carried in his head was a bleak one—the Old Testament God of Abraham and Isaac and David, who took no foolishness and punished true to his word. A vengeful, dusky-skinned Arab with electric eyes and white hair. This God thundered in his mind after his orgasms; this God bellowed in his head when the need arose and Horace had conjured up the pornographic images he had seen of women and men in unholy congress. Is that when the truth uncovered itself and stood naked before him? When the thought of a woman failed to arouse him, and the thought of a man did?

Let's take a trip, said the voice.

What?

Come on. There's a house next door. Come.

The house next door belonged to the Sapphires. Mrs. Daisy Sapphire had been Horace's second-grade teacher. She was a hateful woman, tall, with long stringy black hair, who never smiled and for some reason seemed to derive pleasure in punishing Horace for no reason at all. She even had a strange way of eating, alone at a table in the cafeteria, slicing her hamburgers into neat bite-sized sections with a knife and a fork, picking up the portions with the fork. All the other teachers avoided her.

Her husband was a farmer, a round-bellied, tobacco-chewing, good ole boy whom Horace only saw atop tractors or flat on his back underneath a truck. His name was Mason.

Around their house were nine pecan trees in clusters at each corner of the squarish property. The house itself was a white one-story with a screened-in porch across the front, with a door at the side that led into the kitchen. Off to the left was Mrs. Sapphire's garden, about ten rows of peas and collards and mustard greens, sweet peas and corn, beets, turnips, and squash. A scarecrow hung on a pole amid the corn rows. Horace stood at the edge of the garden, his toes sinking in the moist earth, thinking about Mrs. Sapphire and the second grade.

Well, well, well, said the demon. Do your worst.

Without hesitation Horace dropped his gun and started tearing and digging in the soil of the garden. The goblins and trolls yelled and screamed and chattered. But he was intent on uprooting turnips and young collard plants, yanking up and breaking poles, trampling cornstalks . . . The destruction didn't take long. Then he walked up and down the rows saturating the ruined plants in urine.

The demon laughed softly with pleasure. Now, it said. The car.

The car?

Go to the car shed.

Underneath the shelter sat a 1967 puke-green Buick. Its streamlined design was now laughable, its wide interior an over-statement of elegance, but dusty, dull, and worn with farm life, though it only got onto the road on the occasional Sunday or Saturday.

Let's go, said the voice.

Go?

Yes.

But how?

Look in, said the voice. Look in.

Folks in Tims Creek were used to a sort of unworried trust among themselves. There was no reason to lock doors, no one was going to walk in uninvited; there was no reason to put away your hoe, no one was going to take it without asking; there was no reason to take your key from the ignition, no one was going to crank it up unbidden. The keys hung there, silver in the slight starlight.

Get in, said the demon. We've got places to go before the sun rises.

Horace got in, complying with the voice, finding less and less will to resist it, beginning to find something like pleasure in acquiescing to it. The old door gave a metal groan as he pressed the button in the latch and pulled it open. Inside the car smelled of lavender and corn and faintly of grease. As Horace sat down on the cold vinyl seat, his skin prickled, and he shivered. Next to him sat a hog with unusually shaggy hair, and in the rearview mirror he saw two eyeless women in blue robes, who began to sing: *Michael row the boat ashore, Hallelujah! Michael row the boat ashore, Hallelujah.* Horace pumped the gas pedal once, then twice, then turned the ignition gently, hoping that the car would respond in kind and ignite gently, *Sister, help to trim the sail, Hallelujah! Sister, help to trim the sail, Hallelujah,* but he was jolted by the loud commotion of the carburetor and the sparks and the pistons and the fanbelt and the shaking chassis. And he thought of Mason Sapphire turning heavily over in his sleep and Mrs. Sapphire slowly awakening, thinking, Is that that old Buick, then thinking, Surely not, then upon hearing it being put into reverse and hearing the cogs and gears clunk and the wheels scrunching the gravel in the driveway, perhaps changing her mind, *Jordan River is deep and wide, Hallelujah! Milk and honey on the other side, Hallelujah,* and maybe she woke Mr. Sapphire, but by the time the old farmer opened his ears he would only hear the car as it was accelerating upwards of sixty-five miles an hour down the highway and perhaps he said through the doldrums of early-morning sleep, Well, it sounds like the old sister, but really, Daisy, who would take the old girl? And at two in the morning, *Hallelujah.*

Holy Science

*A voluntary descent from the dignity
of science is perhaps the hardest lesson
which humility can teach.*

—SAMUEL JOHNSON

James Malachai Greene
Confessions

Hers was a large room, compared to the rest of the house. Yet the bed filled it up, and in the still heat of early August she lay there, beneath a ceiling fan that slowly mingled the shadows, telling me tales of my grandmother, my grandfather, and their fathers and mothers. All as I looked about the grey sickroom sitting in an old rocking chair scanning the room for answers. She would cough every now and then, a hacking, violent cough that sent her frail body into spasms. She would laugh while wadding the phlegm up in tissue paper and tossing it into the already full trash can; she would look at me with the largest brown eyes I have ever seen, almost comically so, and then resume her yarn without skipping a beat. The smell of sickness seemed to grow in the room, thick like the smell of chitlins and collard greens, a smell that caused me to remember . . .

Margurette Honeyblue was not extremely old; she told me she would be seventy-three on her next birthday, November the twenty-second ("Your great-granddaddy Thomas Cross, why that man was out plowing the fields on his eighty-second birthday. With a mule! Yes sir. The day he died he had just finished breaking up the new ground over there by the Pickett Cemetery for spring planting! The very day. Eighty-two!") She had no notion she would live to see seventy-three. Back in January the doctors had told her she had only six months ("Nowadays they seems to be telling everybody, 'Six months,' 'Six months.' And the truth of it is: They don't know. They don't know a Goddamn thing—oh, excuse me, boy. I mean . . . I forgets you a preacher and all").

Never large, a tawny, lean tiger of a woman, she appeared now a skeleton, her arms and legs emaciated ("Look here, I can reach my entire hand around my thigh. Just like that. Just like that. Ain't nothing left of me but the skin on the bone. The skin on the bone"). She had lived in the dim light for so long that her already big eyes had a child's wide-open gaze. She looked off in the distance, even at nothing, with a wan and incredulous stare, her huge, beautiful eyes belonging to a gal of eighteen, searching.

The room was clothed in shadows, full of bureaus and borrowed chairs from other rooms to seat the many visitors, the windows open with the curtains drawn. She would fidget in the bed, which would in turn groan only slightly. She would look at the clock by her bedside and holler: "Viola! Viola! Where is you at? It's time for my medicine!"

Mrs. Sarah Atkins was in the room with us. With a burst of energy that seemed to come from nowhere, Miss Margurette leaned over and looked up at Miss Sarah. With a look of almost childish plotting on her face, she asked, "See if there's any water in that jug, honey." She grabbed a pillbox and shook it. It was empty. She frowned, threw her head back on the pillow, and yelled: "Viola! I said, Bring my medicine!"

After a minute I heard the front screen door banging like a shotgun and the approaching bare feet of Viola. She stood there with a look of accusation on her face, not looking at either Miss Sarah or me. "Ain't there none in that bottle?"

"If there was would I a called you?"

Viola teetered back into an annoyed stance. She wore a faded burgundy dress that rode high on her hips. Sweat beaded on her forehead and rolled down the side of her neck, and there was a beer in her hand.

"And then there's them two others I'm supposed to take now. And I needs some water too."

"All right." This time she looked at me. There was something akin to contempt in her leer. But I was used to it by then. Viola Honeyblue Stone gave everyone that look. But my being a minister and a Greene didn't make things any better.

"Oh, Viola." Viola gave her mother a barely audible groan. "Bring me a beer instead."

A wicked smile crossed Viola's face. It was a smirk, really. She looked directly at me. There was a pause as if she were waiting for me to respond, perhaps to chide Miss Margurette —especially on a Sunday.

But the old lady turned to me and Miss Sarah, saying, "Now you all want something to drink?" As if to say without saying, she didn't give a damn who was sitting there. She was going to drink what she felt like drinking even if the good Lord himself was seated there.

Miss Sarah fidgeted a bit at my side. There was a thirsty and expectant look about her mouth. She glanced my way, then cast her eyes down only to look up to Miss Margurette with a new and manufactured concern: "Now, Margie. You reckon you ought to be drinking such in your condition?"

Miss Margurette threw back her head in a laugh punctuated by a wracking cough. "Child, the way I look at it, it don't make no difference if I drinks piss-weak orange juice or gut-rottening stumphole liquor. When it's time to go, it's time to go."

"Go ahead, Miss Sarah." I was trying to be as straightforward and nonauthoritarian as I could—as if I had any authority in that room. "If you want to, just go on ahead. Ain't no harm."

"No harm." Viola chuckled under her breath, and for a brief moment we stared at each other across the room. I heard a small bird flap its wings against the wind right outside the window. How could I communicate that I was not, did not want to be the holy and pious dictator of a pastor they had been used to for all their lives, that my very presence had nothing to do with my condemnation of their way of life, that I couldn't give a flying fuck about the still her husband Lucius had out in the woods behind the house, or how she, he, and her mother sold all sorts of regulated beverages illegally from their kitchen, or that the last time they had been to church was to funeralize Margurette's husband twenty years ago. There was no way to say: I have not come here to judge you. To say: I want to introduce a new way of approaching Christian faith, a way of caring for people. I don't want to be a watchdog of sin, an inquisitor who binds his people with rules and regulations and thou shalts and thou shalt nots. But looking at those eyes so full of past hurt and past rejection and past accusation, I could only smile and let be what was.

"No a thank you."

Viola returned with four bottles of pills and capsules and two cans of beer. She opened one can with a crisp pop, handing it to her mother. The other she gave to Miss Sarah, who quickly opened it, took a brief gulp, and thrust it under the chair, as if to hide it from me. Viola gave her mother each dose, one or two or three pills, Miss Margurette downing them with a swig of beer and finally reclining. She lay there quiet and as still as the bed. A warm breeze troubled the curtains and she gave me a wink, took a deep long breath, and sighed.

Place: First Baptist Church of Tims Creek.
Time: 1:35 P.M., Sunday, June 10, 1983.

Scores of people mill around on the church grounds. HORACE, *wearing a suit, stands at the door to the side entrance, apparently nervous. Two elderly men slowly step out the door. They are talking. They speak to* HORACE, *and he respectfully speaks back, nodding. Finally* JIMMY *comes out, clad in a blue-and-white minister's robe, talking with* MRS. CHRISTOPHER. HORACE *looks up at him, but does not smile or speak.*

MRS. CHRISTOPHER: . . . and such a good sermon today. I declare. We're just glad. Glad to have you here, Jimmy—oh, I guess I should call you Reverend Greene these days. (*Giggles.*)

JIMMY: Oh, Mrs. Christopher, you've known me all my life as Jimmy. No reason to change my name now.

MRS. CHRISTOPHER: Well, I'm glad. Just glad. And I know Jonnie Mae is proud. Just proud.

JIMMY: That she is.

MRS. CHRISTOPHER: Well, I'd better go on and see about Mr. Christopher. But I wanted you to know that I'm just as proud of you as I would be of my own boy. (*She looks at* HORACE.) Why, hello there, Horace. How you doing today?

HORACE: Fine, Mrs. Christopher. And you?

MRS. CHRISTOPHER: Fine. Fine. Good. I'll see you all later.

JIMMY: Thank you, Mrs. Christopher. You have a good day now.

HORACE: Goodbye.

(MRS. CHRISTOPHER *walks away smiling.*)

JIMMY: Well, Horace. How're you today?

HORACE: Fine. (*Pause.*) Jim? Can I . . . can we . . . talk . . . I mean—

JIMMY: Is something wrong?

HORACE: No. No. I . . . I just want to talk.

JIMMY: Okay.

(*Two more men walk out and past the two.*)

HORACE: No. Not here.

JIMMY (*smiling knowingly*): Okay, where then?

HORACE: Over here. (*He points to tree at the side of the church, away from the people.*)

(*They walk over, and stand beneath the tree.*)

JIMMY: Okay.

HORACE (*soberly*): Jimmy . . . I got a problem.

JIMMY: What's the problem?

HORACE: I—

JIMMY (*jokingly*): It's not a girl, is it?

HORACE (*almost yelling*): No! It's . . . well, sort of.

JIMMY: Sort of? (*Pause.*) What's wrong, Horace?

HORACE: It's really hard to talk about this.

JIMMY (*becoming visibly concerned*): What is it, Horace, you're—

HORACE (*quickly*): I think I'm a homosexual.

(JIMMY *pauses; makes no motion, but is obviously thinking.*)

JIMMY: You "think"? Why do you think? Have you been with a man?

HORACE: Yes.

JIMMY (*smiling, puts his hand on Horace's shoulder*): Horace, we've all done a little . . . you know . . . experimenting. It's a part of growing up. It's . . . well, it's kind of important to—

HORACE: But it's not experimenting. I like men. I don't like women. There's something wrong with me.

JIMMY: Horace, really. I have reason to believe it's just a phase. I went through a period where I . . . you know, experimented.

HORACE: Did you enjoy it?

JIMMY (*slightly stunned*): En . . . Enjoy it? Well . . . I . . . you know. Well, the physical pleasure was . . . I guess pleasant. I really don't remember.

HORACE: Did you ever fall in love with a man?

JIMMY: Fall in love? No. (*Laughs.*) Oh, Horace. Don't be so somber. Really. I think this is something that will pass. I've known you all your life. You're perfectly normal.

HORACE: But what if I'm not? What if there is something really wrong with me? I mean . . . can it be okay? You know. To go on . . . being . . . like this?

JIMMY (*rubbing his eyes wearily*): "Okay"? What exactly do you mean, "okay"? Okay to be gay? Well, you know as well as I what the Bible says. But I think—

HORACE: It's wrong.

JIMMY: Yes.

HORACE: What if I can't change?

JIMMY (*impatiently, voice rising slightly*): Horace, you'll cha—Change? Well, there's nothing to change. You're normal. Trust me. These . . . feelings . . . will go away. Just don't give in to them. Pray. Ask God to give you strength and in no time . . .

(*Someone calls him from across the yard.*)

HORACE: But what if I can't change?

JIMMY (*sternly*): You'll change. (*He starts toward the front of the churchyard.*)

HORACE: But if I can't?

(JIMMY *stops and looks at* HORACE, *narrowing his eyes.*)

JIMMY: Horace, you do realize that in the end this is a very serious matter, don't you? Search your heart. Take it to the Lord. But don't dwell on it too much. You'll be fine. Believe me.

(JIMMY *turns and walks away.* HORACE *stands beneath the tree, his hands in his pockets, looking up at the tree.*)

A preacher. A minister. A man of God. In the book of Luke the apostle writes that Jesus returns to Nazareth and reads from the Scriptures during the services, saying that he has come to fulfill them. He tells us that the people in the synagogue were then "filled with wrath, and rose up, and thrust him out of the city, and led him unto the brow of the hill whereon their city was built, that they might cast him down headlong." My grandmother knew this story when she began, in her subtle way, to nudge me closer and closer to the pulpit. But then everybody knew; it's commonly known among Southern Baptists that it's hard to preach to people you know and who've known you all your life and most of your family's life. It is formidable. And it happens rarely. But in this case it was the result of my grandmother's unearthly will. That and the will of a few dead folks.

It actually began with her grandfather, Ezra Cross, who had given the land on which the present First Baptist Church of Tims Creek stands. It was his dream that one of his own progeny would stand before the altar as His, and his, minister. So it was a familial, dynastic hope for the both of them. What better gift to the Lord than *your* begotten son? How fitting. How Godlike. How worthy. And for the sons of slaves and of former slaves, what more did they have to give? Ezra had twelve children, yet only six survived—which was not a great deal in those days. People needed as many hands and backs to work in the fields as they could get. He had somehow amassed over one hundred acres of land, exactly how no one is truly certain. If you ask one person he'll tell you old Grandpap was given the land by his former master; if you ask another he'll tell you he went away and worked and saved and returned and purchased it; yet another will say he stole, killed, and cheated for it. But however he came about it, in around 1875 he had title to more land than most former slaves dreamed of having and he needed all the sons he could get to manage it. There was Thomas, the oldest; Paul Henry, who in turn had nine girls; Louis, who in turn had two sons; and Frank, who was killed before he and his wife could have children. Then there was Bertha and Elma, who both married, Bertha to a man over in Muddy Creek and Elma to an insurance salesman who moved to Virginia.

So it was Thomas, the oldest, who worked the biggest part of the farm. Paul Henry worked another piece Ezra had over the river, and Louis and his sons worked a piece that Ezra and

Thomas bought in the 1880s from old Widow Phelps who had no sons. But it was in Thomas that Ezra put his faith and hope, selecting the spot for the new family home and moving in with Thomas's family when his wife died at forty-eight. Yet Thomas was not as fruitful as either of them would have hoped, producing Ezekiel, the oldest; Jonnie Mae, my grandmother; Jethro; Zelia; and Agnes. Both Zelia and Agnes married and moved away. So before his death, Thomas split the land he had inherited between Zeke, Jonnie Mae, and Jethro. Zeke, being the oldest, was favored with the largest piece, as his father had been; Jonnie Mae received the next largest piece, for she was her father's favorite; and Jethro was given a respectable-sized farm, with the admonition to help his brother and sister and conquer any jealousy he might harbor.

My Uncle Zeke had only one son, Samuel. A big, strong, hardworking, loyal son, but with a spirit as wild and free and untameable as his forefathers. There was no preacher in him. So my grandmother took it upon herself to redeem her grandfather's dream. She married a man named Malachai Greene, from another farming family with an exceptional amount of land for a black family in the 1920s. Their lands combined were equal to her brother Ezekiel's. And as time went on, she and Zeke took on more and more of Jethro's place, a field here, a pasture there.

Now who's to say why my Great-Uncle Jethro took to the bottle? With a brother like Zeke and a sister like Jonnie Mae, I suspect I have some inkling. He and his wife Ruth Davis had twelve children by 1935. Six were boys. By 1950 all the boys who had not moved or run away or had not been drafted into World War II and decided to stay in the service, had taken jobs at Camp LeJeune military base down in Jacksonville. The girls all went North either during or right after the war. Jethro died in 1959.

My grandmother and grandfather had only one son, Lester. The rest were girls—Rebecca, Ruthester, Rachel, and Rose, my mother. Jonnie Mae resigned herself to her task. For many years her husband, Aunt Ruth, Uncle Jethro, Lester, Uncle Zeke, Sammy, and Jonnie Mae herself ran the Cross/Greene lands together. They kept afloat, through war and depressions and recessions and sickness and death and children growing up and walking out. Through it all, in the back of her mind—it amazes and chills me to realize—she had plans still that her issue would stand on the pulpit of her "Grandfather's church," as she would sometimes slip and call it when she forgot herself.

Uncle Lester established early on that he was not preacher material. He and my Uncle Sammy became the family hell-raisers, two handsome, big strong men made to work hard in the field all day; their minds were not on prayer meetings at night. They were loyal sons who apparently never considered leaving the family, but they reserved self for self, never went to church, and drank what they pleased, when they pleased, and with whom. But the community as a whole adored the both of them, admiring their independent minds and charming ways. Both were charismatic in that heroic sort of way, inseparable, swift—often violent. It all changed for Uncle Lester the day Uncle Sammy was shot down in Maple Hill over some foolishness. He lost that fierce independence of mind, that dashing cavalier attitude, and knuckled under to Jonnie Mae's reign. He never became a churchgoer, but he lost the luster and sparkle.

I don't know how Jonnie Mae did what she did, keeping her family together and in one place while others dispersed and seemed to disappear from the face of the earth. Together the family toiled and worked and sent Rebecca, the oldest, to Elizabeth City College for an education. She came back to Tims Creek to teach in the York County Public Schools, and to work to send her sister Ruthester to North Carolina Central, which was then North Carolina College. And Ruthester in turn returned to York County to send Rachel to Winston–Salem State Teacher's College. Already it was the late fifties, and my mother, Rose, a few years younger than Rachel, would be ready for college in a few years. This break would give the family chance to gear up for the final haul, and Jonnie Mae could sit back with satisfaction at having sent all her girls to school, which was a true achievement in those days.

At this point Rebecca and Ruthester had been married for going on a decade. Both were childless. Rachel seemed disinterested in men, and though her mother nudged and pushed and argued and coerced her to find a husband, she never did. They all waited on Rose, the ace in the hole.

But Rose never went to college. She never finished high school.

Rose loved pleasure, a foreign thing to Jonnie Mae Cross Greene. She would slip out of the house with tall country boys trying to forget long days of farm work in their brand-spanking-new Dodges and Chevrolets and Fords, going out to good-time, finger-popping juke joints, places that were no more than old barns and abandoned houses that sold liquor and beer and had a music box in the corner cranking out Johnny Walker and Little Richard and the Ink Spots. I can imagine her now, looking much older than sixteen, her long, slender neck exposed, some potent young man, his callused hands clutching her slender waist, nibbling at her neck, her tongue touching her top lip.

At sixteen she just disappeared. Vanished. At seventeen she returned, broken and pregnant. She bore Isador, and in a year she ran away again, leaving her child, only to return once more, battered and full with another child, Franklin. I don't think it was the children out of wedlock that hurt Jonnie Mae the most—her standing in the community was unbesmirchable, and she was accorded more sympathy for having a wayward daughter than for harboring two illegitimate children in her home. But the loss of power, the blatant disregard and disrespect, shook her. The actual possession of the children soothed her somewhat, but at the same time they were reminders of what she could probably only see as her failure.

They tell me at Franklin's birth Rose decided to change her ways, and wanted to take her children with her, up North. Jonnie Mae inquired after my mother's sanity, coolly explaining that she would have to be moldering in her grave before she would allow that hussy to leave her house with those children. Rose left again. This time it was two years before she returned. With me, a six-week-old infant.

Rose was twenty-four. Finally a little older, a little smarter if not wiser, and I'm sure a little more afraid of life and the consequences of her past actions. There were three children about her feet now, calling her Mamma. She decided to bend to convention and her mother's will and remain at home and work and take care of her children. I'm sure she meant well;

I'm sure in her heart of hearts she had made up her mind to do right. But she had not reckoned on her sisters.

All three had been "good"; all three had married; all three were childless. They were the ones the family had sacrificed to educate. They had come home to tend home, to build nests around their mother's nest, to nurture the family as was the duty they had been taught, as she had been taught. Yet in their eyes Rose had turned her back on the family, flaunted her sins, and smeared their name in midnight gutters and liquor-scented backseats. Did she really believe they would welcome her with honey and sunshine and a roasted calf?

Rose became a pariah in her own home. They treated her as they would a servant girl, humiliating her, excluding her, back-biting, accusing. She lasted about a year and a half, which in and of itself amazes me. She left finally, in stormy fury, rising from the Sunday dinner table surrounded by the entire family, disgusted, hurt, and angered beyond words. She just walked out the door, I suspect, never looking back. She wound up on the West Coast and returned only twice—at the death of my grandfather when I was twelve, a visit that I remember only as swift and veiled—it rained that day—and at the death of her mother.

Anne never meddled in my relationship, or lack of relationship, with Rose. Once or twice, in the beginning, she suggested I at least call, but when she saw my reaction she never mentioned it again. I had no reason, but she never called me either. I cannot say I felt abandoned—I was in more than capable hands, surrounded and protected with love and care and instruction from all quarters. We did exchange obligatory Christmas and birthday cards when I was young, eight or nine, but as I got older even that stopped, and any feeling I might have had for her simply evaporated. There was neither hatred nor sorrow nor pity, merely indifference, icy and void.

Last year, when I finally saw her again after twenty-three years, I was overwhelmed by one thing: I did not know this woman. I had thought perhaps I would have been overcome with a recognition, a primeval, instinctual knowledge. Mother. Mamma. *Mater.* Nothing. All my feelings of Mother were directed to the still woman who lay in state in a bronze and chocolate coffin, her face covered with too much powder, her cherrywood skin too dark, her bold, brown lips almost black, her eyes forever glued shut.

Rose stood at the graveside ceremony as Reverend Raines eulogized my grandmother, reading from Paul's letters to the Corinthians ("Though I speak with the tongues of men and of angels, and have not charity, I am become as sounding brass, or a tinkling cymbal"), a beautiful woman, once blessed with that intangible irresistible nature men call sexy, her skin still richly loam dark, her lips full and insolent. I could easily detect the defiance that had set her against her mother those twenty and odd years ago—all in those lips. ("And though I have the gift of prophecy, and understand all mysteries, and all knowledge; and though I have all faith, so that I could remove mountains, and have not charity, I am nothing.") But her eyes—I could see them even through the veil—bore the consequences of hard living, hard love, hard times. They were lonely, lovely, scorned eyes. Eyes that had learned to look for themselves, and had seen. ("And though I bestow all my goods to feed the poor, and though I give my body to be burned, and have not charity, it profiteth me nothing.") When she began to cry, a calm and low sob, she looked suddenly forlorn and forsaken, a child lost and alone. And even now I cannot believe that no one, not Aunt Rebecca, not Aunt Ruthester, not Aunt Rachel, not Isador, not Franklin, and not I, especially not I, turned to comfort her. ("Charity suffereth long, and is kind; charity envieth not; charity vaunteth not itself, is not puffed up."). Until finally, in a moment of such black tension, huddled over the lowering casket, a thin, invisible line separating the prodigal from the faithful, my Uncle Lester stepped over that line and put his hand on her shoulder. ("For we know in part, and we prophesy in part. But when that which is perfect is come, then that which is part shall be done away.") It was a crude and clumsy gesture, but in all its lack of grace it was full of grace. ("For now we see through a glass, darkly; but then face to face: now I know in part; but then shall I know even as also I am known.") Seeing that, I knew my sin, but was unrepentant.

As the first clumps of dirt thudded atop the coffin I began to think, What a shame. Looking at that sad, tall figure as she bent over to be kissed by my Great-Aunt Ruth and my Great-Uncle Zeke and as she shook hands with a cousin here and a cousin there—never a sister or daughter or son—the magnitude of my crime washed over me. How much I could have learned from her. She had raised her fist to her home, to her God, to her people, and chased after her heart . . . and lived. What had she seen? The scars were evident to me. I saw them in her hands, in her neck, in her stance, in her face. How had it changed her? For she could never return home. What had she come to understand of love and sex and lust and freedom, of violence and betrayal, of evil and hypocrisy, and all the naked pain I am sure she endured? Does knowing those things make living easier? But I would never know, for as Pharaoh I could hear my heart ossifying within my living breast. It would break before it would soften.

It was late September. Fall was coming, and a heaviness was in the trees, whose deep green leaves testified to the season and hung low in the heavy air. The family cemetery was at the edge of a field in the shadow of one of the three family tobacco barns. As we walked from the grave to our cars, she approached me. I searched for Jonnie Mae in her face, and was discomforted that I found only Rose.

"So they tell me you're a preacher?"

"Yes."

"I bet she died proud."

"I bet she did."

She said nothing more, not I'm sorry to hear about your wife, not Goodbye, not Take care of yourself or Fare-thee-well. She merely took one measured step back, looking me up and down, slowly, while pulling on her gloves. She smiled at me and nodded, nodded and turned, walked to a car, a rented Ford, got in and drove away, never looking back, not once.

A preacher.

December 8, 1985
12:30 pm

—But I do love you, Ruth. You know that, don't you? I always did. I always did and I always will.

    —You don't love nobody, you old liar. You never did and you never will. You don't love nobody but self . . . your own self. And you know what? You don't really love you, neither.

She is old now. Once she was young, not long ago, really. Only a few days, it would seem. A few sunsets, a few sunrises, a few childbirths, a few deaths. But she has been old for some time now. This she knows; this she feels; this she hates. When she was young, younger, so full of life and living, so impatient for tomorrow, so hopeful of hope, she did not reckon she would be old for so long.

    Hospitals. Cemeteries are more pleasant. There at least things are real—the ground beneath your feet, the sky above, the trees, the grass . . . but in a hospital nothing is for sure, nothing certain. Everyone is a victim, patients and visitors alike, at the mercy of those people called doctors. People she does not trust.

Asa looks pitiful. It saddens her more than she thought it would, more than she thought it could, to see him here. A light-skinned man all his life, now his skin appeared ashen, sickly, frail. He had been there in bed when they entered, his eyes closed, trembling with every breath, one tube stuck up a nostril, another tube jabbed into his arm—one green, one red. He wheezed as he breathed, and the green tube gurgled like a straw does when you've finished a drink. And the smells—disinfectants, ammonia, soap, urine, and that smell she knows so well, sickness. It has its own smell, sickness, like a dog with its tail betwixt its legs, its head held down, an old dog with droopy eyes and a worn-out tongue. That's the smell of sickness. It is here, in the air, in the sparkling white, hard bedsheets, there, surrounding the gleaming metal railing of the bed, and even about them fancy gadgets and whozits ablinking and abuzzing.

When Asa opens his eyes they are bright white, and she almost forgets that he is here in this place where sickness breeds, where women dressed in white wearing funny white shoes look at you as though you should be in bed. When she sees those eyes she remembers when they were both young, she a new bride, he a cousin of her husband and the best-looking thing she had ever laid eyes on. Is that when it went bad? When she realized she was not content? Was it her first sight of Asa with his broad face and round cheeks, his full lips and smiling white eyes? Now Asa's eyes are rheumy and dark-ringed; they seem to call out in pain, and at the same time betray embarrassment. He had jumped when he opened his eyes, looking puzzled and lost, unfamiliarity surrounding him in an unfamiliar place, feeling, probably, unfamiliar himself, though she figures the feeling of coming death is probably a very familiar feeling, one we begin to acquaint ourselves with the moment we take our first breath. He had opened his mouth, saying something so low no one, not even he, could have heard it; his bottom lip descended, trembling, trembling as though he would burst into tears at any moment. Slowly, shakily, he lifted one hand, to no one of the three in particular, clearing his throat, and said:

"What time is it?"

"It's about one-thirty, Daddy." His daughter, Tisha Anne, stands on his other side, but he does not look at her. He still looks at the three standing by his bedside. Who are they? his eyes ask. Three ghosts? Apparitions? Spirits? Is this death come to take me?

"Asa?" Zeke stands uncomfortably, his face caught in a grimace.

"That you, Zeke?"

"Yeah, boy, it is."

For a minute Asa continues to look puzzled, trembling, looking at the old man, the old woman, the tall man in the center, his hand still wavering in midair as if about to point out something arcane and mysterious. He puts his hand down, closes his eyes, and sighs phlegmatically. His breathing is ragged, as if he had run up many flights of stairs. He asks with his eyes still closed: "That Ruth? That you, Jimmy Greene?"

His daughter answers yes. He falls asleep.

*　*　*

—Woman, you can't throw me out of my own house.

—Oh, yeah. Watch me.

—I live here.

—You don't live nowhere, nigger. You live where you can get your hands on a bottle of liquor. That's where you live; you live where you passes out. But I swear to God you won't pass out here no more.

—Stop, Ruth, dammit. I said stop it, right now. Don't you throw another thing—

—No. No. No, Goddamn it. I tried—Lord knows I tried—but I ain't gone try no more. You gone, Jethro. Gone.

—Woman, I'll—

—And if you ever lay a hand on me, nigger, I'll kill you.

It seems to be that way with old ones: things known and not known are one and the same. They begin to place true importance on something young people, except perhaps the very young, pay no attention to—feelings. When was it? When she was seventy-eight? Eighty-three? Eighty-nine? Suddenly the things she felt became more real to her, as if she could reach out and touch them. Just like the old saying, I can feel it in my bones, she too now could feel things like the coming of spring, or an early frost, or a bad storm, or the creation of a youngin. It was as if, like the blind who hear better than the sighted, she had been given this sixth sense in the place of her failing legs and curved back and stiff, aching joints. She believed it to be no miracle, nor anything important or special. No particular blessing or curse. It was nothing, she suspected, that other old folks didn't have as well.

So it came as no surprise to her when she felt it, heard it. She knew it when she came in. The hospital was made to be reassuring, to give some sort of hope, she surmised—its lobby had been made to look very like an old mansion, with fat columns and marble floors, fine wooden panels and carved ceilings—but at the same time it was modern and fancy, with all sorts of machines lurking in corners. It didn't deceive her none. Not the orderlies rushing about in their whites, not the loud families with their loud no-mannered children, not the patients with prosthetics who ambled about, not the wheelchair-ridden, nor the crutch-laden, not the shiny tiled floors, nor the jerky elevators that tinged at each floor and upset her stomach so. She knew, she knows.

So why is it, Ruth, if you are so firm in your knowledge and knowing, so sure of all these things and not fooled, why is it that you are so unnerved to see your husband's cousin at death's door?

Had he been a good man. Had he been a righteous man. Had he been a loving man. Had he been a man who cared for his children. Had he been a man who looked after his farm properly. Had he been a considerate man. Had he been a lucky man. Had he been a man who would, and could, turn away from a bottle. Had he been a faithful man. Had he been a religious, churchgoing, God-fearing man. Had he been a less handsome man. Had he been a man who couldn't have laughed so brightly. Had he been a solemn man. Had he been a hard man. Had he been a soft man. Had he been . . .

✳   ✳   ✳

So they had come this far . . . for what? To be depressed? To watch a dying man die? To . . .

"Obadiah? Obadiah! Boy, where is you?"

"I'm right here, Maw. Hush, now. Hush."

. . . to pray over, to *attempt* to pray over, a dying man for this . . . this outrage? She wants to scream. She wants to holler, to grab the woman by that little white piece of mess that passes for a hospital gown and slam her up against the wall and yell: Can't you see we trying to pray over here, you no-mannered white fool?

"Obadiah, my teeth ain't in. Boy, where my teeth?"

"In your head, Maw. Now hush awhile."

But the more Ruth thinks ill and hateful thoughts about the old woman in the room with Asa, the more pity swells up in her—no, not pity, something more like sorrow, sorrow for herself, sorrow for Asa, sorrow for Zeke, sorrow, yes, even for that crazy white bitch.

"Don't somebody need to see about that colt? It's cold outside. Go put a blanket around the colt, Obadiah. Will you, son? I'm scared it might freeze to death."

"Maw, it ain't gone freeze."

"Well, I'm gone do it myself. Livestock's too expensive. You work, you toil, Lord knows you do, and you got to take care of what you got even if it ain't much, even . . ." The woman starts getting out of bed as her mouth continues on and on like some never-ending record player someone left on in a room no one could get to. Thin as a pole, with skin the color of dried corn, her eyes are ringed with deep black circles.

"Maw, now just lay down. Please. Just lay down now." The boy she calls Obadiah, if Obadiah he even is, is a thin, lanky child with thin mouse-colored hair and a plain straight-up-and-down face; his teeth are bad. On his face is such a hopeless expression that Ruth is almost moved to go over and comfort him. Almost.

"No. No, I can't just lay down. Sun be up soon. Got to get breakfast. Milk that old cow. See bout them hens." She stops abruptly and turns to her son, her hands still poised at the tubes she fully intends to jerk from her arms. "Did you hear them chickens last night? Bet there was a coon after them." She goes back to unplugging her tubes.

"Maw, now stop that. Stop that, you hear. Quit it."

But she is too quick and has already swung her feet to the side of the bed, making Ruth think, Where do these sick folk get this energy? Is it from their craziness?

"Obadiah, you seen my hoe? Where my hoe? I bet them damn Simpson children come by here yesterday and borrowed my hoe and didn't bring it back nor say hello, goodbye, kiss-my-foot, nor nothing. Just like them. Damn white trash. I got to hoe my beets and my row of butter beans. They bad off with the weeds."

The old woman is pushing to get out of bed as her son, baffled, gently tries to prevent her from getting up. It looks to Ruth, in some funny way, as if they were trying to dance.

"Nurse! Maw, please. Maw. Nurse! Nurse!"

"Lord, Lord." Asa rolls his eyes and purses his lips. "Now I got to put up with this to boot?"

The four of them stand helplessly, staring, as the woman finally frees herself from her son. Like newly freed things she has a wild look in her eyes.

"No, no," she says, pointing toward Ruth. "That ain't the way you iron, gal. Let me show you." And she walks, quick as a bird, toward Ruth, who jumps at the sight. As the woman reaches for Ruth's purse, her son grabs her and begins gently to lead her back to her bed. She does not offer a fight. "But that colored gal don't know how to iron."

"Do you need any help?" Jimmy offers sheepishly, Ruth notes, and after the woman has gotten back in bed.

"No, Reverend. No, a thank you," Obadiah says. "She gets like this every now and then. She gets a little addled every now and then, on top of her heart ailments and all." The lines on his face prove his smile is a lie, and that he is trying to hide his shame. "Nurse!"

The woman sits up on the bed, mumbling about dust; and he goes to the other side of the bed, picking up the pieces of disconnected tube, looking at them, bewildered. He calls the nurse once again.

"Ain't no cause to be so ill, Amos," the woman says to him. "I ain't caused you nothing to fret over. I'm a good wife; I work; I'm a good cook. Oh, yes. A very good cook."

"Nurse!"

Once again, the woman gets out of bed. Her frenzy is beginning to take its toll, her voice getting weaker, slower.

"No, no, no, Mr. Edmund, I don't work in no tobacco no more. I give up after my seventh youngin. No, can't stand it no more, can't stand the sun and the . . ."

Asa lets out a disgusted sigh. "Can't somebody, won't somebody, please, *please*, shut that woman up?" He speaks louder than they have heard him speak since they have been there. "Mister, I know your mama is sick . . ." He stops to cough. ". . . and I mean no harm. But please, sir: Just try to quiet her. I just can't take all that fuss." He looks to his company with that look of personal frustration: "Where is that damn nurse?"

Again the man calls the nurse, his voice now high pitched and cracking.

"Ring your bell." Tisha Anne pours water for her father to drink.

"My bell?" The man's embarrassment saddens and angers Ruth.

"Yes, your bell." Tisha Anne points.

"But I don't see it. A bell?"

Ruth is no longer able to keep still. "The bell over the bed, you ninny!" Everyone looks at her. Has she spoken too loud?

Asa tries in vain to reach his buzzer. Tisha Anne pushes it for him, but he continues to reach in vain.

"No need, Papa. No need."

"And I spect the price of corn'll go up. I bet it will. That's what Amos said he heard down at the mill. Price gone go up. And hogs gone go up too. Yes, sir . . ."

"Maw, be quiet."

"I declare." Zeke scratched his head. "I wonder where that nurse is at."

". . . things is looking up. I spect we'll get ahead for once. For once in our lives. For once. It'll feel good, too. Sure will. Feel good. Feel damn good."

Finally the nurse arrives, a large, dark black woman whose white dress is a little too tight, a little too short for Ruth's tastes. She wonders why such a stout woman with legs that big would want to walk around in such a tight frock. But most importantly she feels relief.

"You all scuse us." The nurse pulls the curtain in a little white square from the wall out around the bed and back into the wall. Ruth listens but hears no struggle, no scream of pain; and quickly, quietly the incessant banter of the woman dwindles, like the sound of a train leaving town.

". . . and I expect to see my grandchildren for Christmas. Yes, I do. Fix them a good dinner. Breakfast, too. Breakfast. Eggs. Good. Sausage. Smoked ham. Eggs. And sausage, and eggs, and ham. Smoked ham. Smoked and eggs . . . eggs . . . eggs . . ."

Ruth looks out the window over the healthy emerald lawn and remembers that it is December, not July, and it is cold outside.

She sighs.

He would come home those nights, those blue nights already filled with cooking and cleaning and bone-tiredness, tiredness that felt like the dirt that accompanied it, and after the children were all put to bed she would wash, and wash, and wash and wash until the dirt was long gone but the tiredness remained and in the end she stopped out of pure exhaustion, and she went to bed, falling asleep as soon as her head hit the pillow, seeing in her mind's eye soapsuds, hoes hitting the earth, the clouds of dirt with weeds, grass, tiny halves of sliced caterpillars; and bugs buzzing, buzzing in her ear; and cleaning chickens, the plucking of feathers, the scraping of pink skin, pulling out the tiny pinfeathers and cutting off their orange feet, and the canning of apples and peaches and grapes and back into the tobacco fields and the barn shelter tying tobacco leaves, bright green, and the smell of tar, black and thick on her hands and dirt, dirt, dirt always dirt, and he would come home, and even though she was too tired to move she would wake and hear him coming up the trail, hear his tired feet (tired from what?) stumbling drunkenly up the steps, hear him fumbling for his keys, hear him drop them so many times, their telltale jangle echoing in the woods and back, hear him fumbling in the dark, through the dark into the room, and she would see him in her mind's eye: his face, not as she knew in her heart it was, with bloodshot eyes, stubbly half-beard, tired cheeks, and a lazy, distant expression, but she concentrated, concentrated on a handsome him, a him on a Sunday afternoon, a green spring, down by the riverside, with white happy eyes and a smile, this she thought as he struggled with his coat, struggled with his shirt, struggled with his pants, struggled with his shoes, and as he climbed into her bed calling Woman, in a vaporous mumble, she imagined the sun brighter, and the water cleaner, and his smile kinder, and when he touched her, grabbed her like a feed sack, rough, she imagined him holding her, tender, and when he muzzled up to her neck and she smelt the hateful rotgut breath, she dreamt, oh so hard, of a clean shirt, a pretty tie, and a fresh white shirt, and when he would roll her over and say, Be good to me, woman, be good, she would think of him whispering sweetly, pleasantly, of silly things, childish things, of promised trinkets and trips and times that would, someday, happen, and when he mounted and entered her with the sigh of a peeing bull, and the pain, the quick, quicksilver pain shot up and out through her loins, and the rhythm, the rhythm, began, and she reached to grab something, anything that was not him, and she tried with all her might to remember that it was love, and that she once loved him, and that she wanted to love him and it turned into a prayer, a funny prayer because it would be lost in the rhythm that stabbed through her, that was both white and black, that brought her joy and pain, joy and pain, joy, pain, but more pain, less and less joy, and hastened within her, inside her, and she did finally grab him, did clutch him and as he called to her, called for her, crying, sobbing, as a baby, as he climbed, from his cradle, oh Lord, she hugged him, she rocked him home, and he called out, Dear Lord, oh Lord, Sweet Jesus, and she loved him, and when he was done, after the world had certainly turned catty-cornered, after she opened, gave, sought, saw, comforted, protected, released, received, after she had been the beginning, the middle, the end, after she had drunk tears, wiped snot, licked sweat, when the world had been righted and all that was left, now, was a calm, still blue, he turned over, without a word, leaving her empty and cold, and commenced to snore.

"Let us pray:
    "Our father, we come to you as humble as we know how . . ."
    The death itself will probably be, will be, swift and merciful. But she hates that he has suffered so. As she looks at him there, his brow furrowed in concentration over Jimmy's prayer, she says her own secret prayer:

Dear Jesus,

Lord, I'm a broken-down old woman, and come a day soon and very soon, you gone call me. And that's all right. Times I sure wish you'd a took me a long, long time ago. But you didn't; and you're God. So I ain't gone tell you your business cause I know what it's like to be about your business and somebody who don't know nothing bout your business come along and fixes to tell you what you done wrong, and how to improve your job and so forth. But Lord, I ain't come to dabble. I ain't come to meddle. No, Lord. I just come to ask you, my God, cause I know, I do know how it must be for Asa to lay up in that bed and just be helpless and in pain. And Lord, I know he gone be gone soon, and Lord, I know he's in pain, and Lord, I know that pain's part of man's plight since the Fall, but Lord. You know. Oh, yes you do. You know ain't many folk been kind to me in my day. My Paw, he tried, cause my Maw, she didn't know how. Many one aunt— but Lord, I ain't complaining, but that man, this man . . . I . . . I . . . think right much of him. He done . . . he done a lot for me. Me and my family. He stepped in when my sorry old husband couldn't and wouldn't do for us. He brought food when most of the folks would just sit and laugh at me. Laugh. And me with eight, nine head of youngins to feed and clothe and train and the man what give them to me out and gone. Out loafing somewhere. Out drinking. But this man. He's a good man. And I ain't, I say, I ain't gone to ask you not to take him, cause I seen enough of this world to know it's probably a welcome relief to get out of here. But Lord, if you please to: take his suffering from him and put it on me, Lord. Put it on me. And let him die in peace.

I hope it ain't much to ask. But it say in the Bible: *The prayer of a righteous man availeth much.* Well, I might not be righteous, Lord, but I'm plain. I'm honest. And I'm sincere.

". . . in that world that will have no end, and where every day will be Sunday.

"Amen."

Amen.

Had he been . . . Had he been . . . Had he been . . . But he wasn't.

—Jethro. Jethro?

—Yeah.

—Come on in and eat your supper.

—I be in directly.

—But it'll get c . . .

—I said, directly, Ruth.

—But, Jethro . . . what's wrong with you . . . you . . . what you crying for?

—Leave me be, woman. Just leave me be.

—Jethro? Is you sick? Is there something the matter? The children . . .

—No. No. No, now leave me be.

—But Jethro, it ain't natural for you to go off crying by yourself. Something's got to be the matter.

— . . .

—You need money? You sick?

—Woman—

—No, you gone tell me, now . . .

— . . .

—Jethro.

—I . . . I didn't want it to be this way.

—What way, Jethro?

—I didn't want you to live in such a bad way. I don't deserve you. You . . . you don't deserve me. I ain't worthy of you, Ruth. And I don't know what to do about it. I just don't. I try to do better. I sure do . . . but I fall. I'm weak. And look at you. Look at you.

—You . . . we'll just have to keep trying hard. That's all. Just keep on. Just keep on and don't quit—

—You a good woman, but you don't understand, do you? You don't understand.

Oh, but I did. I did.

It's hard to look at him. He's so tired. So anxious to take wings and go. She too is tired, has been tired, day in and day out, tired for longer than she cares to remember. Soon, Asa. Soon and very soon. Neither one of us will be tired much longer.

"Well, I thank you all for coming." Asa's eyes are crying, even though no tears happen to fall. "Drive careful, now."

The woman across the way is dozing; her son has gone. A short man, the color of fertile soil, mops the hall floor outside the room. There is something comforting in the slick, wet rhythmical sound of the mop head slipping across the floor. She can smell the ammonia, fresh and new.

It is time to leave.

"Well, Asa," she says, "you rest, now. You hear? Just rest. Everything gone be all right."

"I know it will, gal." He winks at her and smiles. "I know it."

Tisha Anne escorts them down the hall, Zeke in front, Ruth behind, Jimmy on the left, Tisha on the right.

"Papa looks better than he looked in a long time."

"Does he?" Zeke asks.

"Yes, sir. He does."

"Gal, what the doctors say?" Zeke peeks in each room as he walks by, waving and nodding howdy to everyone who catches his eye.

"Now, what you want to know what the doctors say for?" Ruth does not look up, merely turning her head sharply as if listening to the ground.

"Now, Ruth—"

"Now, Ruth, nothing."

"Aunt Ruth!" Jimmy already appears nervous. There's that tone in his voice as though he were talking to children in school and not a grown woman, but she also detects . . . impatience? "I want to know too."

"They say Papa's heart just ain't got the strength to keep on much longer. That's all. He done had two heart attacks, as you know. He's just lucky he ain't had no stroke . . . yet."

"They say it's a possibility?"

"Yes, sir. They do."

"Uh-uh." Zeke shakes his head as the elevator doors slide open, his eyes focusing through the back of the wall.

"Well, you happy now?" As Ruth steps in, the elevator door begins to close on her, and before Tisha Anne or Jimmy can grab it, it knocks into her, sends her careening into Jimmy's arms. And instantly she begins thrashing like a fish out of water, striking him about the arms and chest.

"Aunt Ruth! Aunt Ruth! What is the matter with you?"

"Ain't nothing the matter with me. Just tell them to fix these damn elevators. My stick. My stick. Give me my stick. *I want my stick.*"

Jimmy grabs her by the shoulders and stares into her eyes. "Aunt Ruth, *why are you hitting me?*"

She stops and is aware of everyone staring, the orderlies, a white man in an orange tweed coat and a woman with him, Zeke, Tisha Anne, and she wants to tell him, she wants to spit in his face, yell, scream, and tell him how much she despises him, how much she resents him, his grandmother, his Uncle Zeke, his whole damn family, but she is too stunned by his sudden display of . . . of what? . . . strength?

"Boy, who you think you talking to? One of them snot-nosed youngins from your school?" He looks away, embarrassed. "Give me my stick."

Tisha Anne hands it to her, and when Jimmy attempts to lend Ruth a hand, she merely stares at it and steps into the elevator.

Zeke looks at her, his mouth agape. "Ruth, you didn't have to talk to the boy like that. He was just—"

"Leave me be, Zeke. Just leave me be."

She hates elevators. Her heart is racing, her stomach changes shape. He is not her nephew, he is the nephew of her husband; and his grandmother, the Royal Miz Jonnie Mae Cross Greene, was one of the people who sat back and pointed at her for marrying her drunkard of a brother. Oh, she would help out when

Jethro took to the bottle for too long; oh, she'd give her advice about child rearing—specially since she'd been so successful with her four girls and that boy, Lester, that she made a slave; oh, she'd been a good sister-in-law, but she never respected Ruth. Never treated Ruth like an equal. And she had made Jimmy, her grandson, into her own image. She hated them both. But she was a good woman. Jethro had told her, once.

Back outside the air is warm, yet not warm enough to make her happy. As Tisha Anne wishes them a safe journey home, she stares out past the green lawn, over the rise in the valley, over the rest of that emerald hill, beyond the white gravestones and the high wrought-iron gates, and she notes the color of the sky—dishwater grey. She thinks: I want to die under a blue sky.

April 30, 1984
2:40 am

Horace sat dumbfounded in the puke-green Buick. He recognized the great black asphalt parking lot just off the east wing of his high school. Why was he sitting here? He could not remember what had brought him here or even driving here or arriving. Suddenly he opened his eyes and he was here. Though he remembered remembering, the church, the baptism, the school . . . the garden? It was neither clear nor chronological, and the images, the shards of feelings slicing at his heart caused him more confusion.

But he did remember the voice, and its seeming plan for him. Where was it? He derived something like comfort in thinking there was a power at work, no matter how terrifying. The course had been lain. Decisions were out of his hands. He was now a pawn.

Dousing the headlights, he stepped out of the car, turning around, half expecting to see someone there. Who? Song lyrics jingle-jangled in his head, *Take this hammer, carry it to the Captain* . . . He felt a loss. Why? Baffled, he shrugged, finally turning from the car and walking toward the school.

As he walked across the tarmac trying his best to keep the broken glass, can tops, and pebbles from cutting his bare feet, memories welled up of the mornings in fall, winter, and spring when this parking lot was full of cars. Toyotas. Hondas. Ford Rangers. Old Cadillacs. Those nice Volkswagen Rabbits purchased by eager-to-please parents or Pontiac Firebirds from overly indulgent, well-to-do parents; those pickup trucks given to grandsons by grandfathers who could no longer shift the gears; the Chevrolets, the Mercurys, the Chryslers that doubled as family cars, and those cheap, easy purchases that the thrifty and the hard-working bought with their savings from summer jobs and after-school jobs in the supermarket or the shoe shop or McDonald's. Those assortments of clinking, honking, grinding, guzzling machines were emblems of pride, an accumulated source of self-importance among Horace's peers. People who drove to school were a notch above those who rode the bus, whether they drove a Mazda RX7 or a 1954 Dodge truck, for they were independent. They were one step closer to being grown up.

Horace made it across the parking lot with only a cut or two on his feet. He sat down on a squat pylon among a row that separated the lot from the schoolyard, and examined his feet one at a time, picking out pebbles and such. Once again he sat beneath a high nightlamp, and once again he was oblivious to his nakedness. He looked up at the dim monolith, gray and silent, its windows reflecting the crescent moon, its flat top blending in with the sky.

South York County High School belonged to a different era. Its original hull had been built in the late fifties, with a cafeteria added in the early sixties, a gymnasium in the early seventies, a business annex in the late seventies, and most recently a huge auditorium with a music chamber for the band. It was a streamlined giant in faded beige brick not in keeping with the farms and garages and woods and fields that surrounded it. Since South York's population was over twenty-five hundred, the largest in the county and most of eastern North Carolina as well, the money had been appropriated for building and more building, until it became the pride of the county. Its football teams, basketball teams, track, tennis, and even baseball teams, both junior varsities and varsities, were local favorites. Though the varsity men's basketball team had an ugly losing streak, the junior varsity had been undefeated for six years (everyone blamed it on the varsity coach), and the girls' team had won the state championship twice. The varsity football team had been considered the best in the state for a while, winning the state championship three years in a row; the last few years it had ranked in the top twenty. The top seeds on the tennis teams went on to do well at East Carolina and State; and several members of the track team had won scholarships. "You can tell the caliber of a school," the principal, Mr. Unger, once said at an assembly meeting, "by the caliber of its sportsmen and women." Horace knew his cousin Jimmy would have rumbled, What about its scholars? But Horace had learned, after three and a half years there, that image meant more to these administrators than learning.

—What was that? Listening, he was certain . . . yes—the sound of wings. Flapping. Large wings cupping and beating the air. He jumped to his feet, half filled with terror, half filled with awe. Had the demon decided to show itself! He looked around, peering into the dark, across the fields, into the nooks and crannies of the building, into the woods in the distance, and behind the poles and pillars, the fences and gates—nothing. What had he heard?

To the left he heard footsteps. Without stopping to think he gave chase. He ran around to the front of the building, seeing nothing, but knowing it had gone this way. The lobby, fronted by a glass panel, barred by steel columns and concrete posts, was full of the paraphernalia of high-school patriotism. The school mascot was an Indian, so in the lobby stood a petrified chief, his long-feathered ceramic bonnet touching the floor. The floor itself, an artificial tile made to resemble marble, shone with an unnatural luster. There were the trophies and the plaques and the banners and the state seal; a large rubber tree sat in each corner, not at all in keeping with the modern, academic, polished nature of the hallway.

Horace reached for the door handle, sure the door would be locked, that the being had perhaps walked through it like mist, and with the same surprise as the women at Jesus's tomb, he opened it. He did not consider this to be supernatural; he did not think the demon had fiddled with the lock; nor did he wonder whether Mr. Unger, in his usual disorganized huff, had hurried out of the building without locking the door behind him. He rushed in after the being, ruled more by curiosity than by terror.

Which way? Quiet and shadows confronted him, the regular everyday shadows that curved around corners and stretched out in elongated arcs and bends. Nothing supernatural in these dark, dim walls, the empty staircase, the reflectionless windows, the corridors that gave up no light. He remembered the footsteps he had heard just hours before of the students and their brash loudness and the business of education.

Then the telltale rustle at the top of the stairway. Horace leapt up the stairs three at a time. Again, nothing. A door gently went, Click.

He stood before the door of Miss Clarissa Hedgeson's biology classroom and paused for the first time in this chase. His breath came in short puffs and he wondered what horrid, hideous, malevolent, bone-crushing, evil beast he might meet. What unenviable end might he find? What pain lay here? What torture? He opened the door.

You're late, Mr. Cross.

Sunshine beamed through the windows. There stood Clarissa Hedgeson, wearing her old maid's print dress, her silver steel-rimmed specs, and her authoritarian snarl. His fellow ninth graders all looked up at him, save those who were busy reading the latest Spider-man comic book inside their biology texts, or those who were gossiping in the back of the room, or those who, lost in daydreams of being spies in Russia or of having love affairs in Victorian England, peered out the window to Moscow, to London, to some cool swimming hole.

Well, take a seat, young man. We don't have all day.

No one snickered at his nudity. In fact, he had forgotten his lack of clothing. Clutching his book bag and muttering apologies for his tardiness, he sat down with relief and looked forward to a lecture on cell division, full of questions about mitosis and osmosis and membranes.

Miss Hedgeson droned on and Horace looked around, seeing Gideon and John Anthony and Edmund Clinton, and in a double-minded instant Horace knew that he was here and that he was not here. He looked down, and he was naked in their midst and three years older. They were the same. Not nostalgia, but regret and sadness tugged at him, yet he was still baffled: is this real?

He looked over at Gideon, brown and sweet, as complex as calculus and as direct as a bare fist. Horace remembered romance. He wouldn't call it love, but it had been intense and real.

> *I can't light no more of your darkness*
> *All my pictures seem to fade to black and white . . .*

Had he a chance to do it again, he was certain, very certain, that he would succumb. It was "the magic of the first time" that clung to his mind now, and though fraught with guilt, it had been somehow pure in its sordidness, honest in its awkwardness, innocent in its seriousness. Certainly a thing he could never see again, even if he lived to be three hundred and loved the bravest legion of the greatest empire's warriors.

Don't discard me just because you think I mean you harm
Stranded here on the ladder of my life . . .

How could such a thing be evil? How could he have spoiled such—

Horace. Are you and Gideon ready to give your demonstration?

At first it was to have been Edmund—a swarthy boy of raven-colored hair and olive skin who played on the junior varsity basketball team and who confessed to Horace a deep desire to be a black person—with whom Horace was to work on his experiment in plant tropisms for Miss Hedgeson's ninth-grade biology class. Edmund was much taller than Horace and had, as the old women say, filled out early. His clumsy attempts at black speech and black gestures endeared him to Horace, who had a crush on the boy. At fifteen Edmund had more hair on his body than Horace thought possible. He became obsessed with the dark, mysterious tufts.

Horace? Gideon? Are you ready?

Edmund was incredibly dumb. And though Horace preached and lectured about the growth processes of plants, he could not seem to excite Edmund in the least, nor teach him anything about biology. Edmund was much more interested in Peggy Somers and the Celtics and the new stereo system he had just put in his Camaro. At a very crucial stage in the experiment Edmund decided to opt for the long written report instead of the high-credit experiment, leaving Horace with an elaborate headache.

Horace?

At about the same time that Edmund decided he wanted no part of pea plants, a hungry black snake found its way into Lucius Stone's barn and gobbled up Gideon's project on the growth and development of chicken embryos.

Yes, Miss Hedgeson. We're ready.

In her teacherly wisdom, Miss Hedgeson decided that Gideon and Horace would work well together.

In all there were 128 pea plants—Horace had chosen pea plants because of his admiration for Gregor Mendel. He fancied himself, in some distant way, very like Mendel, a devout monk devoted to the gathering and interpretation of important knowledge, data, secluded, on a mountaintop, the monastery above, simple and stark, made of dull stone hewn from that very mountain, he walking among the pea plants in spring, their white and blue blossoms fragrant, the buzz and hum of honeybees in his ear, brushing the tender green worms away from the leaves, thinking of vespers, St. Benedict, the genetic code—of course, Miss Hedgeson objected to the use of pea plants. They weren't sturdy enough, she said. Horace calmly demonstrated how pea plants were a fine plant to demonstrate the phenomenon—any plant would be, he said in his already notoriously stubborn way. She gave her approving nod with an annoyed smile that Horace had become used to, having become used to getting his way.

Yet Miss Hedgeson would not allow Horace to complete the project alone. She felt it was already too big, if not already out of hand, what with all his projected charts and diagrams, not to mention the paper, the outline of which was too long in the first place, and really Horace, don't you think this all a bit much? I mean . . . Okay. Okay. Of course you know what you're doing. I'm not implying that you don't. But I insist that Gideon join you. There's really no other way. No other way, and no discussion, *Mr.* Cross.

The nature of the experiment was so sensitive that no plants could be moved until the day of the fair. The only thing left for Gideon to do was help draw the charts and diagrams that Horace had planned. And he insisted on coming over to Horace's house to assist in the keeping of the plants.

Horace's first reaction to the whole idea was annoyance: No longer could he be the solemn monk retreating into his garden sanctuary, pious, thoughtful, and alone. Now there was another presence, a presence Horace found disturbing.

Over the summer Gideon had changed. His girlish, cute body had been transformed, much like a butterfly emerging from a chrysalis. Everyone was talking about it. Noticing him. The old women would say, Have you seen that boy of Lucius and Viola's? He done took to growing! Suddenly he was taller than Horace. His arms, which seemed thicker and nothing like a girl's, were falling beside a waist that was bunching itself together into something solid and decidedly manly. His voice was taking a deeper register. It was clear he would follow in the footsteps of his mother and his brothers and become a large man. And even more disturbing to Horace, what had once been annoying indiscretions now appeared intentionally charming; his formerly shrill and high-pitched voice was now honey toned; his "sissified ways" were being called mannerly and intelligent. Horace made an effort to avoid looking at him.

He would be lying to himself if he said he had not been attracted to Gideon, now more so. But admitting this resulted in such overwhelming guilt, he might as well have crucified himself. How? How? How? could he endure working closely with him? Why couldn't the Lord take this bit of torture, this careful trap away? Give him larceny to fight instead. Let his piety be questioned. Try to force him to lie, to worship false gods, to dishonor his mother and father, to covet his neighbor's home . . . but why Gideon?

Then he realized—it had almost been an afterthought—what his family would say about him working so closely with the son of a bootlegger. He knew he had stumbled upon the solution.

Granddaddy, Mrs. Hedgeson says I have to finish my project with Gideon Stone.

So?

You know. Gideon Stone. Lucius Stone's son?

So?

Well, I mean . . .

You mean what, boy?

Well, you know . . . his daddy and all . . .

Uh-huh . . .

They ain't . . . righteous people.

I beg your pardon, son?

That's what you said be—

Come here, boy. Come here.

Yes, sir.

Now, son. Just because folks don't do like I say don't mean I got no cause to judge them. I say things, more than I ought to sometimes, but listen here to me, boy: Don't you ever feel yourself better than nobody round here in Tims Creek, you hear? Nobody, nowhere. White nor black. Folks do what they gots to do, and cause that ain't what *you* got to do it ain't no cause to turn up your nose to them. Now let that be a lesson to you, boy. You go on and do your work with Gideon Stone. It won't hurt nary one of you.

It was done. Locked. Bound. Tied. As if by the hands of the old Arab himself. He could hear John Anthony now: Ole Horace got a helpmeet. They gone tend their little garden together, boys. Like . . . like Adam and Eve—Huh, Horace? You gone name the animals, too? Or do you plan on giving him some forbidden fruit? Maybe even a little pea plant?

The first time Horace was to go to Gideon's house to work on the charts, his mind was not on pea plants. Gideon had behaved himself throughout their collaboration. To Horace's surprise there were no sly remarks, no attempts at touches or any of the abominable behavior he had expected. In fact, Gideon's grasp of the project was so deft it angered Horace. All of a sudden it was Gideon's project, and Horace found himself in the obstinate position of having to affirm that *he* had thought of the project, that *he* had initiated it, that *he* had done the majority of the work, and that *he* should receive the bulk of the credit, and that, in the end, make no mistake, Mr. Stone, this is *my* project.

Lucius Stone's house sat on a path that trailed off from another dirt road, back just beyond a wood. Unpainted and older than Horace could imagine, it was greyish brown with a tin roof painted green. The yard, a bumpy, lumpy stretch from the barn to the woods, was littered with barrels and cans, stacks of lumber for extensions to the house, and cars, at least seven, four of which were tireless and on blocks, devoid of an engine here, a gas tank there, or a backseat there. Chickens ran all about the yard, for Mrs. Stone had said she couldn't eat no store-bought hen—it had to be fresh killed for her. The place sat very near a creek, so the ground was soggy and wet. The entire estate smelled of the creek, of rotting timber, of moss, of chickenshit, of old cars and gasoline and oil.

People were always around Lucius Stone. As Horace walked up the path he could see him sitting on the porch with Mrs. Stone and three of the seven boys—Bo-Peep, the oldest; Bago, the biggest; and Boy-boy, the darkest. With them sat Sam Vickers, still in his Sunday-go-to-meeting suit, and Joe Allen Williams and John Powell in their coveralls. Except for Lucius, everybody had a glass in his hand. Lucius drank from a mason jar.

He was a tiny man with a face like a weasel. Ratty, Horace had once heard his Great-Aunt Jonnie Mae call him. His hair was a dusty grey, and he wore a scraggly beard with no mustache. His eyes wandered around in his head as though he were blind, but when he had your attention he focused like a hawk. Some said his eyes wandered because he was thinking so hard, others said he was just plain touched in the head. That day Lucius fixed Horace clear and true. Everyone else on the porch eyed Horace with unfriendly looks, but Lucius beamed broad, grinning and leaning forward.

"You come to work with Gideon on that project of yours, did you?"

"Yes, sir."

"Good, good." He lifted his head up and hollered. "Gideon! Gideon? That Cross boy is here!" Lucius looked back at Horace with a quick jerk of his head. "He'll be right out. Sit a spell."

No one said a word as Horace moved to sit on the porch, so he quickly said Good afternoon. The menfolk all grunted and mumbled, Hey, and looked away. Viola Stone sat like a rock, her legs gaped open showing her satin panties beneath her orange-and-black dress.

"What you all working on so?" She said it more as if it were an accusation with her barrel-bottom voice, the color of a man's.

"It's a science project for school."

Lucius slapped his knee. "See, now that's good. I tell my boy Gideon to stick with his schooling and not to do like these other ones done—quit school. Mess around with these here cars like that was all there is to life." Skillet looked back at his father, a scowl on his face. Lucius turned to Horace, then to his glass, gulped and looked away. "Now, I didn't get much education. When I was in the fourth grade I—"

"Lucius." Viola looked at him with one eye closed. "This here boy don't want to hear all this foolishness about you and your education."

"Hush, woman. I ain't talking to you."

She frowned and took a swig from her glass.

"See," Lucius smiled, "education is the way this days. Ain't that the truth, boys?"

The men all gave unenthusiastic Uh-huhs.

"Yes it is. The white man got things turned around so that a black man can't get his hands on nothing less he got one of two things: a whole lot of money in the bank or a college degree."

"That's the truth." Joe Allen Williams spoke into his glass.

Lucius closed his eyes and nodded, pleased with his observation. When he opened them he glanced at Viola, who pursed her lips in disgust. He turned once again to Horace and leaned over.

"You understand me, don't you, young fellow?"

"Yes, sir."

"Keep to your studies. That's the way."

Viola arched her back like a cat and scratched it with her free hand. "What's this science project you all working on?"

"It's a demonstration of plant tropism."

"Plant tropism?" Joe Allen chuckled.

"Negro," Viola pursed up her lips again and looked toward Joe Allen, "what you laughing at? You know what it is?" He shrugged his shoulders, embarrassed, and gulped his liquor, turning away.

"Well," she turned back to Horace, sucking her teeth. "What is . . . what did you call it again? 'Trophytism'?"

"Tropism."

"Yeah. What the hell is it?"

Lucius jumped. "Viola, you know who that boy is? Don't talk like that in front—"

"Shut your mouth, Lucius. I'm the one talking to the boy."

"Well, that ain't no reason to cuss."

"I ain't cussing. I'm asking. Now hush up a minute!"

"Woman, don't tell me to hush up."

"Man, will you let me ask my question?"

"Well, ask you damn question, then, Goddamn it!"

"I will—"

"Well, go on then."

"If you'll hush!"

Horace quickly said, "It's the study of what makes plants grow the way they do."

"Is that all? Shit."

"Viola!" Lucius almost jumped out of his chair. Viola lifted her glass threateningly.

At that moment Gideon appeared at the door. "Hey, Horace. Come on in."

Horace leaped up at the invitation, excusing himself, and instantly realizing how prissy and proper his "Excuse me" had sounded to the people there on the porch.

The house, like the yard, resembled a junkyard. Clutter and rubbish, furniture with holes and cigarette burns, and empty glasses all around. The smell was the same as outdoors, a soggy, rotten, mossy smell—except more intense. Suddenly it struck him: there was something arousing about the odor. Or was it the odor? Gideon's room, on the other hand, was neat and organized and clean, almost Spartan. The materials they were to work with were stacked neatly on the bed.

They set to work with the intensity of termites. They spoke little. Horace tried hard, but he could not ignore the situation. He was alone with Gideon. His thoughts strayed. Colorful. Forbidden. Thrilling. They rushed in and out of his mind, a restless army of ideas, possibilities, analyses. Several times Gideon caught Horace gazing at him. Gideon smiled and continued working. He didn't seem to share any of Horace's distraction. Horace could not help but notice Gideon's deft fingers as they worked, their shape, or the rich, coffee color of his forearms, or the fullness of his biceps, or the muscular tension in his legs as he sat crosslegged, or the lines of his neck, equine and smooth, bent in concentration. Horace remembered all the past taunts and jokes he had hurtled at this person before him. They worked on into the afternoon.

At one point Horace shifted his position, and to his embarrassment noticed a tension in his pants. Terror clutched at his heart: What if the house caught on fire? What if my grandfather calls? What if Gideon asks me to another room? He could see images of Viola Honeyblue Stone throwing an entire car engine after him, her face contorted into a mask of hatred, yelling, Faggot!, the other men busting guts from laughing. The more he worried the greater the tension protested, and he thought of ploys he should have tried on Miss Hedgeson, scandals he could have dragged to his grandfather that would have kept him away from this room, this day, this boy.

The embarrassment had subsided by the time he had to leave, but the desire had not. He felt ashamed and wanted to tell Gideon, to ask him if he felt anything too. But knew he dared not. What if Gideon isn't a faggot? What if what we've thought all these years is wrong? What if I'm the queer and he's straight as an arrow?

Gideon rose, a look on his face unlike the one before, calculating, devilish, and sly. Had he seen it?

"I'm glad you could come by, Horace. We got a lot of work done."

He stood there, Gideon, with that efficient, choirboy look on his face, and Horace could not think of what to say, to do.

Gideon put his hand on Horace's shoulder, winked and said: "I'll see you later." He squatted and began putting away sup-plies. Nothing more.

That night Horace dreamed. Not that he had never dreamed of men and boys before, but that night he dreamed of a par-ticular boy and was filled with a warm and tender feeling. There was also the terror, the familiar question he had refused to acknowledge. It was a horrible voice saying: You must cease this sinful thinking! Are you mad? Do you realize what will happen? But he could not help it, he was not willing to part with this strange new feeling. And as for the danger, the real danger, it only made his obsession seem all the more worthwhile.

He began to behave nicely toward Gideon. He would walk with him to and from class (it was no longer a stigma to be seen with "that Stone boy"), and they spoke of *Star Trek* and science fiction and horror novels. Just being around this seem-ingly new person made Horace glad. It was as if he had met someone entirely different. Where was the sin? he thought. Each night he would resign himself to tell Gideon he loved him. And each morning when he looked into those brown eyes and saw those strong teeth, he would become afraid, afraid of what he would say, afraid of what it meant. Afraid that Gideon would laugh at him and tell everyone and make a fool of him. It was then that he would realize that he was different and vulnerable and that the simple joy of being in love and expressing it with straightforward passion was denied him, and he would retreat into an indigo funk, to be rescued only by the thought of Gideon's remarkable presence. The little things—Gideon's laugh, Gideon's smile, the way Gideon would phrase a word, the way he would cup his chin when he was pensive . . .

But Gideon gave no indication that he too was infatuated. He seemed so self-contained, almost aloof, which was something that often infuriated Horace. Gideon didn't appear to need anyone or anything, just his music, his books. He had been taunted and excluded for so long that he had built a world of his own within himself. Other people simply did not matter to him. His new-found popularity, this sudden attention he was getting, made him even more withdrawn. But Horace was an exception: He was fond of Horace, and this made Horace bold and hopeful.

Horace wrote a letter. Actually he wrote about twenty-three letters. By writing and destroying and putting away for a while and starting over from scratch, thinking, No, I can't say that, I won't say love, I'll say . . . like strongly? really like? love? he finally finished and stuck it into Gideon's locker. It consisted of three paragraphs:

First it swore Gideon to secrecy, and explained how much nerve it had taken him to actually write down what he was about to say and then to deliver the epistle, and exactly what he had to lose in reputation and peace of mind if such information as he was about to disclose ever got into the wrong hands.

Second, he said that Gideon was the first and at present the only person he had loved (yes, loved) and he was both confused and happy and frightened.

And third, he admonished Gideon to respond in some fashion, soon, once again reminding him that his reputation, his very life rested on Gideon's goodness.

That very day in the cafeteria Gideon came upon Horace, who was sitting alone. Horace's heart beat so that he was sure he might pass out; sweat beaded his forehead.

Gideon sat down and took a bite out of his hamburger. "You're something else, Horace. You know that?"

Horace's insides felt as though he had just fallen from a four-story window. He was certain that Gideon was going to betray him. He became instantly angry, thinking himself the biggest of fools. "What exactly do you mean by that?"

"I mean, I've had a crush on you since the sixth grade." Gideon winked at him and continued to eat his hamburger.

Learning for the first time what it meant to be speechless, Horace stared at his plate. He could not finish eating.

The first time they kissed was during a football game when they slipped to the other side of the school. They stood in an unlighted and deeply recessed doorway. Horace was certain Gideon had done it before, he did it so well. But Horace could not bring himself to ask.

This began right before Christmas vacation of their freshman year, but it was not fully consummated until just before summer vacation. One Saturday Horace's grandfather was to be gone all day. Gideon came over.

"Are you scared?" he asked Horace.

Yeah.

If there had been any doubt about how he felt, or any notion of turning back from his reprobate mind, that experience expanded his knowledge of himself and stalled any such thought for quite some time. It had been somehow necessary, that touching, that closeness, that body heat, that caressing.

For the first time he realized the difference between knowledge and experience, and that there is more than one way to know.

So, Horace, said Miss Hedgeson. To sum up. Tell us, What exactly, is tropism?

An orientation of an organism, usually by growth rather than by movement, in response to an external stimulus.

Horace looked around and the room was dark, unpeopled; he heard the faint split-second echo of his voice as he sat there, his bare bottom on the cold chair. He began to feel silly—silly, he was sure, the way a man about to be hanged feels silly, with a rope about his neck. He stood, looking around the empty room, half hoping to see someone there. Seeing no one, he picked up his gun and stepped out the door. He walked down the hall, past Mrs. Clark's room, Mr. Potter's, Mr. Johnson's, and Mrs. Garcia's, where he had studied English, history, and Spanish. As he walked down the stairwell at the end of the building, his feet smarted against the cold steel steps of the stairs. He began to sneeze, his body chilled by the reentry into the outside, though it was no cooler than earlier.

Along the great rectangle of a building, leading from the school to the gymnasium, was a long, covered walkway. As he walked along he kept his eyes and ears open for the mysterious presence. Horace could hear the sounds of students walking to and fro, the clamorous electronic school bell announcing the end and beginning of classes, one guy running after another, laughing and out of breath, who has told his girl friend that he saw him with another "babe," the sound of two girls arguing over the outcome of their favorite soap opera, the sound of lady teachers, their high heels clicking, on the way to the principal's office . . .

What had changed him? Could he have swung so far in such a short time? The summer that followed that first year of high school did something to Horace. Suddenly he became fully aware of his responsibilities as a man, and the possibilities of his being a homosexual frightened him beyond reason.

His grandfather began to take a special interest in him, encouraging him to think about sports in the fall, asking him about girl friends. He would ask Horace to drive him around, showing him off as his near-about grown grandboy. Look a there, don't he look a lot like Sammy? He sure does. Wants to be a scientist, he does. Don't know nothing about it, but spect he'll do fine. Why, he's a Cross ain't he? We always do fine when we sets our minds to it. Yes, we do. A fine boy. Right fine, indeed.

Conversely, Horace became very fond of his grandfather, noticing his age as it gracefully overtook him. He noticed him falter a bit more when he walked, his shuffle getting slower. He noticed how his back, still straight, had a little more of a forward lean to it. Some Sunday mornings his grandfather asked him to shave him. On the back porch Horace would lather up the sagging brown face and slowly, tenderly pull the old safety razor across those brown jowls, paying particular attention to the folds of flesh and the stiff bristles he might have missed. His grandfather would chuckle and look at himself in the chipped and slightly distorted mirror, feeling his face after splashing himself with water from the basin. He would wink at Horace and tell him, Much obliged.

How could he tell his grandfather that he was not like him? How could he even consider telling him? How would Ezekiel Cross respond if he knew?

The tennis courts and gym were before him, and he sat down at the end of the walkway, thinking of his grandfather. Early that summer he and his Uncle Lester painted both Zeke's house and Jonnie Mae's house. He remembered the paint white and gleaming, sliding over the sides of the house as easy as light slides across grass in the morning. His grandfather sat under an apple tree, his legs crossed, watching, rubbing his chin, and giving his usual advice.

When they first started, Horace—in the words of his grandfather—got more paint on himself than on the house. But as time went on he got better, finding the hidden rhythm of the brush, the natural lay of the wood.

People would pass by on the road and stop a spell to talk awhile with Zeke, and to see what the two men were about. Zeke sat there, one eye on Horace, the other on Lester, sipping at a Coke, and regaled them with tales of when he was younger.

"You didn't do that, now did you Cousin Zeke?" Six men gathered about him, sitting under that apple tree.

"That I did. Like I said, I wont but fourteen or fifteen—not even Horace's age. I took that gun and I said, 'Mister, now you think you gone take my money, but you owe me two dollars and fifty cents and I aims to take it'—and you know two dollars and fifty cents was a right smart sum back in them days."

"Yeah, it was."

"And he looked at me and said, 'Now, nigger, a little colored boy like you, pulling a gun on a white man is a good way to get yourself kilt.' And I looked him square in the eyes and said, 'Feller, I done worked in your fields for thirteen days. You keep telling me: I pay you end of the week. I pay you end of the week. End of the week come . . . you don't pay me. I ask you when and you say: Gone away from me, boy. I ain't got time for you. I got other things on my mind.' I stuck that gun closer to his face and said, 'Now you think on this a spell.'"

The men slapped their knees and hollered, saying, "No, you didn't do that, Bro Zekiel? No, you didn't."

"So did you take the money, Zeke?"

"Man, yes I did! I took every penny he had." He smiled and rubbed his chin. "It amounted to about ten dollars, and I left. I was smart enough not to go home, but I was dumb enough to go down over to Pickettstown, calling myself hiding out."

"So he put the law in behind you?"

"Yes, sir. You know he did."

"And did they catch up with you?"

"Oh, yeah."

"Well . . . what did they do to you?"

"Well, I tell you. They took me down to the courthouse in Crosstown and they locked my butt up for true. And you better believe this here was one scared Negro."

"They ain't beat you or nothing, did they?"

"No, they roughed me up a right smart, but they didn't punch me or kick me or lay into me with a stick or nothing like that. But it won't pretty. So they sent for my family. And Paw and old Uncle Paul Henry, Paw's brother—you remember him don't you, John? Yeah, he died before Grandpaw did. Back in '49 I believe it was . . . Well, anyway, I stayed in that jailhouse for a whole day. They brought me before the judge, old Judge Flint was his name. I'll never forget. Not till the day I die. I declare I ain't never been that scared in my life."

"Never, Uncle Zeke?"

"Son, not to my recollection. I was one scared soul.

"So, old man Flint he said to me, 'Now, boy, you know you done wrong, don't you?'

"I say, 'Yes, sir.'

"'Now if you was older, you know what would of become of you?'

"I say, 'No, sir.'

"'Now, yes you do, boy. Armed robbery, why, that's a felony. Didn't you know that, boy?'

"I say, 'No, sir.'

"'Well, if you man enough to tote a gun, I spect you man enough to know the law. Now ain't that a reasonable assumption, boy?'

"I say, 'Yes, sir. I reckon it is.'

"Then he got right quiet and leaned forward, looking over a pair of them half glasses, you know, and he say—and his voice was deep, deep, and when he said this his voice got deeper still—and he say, 'Boy, I could lock you up till doomsday.'"

The men all shook their heads. "Uh-uh-um."

"He looked over to Paw and said, 'Boy, this youngin of yours is got to learn his proper place. And respect for the law. I'll let him go, but you know we can't let little black boys run around pulling guns on grown white folks. We just can't have it. What kind of country would this be? Now, like I said, I'll let him go, but you and that other one there with you got to whip him, right here, before this court, before me. And you be sure to whip him good, too.'

"Well, they done it. Uncle Paul Henry, he didn't do too much damage. But let me tell you, old man Thomas Horace Cross, I declare, he put one hurting on this behind. I spect it was cause they made him cough up twenty dollars."

"Bet you didn't do that again."

"Well, let's say I got more sense than to get caught after that."

The men all laughed. His grandfather took a swig from his Coke bottle, and Horace glanced back at him. Zeke wiped his mouth with the back of his hand and winked at Horace. "Boy, ain't you missed a spot right there by the window, there?"

"Yes, sir, I reckon I did."

"Well, get it then."

"Yes, sir."

All the men were looking at him and Lester. The fumes of the paint were making him giddy.

"Now, I remember the time . . ."

Horace stood and walked forwards toward the gym. It was not open, so he looked in through the windows, not seeing very well. He walked around the side of the building where the football bleachers sat and back around to the side of the gym where the football team exits onto the field. Those doors were also closed. Horace sat down, this time in the dirt, picking at the grass.

He began to think about the voice, wondering whether it had indeed left him. He wished it would return and take him away so he would not remember that day. Especially not here, especially not beneath those very windows where he had made the decision to fight this disease, as he had come to think of his sexuality.

He did not like football, nor did he think he could actually join the team that fall, especially since the team had been chosen in the middle of the summer. So he decided he would run track instead, and had no trouble joining the track team. He began running on his own, thinking that it would make a man of him if nothing else would. Horace decided to become a jock, to get rid of his bookworm image and finally go for broke in the social world of the high school.

It was not difficult. He became president of the Spanish Club, vice-president of the National Honor Society, associate editor of the newspaper, president-elect of the Science Club. Now there was no time to consider the problem that had propelled him into this frenzy of activity. He rarely spoke to Gideon, who was baffled by Horace's new aloofness. And perhaps most peculiarly, Horace began to hang around those white students known as "the beautiful people"—the folks with the money, the looks, the brains, and the attitude to be successful, as they saw it. To them Horace was something of a curiosity; his high academic standing, his newfound activism and athleticism gave him a special token place in their number. He was criticized sorely by his fellow black students for getting an attitude, for being an Oreo, for joining this snobbish circle. But he did not dwell on it.

Now he was a legitimate jock and could hang out with the football players and the basketball players and not be put down for his lack of hip and cool. The tall basketball players and the large football players joked around him and considered him one of the fellows. An okay dude. And most importantly he finally began to think about getting a real girl friend, knowing that now it was more than a possibility.

Had the sinful thoughts left him? Had he become normal? Had he changed? There was nothing to change . . . his mind said. You're normal. Of this he had become convinced.

He went to parties. He began dating girls. Gracie Mae Mayfield became his steady. He even had sex with her a few times. When she told him she just could not do it anymore and she hoped he understood, he was relieved. But he didn't think anything of it.

Then one day he had stayed very late after school and had run an extra mile, walking back to the gym to change. One of the members of the football team, Rick Peters, a huge blond boy whose father was a lawyer, had invited Horace and Gracie Mae to his birthday party that Sunday. Horace was pondering his feeling about Rick, telling himself that the sensation he felt in his stomach was camaraderie not attraction, admiration not lust, that Gracie Mae excited him, Rick merely, merely . . .

"Hey, Horace. How's it hanging?"

The gym, a low-ceilinged space, was empty, echoing mutedly against the tiles and cinderblock walls, and only Gideon stood at the end of the corridor by the boys' locker room. He stood there smiling, devilish, and cunning. His neck, the neck Horace knew all too well, curved in its brown and seductive way; Gideon's very stance smelled of sex to Horace.

He wanted to yell at Gideon to go away. "Hi," he said coolly, and walked swiftly toward the locker room without looking at Gideon. Gideon followed him in. Horace wanted to say something about this being a men's locker room, but decided just to dress and go. Dress and go. And ignore him.

"Horace, what is the matter with you? Why have you been avoiding me? Man, I don't want any trouble. I just want to know."

Suddenly a part of Horace became aware of the locker room, of the musky, funky, sweaty, pissy, sweatsocky, jockstrappy-smelling room, and he knew that he was lying and that made him angrier. "I want you to leave me alone, Gideon."

"I beg your pardon."

"I said . . . I'm saying . . . Gideon, what we did. What you do. It's wrong."

"Wrong?"

"Yeah. Wrong." He thought of holding Gideon, warm and smooth in his arms; he remembered the heat, the taste of his mouth, the feel of his hair, his scent. And he thought, Which is more wrong, sex with a man, or lying? "Yeah, wrong."

Gideon stood, stunned. After a spell he smiled. "Okay, Horace. No sweat. No sweat, at all." Gideon turned his back to go, but stopped.

"It's just wrong, Gideon."

Horace had taken off his T-shirt, his back to Gideon.

"My, oh my, but you have been doing some developing." Gideon stepped toward Horace. Gideon walked up behind Horace. His hands glided over the width of Horace's shoulders as though he were checking a wing span.

"Don't touch me."

"Oh, come on. Nobody's here." Gideon wrapped his arms around Horace's waist, placing his head on his shoulders, and releasing a catlike sigh.

"I said, quit, you faggot." Horace grabbed Gideon's hands and forced him back.

"Oh, Horace." Gideon was almost laughing, and the fact that he thought Horace was kidding made him angrier. Once again he reached for Horace, this time for his hips. But Horace grabbed both hands, firmly, hoping he would cause him pain.

"I said quit, damn it." His teeth were clenched.

They stood before one another. Slowly, it seemed, Gideon became aware of Horace's seriousness.

Gideon snatched his hands away. "So, who pissed in your cornflakes, Cowboy?"

"Leave me alone, Gid. Just leave me the fuck alone."

"Oh, come on, Horace. What's gotten into you?" As if nothing had just happened, Gideon grabbed Horace by the wrists, and winked slyly, grinning. "Come on, let's do it here. Right here. It'll be great. No one's here. Nobody will know." He began pulling Horace toward the showers.

"Gideon!"

"Come on. It'll be a turn-on."

"Stop."

"Oh, come on. I know you'll like it. You want to. Come on."

Horace hit Gideon. Full square in the mouth, so quickly he himself did not realize what he had done, so hard he could not doubt he meant to do it. But had he wanted to hit Gideon, or himself for not wanting to hit him? Gideon staggered; blood appeared on his lip. Tears welled up in his eyes, along with disbelief, rage, disappointment, betrayal, hurt. His open mouth formed an almost comical and silent O.

Horace noticed the blood and felt sick. Suddenly he wanted to rush to him, to grab him, to kiss him, to rock him and beg him for forgiveness. But he would not. Ever. And he steeled his jaw and looked away. "Sorry. But you wouldn't stop."

"Bastard. You fucking hit me."

"I can't, Gid. Not anymore. It's just wrong."

"Why did you fucking hit me?"

"I told you. You shouldn't have grabbed me."

"You didn't have to hit me. Damn you." His voice was pain. Not like pain. Not full of pain. The thing itself. Pain. Horace felt sorry, so sorry, for causing this pain, and he knew it had not come from his fist alone. He never suspected he could inflict such a thing on another. He imagined another world, another place, in which he could gladly have complied with Gideon's wish and fallen into lusty, steamy, lascivious abandon—but no.

"I'm sorry."

"Go to hell." Gideon went to the mirror and dabbed at the wounded lip. Sobs threatened. He rinsed his face with water.

"Gideon, please understand . . . I—"

Gideon spun around, and Horace tensed. Gideon had the mean, evil look of a hungry jackal. "Fuck you, Horace Cross." He snatched up his books. "Damn you."

"Gid—"

"Don't 'Gid' me, man. I'm going to fix your ass. I know what you're thinking. I see what you think you're doing with your 'new' friends. But remember, black boy, you heard it here first: You're a faggot, Horace. You know? You're a faggot. You can run, you can hide, but when the shit comes down . . . you suck cock, you don't eat pussy."

"You're sickening, Gideon."

"I'm sickening. At least I know what I am."

"Go to hell, Gideon."

"Hey." Gideon raised his hand in resignation. "Just like old times." He touched his busted lip and gave a mocking wink. "Love you, baby." He turned and walked out, leaving Horace with himself, with the smelly ghosts of the men who, for all these months, he had told himself he did not lust after, with the realization that it was a lie and that soon, soon and very soon he would fall, and fall hard.

Wait . . . he heard them again, the beating of wings, and he imagined them mauve and full, he could see them in his mind. They stopped. Over by the football field. Horace hopped up and ran, his genitals flapping against his thighs.

At the gate to the fence around the football field Horace stopped. There through the bleachers he could see it, standing in the middle of the field. It was obscured by shadows, but it clearly was a manlike figure, dark, clad in what appeared to be thick, black robes. On its head was a helmet that shone silver, and it carried a huge scimitar that carried the faint glint of moonlight. And the wings. The curve of the wings' shoulders stood at least two feet above the head; the longest feathers almost touched the ground. The hand that did not grip the sword beckoned to Horace, Come, come. Horace could hear the whispers of many voices in his ear, whispers whispering, *For behold, the day cometh, that shall scorch as an oven;* whispering whispers, *and all the proud, yea, and all that do wickedly, shall be stubble,* Come, come. Horace, afraid to do otherwise, stepped forward slowly. Come. The voices whispered whispering, *But unto you that fear my name shall the Sun of righteousness arise with healing in his wings,* whispered, whisperings, whispered, Come.

Horace heard a car door slam, and, startled, turned to see two cars over by the tennis courts. Out stepped five men, youngish looking, perhaps still in high school. They were white. Horace froze on the twenty-yard line; the specter stood at the fifty-yard line, motioning. Come. Come. Horace saw the two six-packs of beer they put on the top of the car. They snapped the cans out from the plastic loops that held them together and gulped down the beer. Charlie Daniel's Band blasted on the radio. He could make out only bits and snatches of their conversation:

"You know that ole Ford truck of my daddy's?"

"Uh-huh."

"Well, last night I raced it against a brand new turbo-charged Trans Am. And won."

"You's a lying."

"I be damned if I am."

"No, Pernel, I believe him. Them new cars ain't got the pickup it takes to stick with them oldens."

"Shit."

In Horace's ears whispers whispered whispering: Come. Come. The angel merely held out its hand, now, leaning forward. Horace took another step.

Then: "Wait a minute. Do you see something over there?"

"What the hell is that?"

"What?"

Headlights. Horace stood as still as a caught coon.

"A naked nigger."

"With a gun?"

"What the hell—"

"Get him!"

The dark figure was gone, vanished, it did not take to the wind, its large wings extended, beating the air without mercy. It simply ceased to be there. And there stood Horace, the object of a few things that would not simply be gone.

He dashed for the parking lot and the puke-green Buick. He heard the footsteps of the men just behind him and remembered from track not to look back. His testicles began to ache from flapping so hard between his legs. He heard a car starting up. The headlights swung around onto him; his shadow stretched before him, ghastly and distorted. He heard somebody say, "Jesus." There was a low fence before him and without hesitation he leaped, leading with his right foot, leaning forward, the gun clutched tight in his hand. He cleared it gracefully, but he landed wrong on his right foot, and a pain shot through his entire leg. He heard somebody say, "Christ!" Ignoring the pain, he bolted for the car, which was a few yards away. The car door popped when he opened it, and as if to the rescue the voice came from out of nowhere saying: The gun, fool. Use the fucking gun.

Horace leaned over the car door and took aim at the fellow in the lead. He shot just before his feet, the bullet biting into the dirt. Somebody said, "Lord! That nigger's crazy!"

He shot again, this time hitting the second in the foot. "God-damn!" the man howled and hit the ground, clutching his foot.

Horace slipped down into the car seat, the coldness of the vinyl shocking him. He could hear the roar of the car coming to block his departure. He patted the accelerator. Turned the key. The car didn't start. He turned the key again. The engine turned over. He slammed the gear into reverse and wheeled behind the car that was expecting him to go forward. He heard a rebel yell, and his blood ran chill. The other car was coming. A Ford. Horace could see the headlights. He jerked the car into first, swerving around the approaching car, which barely avoided the other, a Chevy. They both swung around after the Buick. The Ford at his left. Horace went to the right. The Chevy zoomed in from the right. He skidded left. The Ford came back from the left. Just like in the movies, he slammed on the brakes. Put the car into reverse. Arced around, bashing into the Ford. He shifted to first just in time to move away. The Chevy rammed into the Ford.

Not looking back, Horace zipped up and out of the parking lot, out the gate of the driveway, the tires making a screeching sound as he hit the highway and flew down the road at eighty miles an hour, listening to the demon laughing in his head, wondering exactly what that dark figure had actually been. Wondering if, perhaps, there had stood his salvation.

Old Demonology

. . . And so forth.
Not that success, for him, is sure, infallible
But never has he been afraid to reach.
His lesions are legion.
But reaching is his rule.

—GWENDOLYN BROOKS

James Malachai Greene
Confessions

"Look at me."

There really are no words to describe how she made me feel. Not that the words don't exist . . . it's just that the words leave me. I am incapable of fixing the right words to the right feelings and the images and the reasons; she was neither cause nor effect for me—she was total affect. Affection.

"What do you see?"

The light of the room, dim, would envelop her, surround her like the glow of a lamp. The air, no matter the time of year, no matter the weather, in that room, would be thick and hold just the hint of musk from armpits and pubic hair, my musk, her musk mingling together with her perfume, her fragrance, lightly sandalwood and cinnamon, sweet.

"Do you really see me?"

The hold she had over me was oriental, like a geisha's. I was her thrall. Her handservant. But she was my possession.

"Me?"

The way she would hold her breast, cup it as though she were about to coax milk; the way the nipple looked, deep brown and round against her sand-colored skin; the way it would perk up in my mouth, my tongue sensing the twitching and the hardening, softly; the sounds of her ooos and aaas; the way her tongue, a fat pink snake, would coat her upper lip with a sweet venom; the way her body felt, smooth, soft, and brown.

"Do you?"

My tongue knew every crevice of her body from the indenture at the base of her neck to the mole on her left shoulder, from the birthmark on the inside of her left thigh to the curve of her waist just above her hip to the tendon's flex just above her heel; from the taste of the juices of her mouth to the lush redness between her legs.

"Do you even want to, really?"

Inside her was another world. Her legs folded behind me, her breath in shorter and shorter puffs, tickling my ears. The total, the sum, the smell of our bodies, the room, the heat we created, expended, the sounds, not just of our breathing, but of the clock on the wall, the house settling, mice in the garret, the taste of her saliva and my saliva and old tea and wine, all seemed to add and add, the intensity beginning to glow. There are times that one extra caress would take me away, send me over the edge, as though I were outside my body watching two undulating forms violently trying to become one, groping deeper and deeper into one another's soul until . . .

"Are you even capable?"

The metaphysical poets called it a little death. I think they were right.

I have lied. To myself. When Anne died, things were not "idyllic" and pastoral and perfect. Memories have a way of censoring themselves, calling up only the sweet, the pleasant, the joyful . . . rarely the pain or the hurt or the uncertainty. "Things" had never really been so smooth or so dear. Perhaps for Anne. But the truth is I'll never know. And therein lies the problem. I believe she was completely unknowable. That lack of knowledge hurts. Even now. I would talk to her, intimately, revealing, confessing, explaining as though she were the perfect Mother of Jesus, and she would hold and coddle and comfort. But she never confessed or revealed to me. She would talk—oh, she was a master of small talk, of conversation, of changing the subject, of evasion. I knew I didn't know her. I would think: But how much does any man know his woman, or a woman her man? And I would convince myself that it is normal to have that distance, for one-sided relationships to exist. But she could also be cruel.

It took a long time for me to actually "come to God." I had accepted that I had the Call from my teenaged years, sitting on a mourners' bench during a revival meeting, weeping real tears of fear—for I had a fear of God then, not a love, just that Old Testament awe of the Most High, and I believed in him as firmly as I believed in spring and autumn, as firmly as I believed in the power of fire and the cold death that awaits beneath the ocean. "He's real," goes the song, and I sang it with true conviction.

I was baptized at thirteen, given the right hand of fellow-ship, joined the usher board, worked on this committee and that, studied the Bible with a true verve, reading it over and over, much to my grandmother's pleasure. I became the model Christian in the eyes of the congregation of First Baptist. Visiting the sick, teaching Sunday school, all with nods of approval from the deacon board and the mothers of the church, all with a stern look of approval from my grandmother.

By the time I was fourteen, Isador had gone off to school. Franklin had proven to be a serious student, a hard worker in the fields, and an excellent athlete, respectful and dutiful. But in the end, just like his uncles, he loved women more than he loved the Lord. So I became the pious one, the holy one. This drove a wedge between us as he started high school and started going out on dates, while I, the Bible-studying, humble little brother, remained behind. He couldn't tell me the dirty jokes he and his friends chuckled over, or the nasty pranks they had pulled, or exactly what he did to those girls he took out in Malachai's old blue Ford. He never tried.

Going to college, however, turned the tables for me, something no one seemed to have considered. Most families worry about sending their children off into the world, but my grandmother, who had seen so much disappointment and failure, had put her unflinching and stolid faith in me and I knew it. And she knew that I knew it, having no reason to doubt me, convinced that her hour was near. Yet when I stepped through the gates of those hallowed halls at North Carolina Central, I became acquainted with the intoxicating rush of freedom. I was far from the roving eyes of the deacons and deaconesses. I was in my own hands.

Looking back, I see my escapades were relatively innocuous, no different from the average freshman debauchery, but at the time I was sure I was the antichrist come, and was perfectly happy to be so. I slept with anything that was willing. I got drunk almost every weekend of my freshman year, many times during the week as well—until I almost flunked my freshman courses. And I went on, from every pillar and post that held something titillating, my only regret being that my aunts and my grandmother never seemed to suspect that I was a hypocrite, a liar. For when I came home I still read the Scriptures in church and taught Bible school, only to return to school and recruit the first co-ed who gave me a willing glance. I realize that this was the true sin.

I met Anne during the second semester of my sophomore year. I didn't sleep with her for almost two years; bedding her had not been my original goal. She fascinated me. She was one of the militant leaders on campus. This was 1971, the immediate aftermath of the civil rights movement and the student uprisings of the sixties. And though we didn't realize it then, students were becoming less radical, less questioning, less vocal. So Anne stood out, shockingly.

I felt something like defeat the first time I saw her. There had been nothing in my life to compare to this dashiki-garbed, lemon-skinned, Afroed radical. I amused her at first. She was from the privileged black bourgeoisie of upstate New York. Educated at a fine prep school, having spent a year studying in the south of France before college, she defiantly chose North Carolina Central over Wellesley and Sarah Lawrence. To her I was a smart, though naive, country boy, with fresh chickenshit between my toes, hayseeds in my hair, and hands callused from hoeing. The genuine article. Big, strong, black, and painfully sincere. Though I had become adept at the biting and sucking and kissing involved in the more direct contacts with the fairer sex, I was clumsy and inept in expressing anything as subtle and strong as the emotion I held for her. I was not in love at the time, but bound by admiration, wonder, and awe.

She kept me around. To talk to. To demonstrate her willingness to associate with those of less sophistication and worldliness. She wanted to hear every detail of my growing up, how my family lived, what we ate. I would follow her to her meetings, to her rallies, to her events. Almost a lapdog. She was sleeping with other men—sometimes I was convinced with a multitude. Yet I went for months before even attempting to kiss her. I had stopped sleeping around, and returned to an almost chaste soul, my worship now being this mysterious force named Anne Gazelle Dubois.

One autumn day, one of the few days in which there were no meetings for her to rush to, she turned to me as we stood beneath a huge cottonwood tree on campus and asked, "Why haven't you tried to screw me?"

I didn't know whether to laugh, cry, or just stare. She had light brown eyes and sometimes she focused them with such unbridled sincerity that they belied her canniness. I kissed her long and hard.

"So you aren't a faggot?"

I chuckled.

"Good."

The first time she took me into her bed I was impotent. "Are you sure you're not a faggot?" she asked. We laughed at the entire situation and went out for Chinese food. I never had that problem with her again.

But she never truly gave herself to me, never opened. Especially not then. The people—the people were her mission, her conviction, her life. This was her ambition, her raison d'être. When I confessed jealousy she accused me of weakness, of being out of step with the movement, of losing perspective of the way of hope for "the people."

"That's bullshit, Anne. I love you."

"'Love'? Come on, preacherman. Don't you see? Your idea of 'love' is a foolish Western concept the white man has created to enslave—who? Me. Woman. No, sir, Mr. Man, I'm my own woman."

"Anne, I love you."

"Yeah, I love you too, little boy."

"I love you."

"You've got my body, Goddamn it. You have my friendship. Leave my fucking soul alone!"

Was it beauty? I often ask myself: Was it the fact that she was so light and I had become enamored of the situation—as Franklin says, some psychological impediment? Did I want to sleep with a white woman, and found in her a way to have both without paying the price? I stopped seeing her. I stopped seeing anyone. My relatively short life as a Casanova was over. I took my heartbreak to be God's way of calling me back to the roost.

After receiving my education degree and my teacher's certificate, I told my grandmother and my aunts I would stay in Durham for a while, teaching, and that I had decided to attend seminary before I sought ordination as a minister. I was certain my grandmother would cry; I'm sure she did, but not in anyone's presence. She began telling people that she had known it all along, I knew that boy was going to make a preacher. I knew it. My aunts cooked cakes and pies for me.

I taught in the Wake County Public School System first in Raleigh, then in Cary, and remained in Durham, taking a few night classes and summer courses at Southeastern. But there was little joy in my life, I realize now; it was more the life of a monk. Existence in that grey industrial tobacco town depressed me, causing me to fear growing old and alone, even as a preacher. I had no desire to see women.

One day, coming out of the bank, I saw her. I had been sure she had fled the town upon graduation, gone to Spain or Brazil, forsaking and forgetting her heated speeches of two years ago. I asked her to have a hamburger with me. She agreed.

"Changed your mind?"

She had become a social worker. Placing and overseeing the care of foster children in Durham county.

"No. Have you?"

Something about her seemed older, less reckless, yet no less potent. In fact she seemed to have grown in determination.

"Well, preacherman. You know what I found out?" She put out a cigarette. "Some men ain't worth the trouble. Some men are."

"Had some trouble? Some guy mess you over?"

"Everything is fine. Now. You know how it can be."

"Do I?"

"I think you do."

"I'm sorry."

"Don't be sorry. I'm the fool."

But I became her fool all over again. Gladly. Isn't it amazing? How so little a thing can change your whole view of things? No longer was Durham grey, and no longer did the prospect of growing old fill me with dread. I saved enough to quit teaching and went to seminary full-time to complete my third year. Anne and I were married in Tims Creek, a place she fell in love with and insisted she must live in, much to her parents' active disdain. Her father was a doctor, transplanted from Oklahoma; her mother, who could easily have passed for white, was an art historian who worked as an assistant curator for a small university museum. She prided herself on being able to trace her lineage back to Thomas Jefferson, something Anne abhorred. Her parents did not approve of me. I was too dark, too poor, not Episcopalian, not traveled, not right—Anne loved it. And my family loved Anne, and was doubly proud that I had snared such an attractive fish, though I suspect they doubted she would be happy living in Tims Creek. They were prouder still the day I was ordained at First Baptist.

There was yet another two years in Durham as I went back to graduate school for my masters in education—ministers of small Southern churches don't earn a real salary, and it was going to be necessary for me to have another, complementary profession.

Yet through all the success I don't think there was ever a moment I felt I knew Anne, and I was always vexed by her self-contained ease.

Then one day I was not feeling at all well and left school early. It was about three o'clock in the afternoon, the middle of spring, cars and trucks honking horns, students from the universities milling around town. I was as innocent as a lamb, as unsuspecting—though underneath my consciousness I probably did suspect. I walked into the house, expecting Anne to be out in the field, but there were signs that she was home. There was a jacket across a chair in the kitchen, a worn, dusty denim jacket. I could picture the man it belonged to, tall, big, maybe a slight pot belly. A worker, maybe a loader at the tobacco factory, or maybe a truck driver. I still don't know, nor do I truly care, who he was. Nor do I know whether I did the right thing, really. "The right thing." As if there is a right or a wrong when you are placed in such a situation.

I walked into the bedroom, without warning. Just walked in. I was already despairing, yet I hoped against hope that the jacket belonged to a plumber or an electrician or a delivery boy, though I knew no pipes were broken, no wires needed repair, and there was nothing to be delivered. But I could not live with an iota of doubt, not a chance. I had to know. So I walked in, plainly, calmly, and witnessed my evidence.

The man was putting on his pants, in no tremendous hurry, which spited me even more. He was in many ways what I had pictured, older, grey hairs gnawing at his scalp. He didn't look at me. Anne did. She looked directly into my eyes, neither smiling nor laughing nor crying. She just looked. There was no indication of regret. She just looked.

I turned without saying a word and walked out the front door. I sat down on the bottom step, feeling the illness that had sent me home originally. I saw the neighbor lady, a middle-aged Polish woman with steel-grey hair, bringing home her groceries. Buses passed by; a stray dog stopped in front of me and sniffed before running along. It was a miraculously beautiful day; the heavens were clear and blue, with thin clouds drifting high, high above. Only the smell of tobacco in the air mixing with automobile fumes and the distant hum of the interstate reminded me that all was not glory and wonder.

I sat there for hours. I suspect my cuckolder left via the back door. I don't know. I didn't care. At one point my paralysis began to worry me. But I literally could not do anything about it. Finally I felt so ill I had to go in. She sat in the chair over which the jacket had been draped. She put out her cigarette.

"Is it so bad, really?"

I wanted desperately to lie down. I could feel myself swaying. I had no intention of discussing anything with her. I stood at the door to the bedroom and stopped. I realized I was not going to sleep in that bed.

"Is it really so bad?"

I looked at her and stumbled toward the guest bedroom, closing the door behind me. The bed was cluttered with junk, clothes, yarn, needles, wrapping paper. I pushed it all to the floor and literally fell on the bed face first. There was a knock. I said nothing. Another knock. "Jimmy?" I said nothing. The knob turned.

"Jimmy. I'm . . . I know you don't want to hear any contrite remarks. And I know there's nothing I can really say. You know I love you, don't you? Jimmy, he was nothing to me. He is nothing to me."

I did not stir.

"Damn it, Jimmy. Say something, you Goddamn pussy!"

I sat up, my face covered with sweat, and looked at her, the representative, the symbol of all I held dear in the world, the very personification of my faith, my respect, my reason, here, before my eyes was my own fallibility, my own weaknesses and strengths, color began to fade in the world, and I knew distantly that I would grow old and grey and that there was not a damned thing I could do about it, and that I was small and vulnerable and bruised oh, so easily, and that the things in which I had put my trust were only as strong as the trust I had put in them, and that ultimately I was alone and unknown and unknowable, just as she was unknowable, alone, across the room at that moment puzzled by my silence and afraid, and I opened my mouth, and released my fear, my pain, my hurt in mounds of stench and food all over the clothes and yarn and needles and wrapping paper.

"Oh, my God. Jimmy."

Place: The dining room in the home of Jonnie Mae
   Greene.
Time: Thanksgiving Day, 1983, 5:15 P.M.

EZEKIEL CROSS *sits at head of a long table;* REV. HEZEKIAH BARDEN *sits to Zeke's left;* JIMMY GREENE *sits on the right;* LESTER GREENE *sits in the middle;* JONNIE MAE *sits on the opposite end to* ZEKE. RACHEL,

REBECCA, *and* RUTHESTER *go back and forth in the kitchen bringing out dishes and plates. The table is set with white linen and covered with food; a plump turkey sits in the middle. The room is full of family pictures. Old sepia-tone photographs of stern-faced men and women, all unsmiling. Polaroids. Graduation portraits. The voices of the three sisters husbands are heard, faintly, from the kitchen.*

ZEKE (*to* REV. BARDEN): But I don't necessarily believe we should be raising money for that purpose. A church's first duty—

JONNIE MAE: Zeke—excuse me, Reverend, for interrupting—but Zeke, where is that grandboy of yours? He knows we start Thanksgiving dinner at five sharp.

ZEKE: I don't know, Jonnie Mae. He said he had to do something with his friends. Said he'd be here on time.

JONNIE MAE: Well, he ain't. "Friends." You mean them white boys he been hanging round with?

ZEKE: I spect.

JONNIE MAE: Zeke, you better have a talk with that boy. It ain't doing him no good to take up with them boys like he's doing. People start to talk. And I don't like it.

ZEKE: Well, I aim to.

RUTHESTER (*placing the cranberry sauce next to the turkey*): Well, you all had better start now. It'll get cold. We don't want that.

BARDEN: No, ma'am. We don't want that. Do we, Reverend? (*He winks at* JIMMY.)

JIMMY (*slightly preoccupied*): No. No, we don't.

JONNIE MAE (*checks the clock*): Well, may's well go on and start. Horace should know better than be late like this. (*In a sunnier tone:*) Reverend Barden. Will you do us the honor?

BARDEN: Why, of course, Sister Greene. Let us pray: Our Father, we come before you today as humble as we know how. You've brought us through another year, and we are thankful that you have allowed us to work and prosper and praise your holy . . . (*Continues to pray.*)

(*Door is heard in the background.* HORACE *enters. There is an earring in his left ear.*)

HORACE: Sorry I'm—

RACHEL: Ssssh!

(HORACE *realizes* BARDEN *is praying and bows his head.*)

BARDEN: . . . in that world that will have no end. We pray in Jesus' name.

ALL: Amen.

HORACE (*moving toward his place at table*): I'm sorry I'm late.

JONNIE MAE (*reaching for the plate of candied yams*): You *should* be sorry. Your aunts work hard all day to produce this fine meal, and you ain't got respect enough to show up on time.

HORACE (*looking sheepishly toward his aunts*): Sorry.

JONNIE MAE (*to* JIMMY): You gone carve the turkey, son? (*To* REBECCA:) You looking after that cake? It should be about ready, don't you think? (*To* HORACE:) And where were you all—

(JONNIE MAE *sees the earring in Horace's ear and dropped the spoon and a dish of corn onto her plate, causing everyone to flinch and look up.*)

Good Lord, boy. What have you done?

(*Everyone looks at* HORACE, *puzzled.*)

HORACE: Ma'am? I—

JONNIE MAE: He has pierced his ear! Pierced his ear. Boy, have you lost your mind?

HORACE: I—

ZEKE: Well, I be dadgummed. You are crazy, aren't you? What got into your head to do such a th—

RACHEL: Horace, how could you, you should know—

REBECCA: You ain't got a lick of sense, have you?

LESTER: Well, I kind of like it, my—

RACHEL: Shut up, Lester.

JONNIE MAE: A pierced ear.

(BARDEN *sits back and grins, shaking his head, amused.* JIMMY *seems bewildered by the reaction of the women.*)

REBECCA: Why would you do such a fool thing?

(*Everyone looks to* HORACE *for an answer; he unsuccessfully tries to suppress a smile.*)

JONNIE MAE (*gravely*): Wipe that smirk off your face, young man. This is not a laughing matter. You may think it is, but I think it's downright disgraceful.

RUTHESTER: Why, Horace?

LESTER: Well, if you asked me—

RUTHESTER: Nobody asked you, Lester.

HORACE: All the guys. That is . . . the group, the boys . . . I . . . we—

JONNIE MAE (*to* ZEKE): Uh-huh. You see, Zeke? You see? What did I tell you? Now it starts this way, but how will it end? (*Stands.*) No better sense than to go on and follow whatever them white fools do. You'd follow them to hell, wouldn't you? I—

RUTHESTER (*moving to comfort her*): Mamma, it ain't that bad. He just—

JONNIE MAE: He *just* pierced his ear. Like some little girl. Like one of them perverts.

JIMMY: Mamma, it's really not that big a deal. Boys pierce their ears nowadays all the time. It's not thought of as—

LESTER: It reminds me of—

REBECCA: Hush, Lester.

JONNIE MAE: No big deal? Don't you see? Zeke, you got to put a stop to this now. Who knows what them boys will have this fool doing next. Having him out stealing. Wind up in jail. Dead. And them sitting back laughing at him.

RUTHESTER: Mamma, you should sit down now and eat. We can talk about this later. You don't want your food to get cold.

(JONNIE MAE *mumbles to herself and sits.*)

ZEKE: Take that thing out of your ear, boy. I ain't gone stand for it.

HORACE: But Granddaddy, I just got it put in. I can't just take it out.

ZEKE: I said take it out. Now.

HORACE: I can't.

ZEKE: Boy, don't you back-sass me—

HORACE: But—

ZEKE: Out.

JIMMY: Uncle Zeke, I think what he means is that he'll have to wait a bit before he can take it out. The lobe has to heal.

ZEKE (*to* JIMMY): You may think this is funny, Jimmy, but I don't. (*To* HORACE:) It's coming out. And those friends of yours. This group. No more. You understand me? You're to leave them alone and they're to leave you be.

HORACE: But—

ZEKE: Now eat. We'll take this up later.

JONNIE MAE: That's the way it's got to be.

REBECCA: But Horace, you have to admit you do spend too much time with those boys.

JONNIE MAE: Any time is too much time. He don't understand. He just don't understand.

HORACE (*testily*): Understand what? Try me!

(JONNIE MAE *is taken aback at being questioned, and everyone looks at* HORACE *in disbelief.*)

RUTHESTER: Horace!

HORACE: But they're my friends.

JONNIE MAE: Friends? Friends! My God, the day that one of my own people would defend a white man at my table!

HORACE: But they're different. They aren't from around here. They—

RACHEL: They're white, ain't they?

HORACE: Yeah, but—

REBECCA: You black, ain't you?

HORACE: But they don't—

RUTHESTER: He's just foolish. He just don't understand.

HORACE: They—

REBECCA: After all the white man's done to us, you gone take up behind him and do everything he tells you to do. Boy, I thought—

HORACE (*angrily*): You all don't understand! You're all bigots! You don't know them! You—

(JONNIE MAE *raises her hand in a sharp motion and* HORACE *instantly, instinctively, stops.*)

JONNIE MAE (*calmly*): Young man. I do believe you have forgotten yourself. (*Pause.*) This is your family. We are the ones who worked hard, looked after you. Remember? The ones who want to see you grow into a fine young man. Somebody who's gone make us proud. You have no idea what hard is, young man. You have no idea what bigotry is. No idea what prejudging is. No idea what hate is.

HORACE: I—

JONNIE MAE (*impatiently*): Let me finish. Do you have any idea how many white men have called me girl and aunt? Out of disrespect? Out of hatefulness? How many white men called your late Uncle Malachai—God rest him—boy and uncle? Do you? And that's just the beginning. Don't you even get the idea in your head to call me a bigot, boy. I don't qualify for prejudice. I know all the facts already. (*To* ZEKE:) Well, you see? You see what I mean now? You see?

ZEKE (*to* HORACE): Well, I do believe you have lost your mind. Get up. I think you have forfeited your Thanksgiving dinner. Ain't got no thanks in you, have you? No, I don't reckon you do. You have not behaved like a gentleman. Your aunts, who've been good to you all your life, and good Reverend Barden here, have had to witness something they shouldn't have. Now you apologize and go on home. Just go on home. And we'll discuss this later. Go on, now. I mean it.

RUTHESTER: Oh, Uncle Zeke. He—

ZEKE: He's got to leave.

(HORACE *stands in silence and exits.*)

ZEKE: You work. You talk. You try your darndest, and they just go astray.

BARDEN: You can raise them, but you can't think for them.

JONNIE MAE: That's so true. I know. Lord knows I do.

JIMMY: I'll have a talk with him.

RACHEL: What will you say to him?

LESTER: Well, I think . . .

JONNIE MAE: Eat your dinner, Lester.

That is what finally got to Horace, isn't it? I keep asking myself. He, just like me, had been created by this society. He was a son of the community, more than most. His reason for existing, it would seem, was for the salvation of his people. But he was flawed as far as the community was concerned. First, he loved men; a simple, normal deviation, but a deviation this community would never accept. And second, he didn't quite know who he was. That, I don't fully understand, for they had told him, taught him from the cradle on. I guess they didn't reckon the world they were sending him into was different from the world they had conquered, a world peopled with new and hateful monsters that exacted a different price.

What has happened to us? Can I cry out like the prophet Jonah and ask God to guide my hand and direct me toward the proper remedy? Once, oh once, this beautiful, strong, defiant, glorious group could wrestle the world down, unshackle themselves, part seas, walk on water, rise on the winds. What happened? Why are we now sick and dying? All the sons and daughters groomed to lead seem to have fled . . . How, Lord? How? The war is not over. The enemy is encamped over the hill. With the morning they will come storming over the wall. They will pillage and plunder, rape our wives and children, destroy our crops, empty our storehouses, deface our holy temple. How, Lord? How? How can we defend ourselves and grow strong again? How can we regain the power to lift up our heads and sing? When will the Host of Hosts visit us with favor and strength?

Jonah. It seems so easy to hide, so easy to die. I see now that not only is life a struggle, it is a war. And it is not enough merely to fight the good fight.

Anne was diagnosed as having a malignant cancer of the pancreas. It was found in April; she went into the hospital for the last time in May; she died in the early part of June, not because of the cancer, ironically, but because of a problem with her lungs during the operation. She was thirty-seven. Strangely enough, it hit my grandmother the hardest. Perhaps she wanted to see grandchildren. Perhaps she had loved Anne more than I knew. Perhaps it was just the idea that Anne was seemingly so good, and so young.

Jonnie Mae herself died last year.

I have never lost my fear of the dead. No matter how many eulogies I preach, no matter how many funerals I attend, perhaps no matter how old I get, I will fear the dead. In my dreams the dead rise, and they wear armor and are armed with bows and arrows and swords and guns and knives. Perhaps the fight goes on. Perhaps the war will be won.

The waitress wore a button that read "Sue" on the left breast-pocket of her fine, white polyester uniform. Jimmy couldn't help smiling in disbelief at the way she smacked her gum and threw her hips out like a floozie, wondering if she realized how much of a caricature of herself she appeared.

"So folks, what's it going to be, huh?" Her impatient manner made Jimmy wince, the way she rolled her eyes and refused to look at them. She flipped a page on her little pad and stood there, poised with her pencil, smacking her gum, and staring out the window.

"What you gone get, Jimmy?" Zeke had to put on his glasses, a huge pair of hornrims, to read the catsup-stained menu.

"Well, the hamburger platter looks good to me."

The waitress began to scribble. "You want home fries or regular?"

"Regular. No. Make it home fries."

She poked her tongue in her cheek, shot him an almost sinister glance and, flicking her hair back with a horselike motion of her head, began to erase.

"I reckon I'll get that too. You all do cook your meat clean through, don't you?"

"What you mean 'clean through'? We cook it, ain't that enough?"

"Well, I mean, there ain't no red juice squirting up. Don't like my meat like that. Makes me sick to my stomach. Rather have it burnt."

"The meat's kind of thick," she said in a deadpan voice. "It's hard to cook it all the way through without burning it."

Zeke frowned. "Okay then, I'll take a plate of your barbecue. You all kill the hogs yourself?"

"No. You want slaw, tater salad, or french fries with that?"

"Oh, let me see. Slaw, I spect. No. No. I'll take your tater salad. You use eggs?"

"Eggs?"

"In your tater salad?"

The woman poked her tongue in her cheek again and turned around toward the kitchen and hollered. "Ernestine, we use *eggs* in our po-ta-to salad?"

"Yes, I do, hon."

"Yeah, we do."

"Well, I don't want that, then. Don't like no eggs with my tater salad. No, gives me gas. No. French fries, huh? I don't like them so much, but . . . No, I'll take the slaw. How fine do you grind it?"

"Jesus."

"I beg your pardon, Miss?" Zeke squinted at the woman over his glasses.

She rolled her eyes. "Yeah, it's grated."

"Well, I'll take the french fries, then."

The woman gave another impatient sigh. "What you all want to drink?"

"Tea."

"Both of you?"

"Yes," said Jimmy.

"And you, ma'am? What can I get you?"

Ruth had been studying the menu in silence. In fact, she had said not a word since they had left the hospital except: "I'm hungry." And when Jimmy had pointed out this Roseboro cafe, she had said, "Fine." Now she frowned. "Now I see seafood platter here. Tell me: Is the fish fresh? Cause that's about all I see up here I want to eat."

"It's about as fresh as we can get it."

"How fresh is that?"

"Ma'am, I don't know."

"Well, you ought to know."

"You want me to find out?"

Ruth made her regal dismissing wave. "No, no, no. I'll get something else." She rustled through the folded sheets, turning the menu over and over, mumbling to herself. "Ain't nothing up here I want." She continued for about a minute. "What kind of 'salad' is this? Mustard greens? Turnip green? Something like that?"

"It's lettuce and tomato with cucumber and your choice of Thousand Island, French, or Italian dressing."

"No, no." Ruth poked her bottom lip out and continued to rustle.

"Aunt Ruth?" Jimmy was becoming more and more annoyed by the waitress's rude manner, despite realizing that her impatience was now, perhaps, becoming justified. "Why don't you try the steak and potato special?"

"What's so special about it?"

"The price." The waitress stuck her pencil behind her ear. "Listen, hon. I'll come back in a minute. What you want to drink?"

Ruth locked eyes with the waitress, obviously prickled at the way the woman had said "hon."

"Just give me a glass of water. If you please."

The waitress, a mocking smile on her face, and pulling her short dress down, wiggled away.

"I don't want none of this mess. White folks don't know how to cook no how."

"Aunt Ruth, I asked you if this place was all right, and you said it was." He became conscious of the whining tone in his voice and hated it.

"Where is she? I'll order something, anything, so we can get some food and get on out of here, cause I'm ready to go home."

The waitress returned with the two teas and water. "You ready now?"

"Yeah. Give me that beef stew. Nobody can mess up a beef stew, to be sure."

The waitress smirked and scribbled.

"This tea ain't sweetened!" Zeke made an ugly face. "Ain't you got no sweetener?"

The waitress reached over the table and pieked up a hand-ful of white packages of sugar and pink packages of Sweet' N Low, dropping them in front of Zeke's glass. "Best I can do." She pivoted and walked away.

Zeke stared at the woman and sneered. "Bitch."

Jimmy, only mildly startled, looked at him. Ruth, also taken off guard, let out a brief Hah, though she did not look at him. Jimmy realized it was more of a mock than genuine humor.

"Try the Sweet'N Low," Jimmy said, emptying some into his own glass. "It dissolves better."

As Zeke picked up one of the packages, the gravity began to lift from his face. "You know, this reminds me of the time—"

"Oh, Jesus, not another one of them lies you pass off for stories." Ruth stared out the window, her mouth set with the minor annoyance one might expect over a cat.

Zeke's mouth dropped open in disbelief. "Now, Ruth. That wont a nice thing to say."

As if pondering she said, "No, it wont, now was it."

Taking a moment to recover some of his dignity, Zeke had a swig of tea. "What's been ailing you, Ruth? You been as evil as a wet hen all day. What is it?"

"'Evil'?"

"Yeah, evil."

"Cousin Asa sure looked bad, didn't he?" Jimmy put his hand on Zeke's, but Zeke turned and gave him a serious glance, shaking his head, No, not this time.

"What ails you, Ruth?"

Ignoring Zeke, she looked to Jimmy. "Yeah, Asa did look pretty bad. Pretty bad indeed."

The waitress brought the food, the aroma reminding Jimmy that he was genuinely hungry. As soon as she had placed the food down he began to eat, and then realized that he, the preacher, had forgotten to pray. Zeke raised an eyebrow.

"Uncle Zeke. Will you bless the food?"

And Zeke gave a short thanks.

"Uh." Ruth grunted and made a disgusted face. "No. Can't eat this mess. Call that hateful gal back here."

"Everybody hateful but Ruth." Zeke put a forkful of barbecue in his mouth. He and Ruth looked straight into one another's eyes for the first time that day.

Jimmy raised his hand and flagged the waitress. "Now, Uncle Zeke, please don't start picking at Aunt Ruth. She's upset. I guess she is upset at seeing Asa in the hospital and—"

"No, no." Ruth wiped her mouth with her napkin. "Let him. Let him mess with me if he thinks he's man enough."

"Yeah, you know enough about castrating men. Don't you, Ruth?"

"Oh, really now. Stop, you two. This is embarrassing." Jimmy wiped his face. He was sweating.

"Watch yourself, Ezekiel Cross. You just better watch yourself."

The waitress came back. "What's the matter now?"

"I can't eat this." Ruth pushed the plate toward her.

"What's wrong with it?"

"Ain't no seasoning to it. The meat's done been cooked to death. It's old. Ain't fit for hogs."

"Now, Ruth—"

"Don't you 'Ruth' me, Zeke. You all always trying to tell somebody the way to talk, the way to dress, the way to live. Well, I'm my own person. Hear me?"

"Ma'am?" The waitress was leaning over her like a cat about to pounce.

"You gone regret talking like this, Ruth."

"I'm old enough to pay my own debts and favors. You ain't got nothing on me."

"Ma'am."

"Well, woman. I knew you was ornery and mean, but I never knew you to be downright dirty."

"See there. That's the way you all operate. Twist things around your way. Make right wrong and wrong right. I—"

"Ma'am!"

"What!"

The waitress stood up straight. "Do you want to order anything else?"

"You all make apple pie?"

"Yeah."

"Well, bring that."

The waitress shook her head and walked away. Jimmy thought hard of something to change the subject. "I heard it was supposed to snow tonight. Wonder if it will?"

Without acknowledging Jimmy, Zeke pounded the table, making the silverware tinkle. "See, Ruth. You're just inconsiderate. That's the problem."

"You got some nerve, Negro, declaring me inconsiderate. The problem is that you, and all you Crosses, is too high and mighty for your own good. That's the problem."

"I heard," Jimmy tried, though he felt silly and an outsider, "that they were going to build a new addition to the community center over near Dobsville."

Zeke smiled and ate another mouthful. When he finished chewing and swallowing he pointed the empty fork at Ruth. "Go on. Go on and do it again. You done it before. Blame me. Blame my whole family. Blame the whole wide world for your ills. You know you the cause for most whatever bad come your way, Ruth. And you know it's true. Don't you?"

"You better lay low, Ezekiel Cross. You treading dangerous ground."

"Ain't no more dangerous than you already made it."

"Leave me lone, Ezekiel. Leave me be."

"You the one pick the fight, gal. I spect I can wind it up if I pleases."

They were becoming so loud that the entire restaurant could hear. People were arching their necks in the direction of the table. Some were shameless enough to turn around. At this point Jimmy felt he should stand, lifting his hands in the air like a boxing referee, shouting: "Uncle Zeke. Aunt Ruth." But already it was as if he were in another room.

"See, I know what you trying to lay blame to, Zeke. You good for dragging such mess up at a time like this. And got the nerve to call somebody else evil."

"Yeah, I called you that. I ain't never seen you do nothing to prove me wrong."

"See, you keep trying me. You keep on."

"No, you the one, Ruth. You the one."

Jimmy noticed his palms were sweating. "Come on, now, you all—"

"Shut up, Jimmy." Ruth was no longer smiling. "Just be yourself still."

"It's all right, Jimmy." This time Zeke patted Jimmy's hand. Ruth watched him and smirked.

"Go on and say it then." She narrowed her eyes.

"Say what?"

"You know what you all fixed me with. Made me guilty, whether I was or no."

"See, you the one bringing it up. Cause you know it's true. You—"

"Ah-hah. I knew it. You shameless old goat."

"It's true, Ruth. You may as well own it."

"He was your brother. Your kin. You knew him before I did—"

"That's right, Ruth. That's right. And I know that before you he never touched a drop of liquor. He was a good man till he laid eyes on you."

"Well, you'll see yourself one day, Ezekiel Cross. See what you and your family, your evil family have wrought. And it wont just on Jethro. It's on Lester. It's on this boy here. It was on your grandboy. You all is something else."

"Watch your step, Ruth."

"I ain't watching nothing. Oh, you something else. Look at you. Set yourself up as God's holy counselor. Heaven walking on earth. Jesus himself. That what you plan to do on your ninetieth birthday, walk on water?"

"'And they will talk about you despitefully.'"

"That's right. Go on and quote the Bible. You don't live it."

"'Do not judge lest ye be judged.'"

"You're so full of yourself, Zeke. See, cause I know. I was there. I know how you turned your own brother away from your doorstep, him sick and in pain."

"Lies."

"You and your sister. Him sick and in the bed for months, and neither you nor that sanctified sister of yours set one foot in the house to see about him."

"Don't talk ill of the dead, gal."

"Piss on the dead."

"You a hateful, wicked old witch, Ruth Cross."

"I ain't no Cross, damn it. I'm a Davis. That's what I was born, you old fool."

"Don't call me old, you broken-down old heifer. Look at you. You the one old."

"Hypocrite!"

"Liar!"

The waitress came with the apple pie as Ruth struggled to get up. "I ain't hungry." The waitress grimaced, and Jimmy noticed a twitching in her forearm as if she were refraining from throwing the pie at Ruth.

Ruth finally stood after a great effort and peered down at Zeke. "The truth will come to the light." She turned to Jimmy. "Boy, I'll be in the car." And she turned as swiftly as she was able and hobbled toward the door. Jimmy realized that everyone in the cafe was aware of Ruth's departure, watching her painful progress. A white man sitting near the door opened it for her. Slowly, she disappeared, her back undulating in turtlelike rhythm.

Jimmy sat fingering his tea glass. "I'm ashamed of you, Uncle Zeke."

"You? Ashamed of me? Boy, I—"

"Now, listen, Uncle Zeke. Aunt Ruth got her ways, I know it. But she's been through a lot. You of all people should know how to show some compassion. Some understanding."

With disbelief Zeke regarded Jimmy. He sat back and spoke slowly. "'*She's* been through a lot'? What about you? What about me? My Lord. I declare, I'm tired, just tired, of putting up with that old crow's acid ways. 'She's been through a lot'? Shoot." He reached for his glass.

Jimmy stood, dejected. "We all have." He reached into his pocket, dropped a twenty-dollar bill on the table, and walked out the door thinking, being the minister, he should perhaps have been more stern with his great uncle. Wondering how.

By the time Jimmy got to the car, Ruth was already sitting there in the backseat staring straight ahead. As he stood there, before the door, before her, he realized once again that he had no idea what he should say to her, how he should say it, or if, indeed, he should say anything at all. But he felt, somewhere in the place that spurred him on as a minister, that he should speak. So he opened the car door. She would not look at him.

"You okay, Aunt Ruth?"

She looked down at her hands. He watched her exhale while rubbing them and shake her head. Finally looking up, she smacked her mouth as though she had gleaned something of great importance. "When we going on? It's going to rain soon."

"You reckon it will?"

"I reckon it will."

Without slamming it, he closed the door and looked around him. This was a small town with a filling station, a tiny grocery store, an antique shop run out of someone's home. A post office. Smaller than Tims Creek. He got into the driver's seat.

"I expect Uncle Zeke will apologize."

"Do I care?"

"Now, Aunt Ruth. It ain't Christian to hold grudges and to carry on like the two of you been doing. I expect you two to do the right thing."

"*You* expect?"

"Shoot." He chuckled and looked back at her. "You two should be setting an example for me." She gave him an unflinching and icy stare. Closing her eyes, she turned away.

Jimmy began rubbing his temples. He was getting a headache.

Zeke shuffled out of the restaurant, picking his teeth with a wooden toothpick. He got into the car with a grunt and rubbed his thigh with one hand, continuing to pick his teeth with the other. "Well. We ready to go?"

Jimmy's hand paused at the ignition. The right thing, he thought. He turned back to them both. "Now look at you. Look at you both. I declare. It's a shame. You know I've been proud of you both all this time. Proud of the way you've . . ."

"Lord, boy." Ruth's stare was still icy. "I ain't in the mood for no preaching, now. Just drive me home. I'm ready to go to bed."

"But Aunt Ruth, I mean it. I—"

"Boy, don't waste your time. You heard her. Trying to talk to her is like trying to get through to a stone wall. She—"

"Ezekiel Cross, you just keep your mouth closed."

"You close it if you want it closed, you—"

"If you don't believe I'll try, keep talking, you—"

"I—"

"Listen to you! Listen to you both. A deacon and a mother of the church." Jimmy put his elbows on the steering wheel. "I don't believe it. I just don't believe it. That two people who've lived as long and who have been through as much as you two can act so petulant and childish. It's ridiculous."

Zeke rolled his eyes and exhaled mightily. "Okay, I ain't behaving like I ought to. I beg your pardon, Ruth. I—"

"You don't have to beg no pardon from me, mister." Ruth raised her hand. "No. Cause the truth will come to the light. One way or the other. I'm right in my soul, but—"

"Well, I tried, damn it. Ain't no talking to her."

"That's right. Ain't no talking to me."

"Fine."

"Fine."

They both stared out of their respective windows, resolute in their steely silence. Jimmy looked from one to the other, dumbfounded. Deciding there was little he could do, he settled himself to drive and turned the ignition.

The engine made no sound. He tried again. The only noise he heard was the passing of a Mack truck on the highway, the gentle whistling wind, a door slamming, somewhere in the distance.

First one, then two, then three drops of rain fell onto the windshield.

✳ ✳ ✳

"Yeah, they'll go on you anytime. And not one bit of warning, neither."

The mechanic hunched over the engine like a mother hen over her brood, implicitly knowing each one, personally, privately, and with tremendous respect for each. Maybe, Jimmy deduced, even with a little love.

Through the rain Jimmy had run to the filling station, where the mechanic told him languidly that the wrecker was out. Jimmy suggested that they might roll the car into the garage since it was only a few yards away. The mechanic spit—he had a big chew of tobacco in his mouth—wiped his mouth and nodded.

With water pelting down on them in the cold air, they pushed the car, with the two people in it, into the mechanic's garage. The mechanic, a short, roly-poly fellow with greasy black hair and green eyes, rapidly diagnosed the problem and spat out his entire wad of tobacco.

"Now, yesterday," he said, reaching for a Coke, "yesterday, you'd a been in trouble, see." He took a swig of the soda, swirled it around in his mouth and spat that out. "Cause I don't carry the part." He wiped his mouth with the back of his hand. "Only started making them in '79." He took a few more swigs of the soda and swallowed them. "But you're lucky, see. Cause I'm farsighted." He fished in his pocket and emerged with his tobacco pouch. "See, I knew a feller, all duded up in his suit, driving his new Oldsmobile, would stop by Roseboro one day. Stop to eat at the cafe. Get out. Get in his car, and bang!" He pinched up some tobacco and stuffed it in his jaw and stuffed a little more. "His car wouldn't start." He winked at Jimmy. "But like I said, you're lucky. Cause the part come in today."

Jimmy sighed.

"But it'll take pretty near two hours or more, cause I got to finish another car before four o'clock. So have a seat inside."

The three went inside. A dingy place, the interior of the filling station. Full of items. Behind, above, in front of the counter. Near the wall, against the wall. Rows of candy and cigarettes and car fresheners shaped like cats. Bubble gum and lighters and lighter fluid, Moon Pies and keychains and batteries. Cheap watches. Penlights. Car oil. Condoms. They sat on two car seats taken from long-dead cars across from a glass-topped cooler containing brown, orange, lemon, lime, and red-colored sodas in bottles and cans. Ice creams as well. In the corner perched a video game machine; a child flipped and popped the switches. A woman with greasy black hair like the mechanic's sat at the counter reading *True Confessions* magazine and eating a banana.

"Now it is a miserable day, ain't it, you all?" She eyed them brightly.

"You can say that again." Ruth looked at her almost smiling, Jimmy noted, though not smiling.

"Where you all from?"

"Tims Creek." Zeke was still peering at the rain through the dirt-streaked windows.

"Yeah? What brings you over this way?"

"Got a sick cousin over Fayetteville way."

"He ain't bad off, is he?"

"Yes, ma'am." Zeke rubbed his hands. "He is."

"Well, that's a shame." For a moment she stared forward with a blank look on her face. The only sounds were the falling rain and the game in the corner with its zapping, buzzing, and blaring.

"I think I'll make us a pot of coffee." The woman slapped her hands together the way a carnival barker would before asking you to step this way. "Care for some?"

"Why, yes, thank you." Jimmy was genuinely glad, for though it was warmer inside, it was still cool.

"Yes, that would be nice." Ruth again, surprised Jimmy. She looked at the little girl and the machine.

"What is that thing?"

"It's a video game." Jimmy was sure she was about to be vexed and demand the child quit keeping that fuss, but her face was placid, and her voice did not seem in any way annoyed. If anything, she was curious.

"It do make a lot of fuss, don't it." She leaned towards it.

They all sat in silence, watching the child play the game. The sound of the coffee machine was barely heard under the din.

"Well," the woman said as she brought them cups of coffee, "I don't particularly like it, but Amy, she's pretty good at it."

The girl turned to look at Ruth, and to Jimmy's surprise, and without a doubt to Ruth's, she winked at Ruth. At first Ruth was taken off guard. Then she smiled and sipped her coffee, closing her eyes. "That's a mighty good cup of coffee, Miss. Thank you."

"Oh, you're welcome."

"Oh, yes." Jimmy reached into his pocket. "How much is it?"

"Don't worry." The woman stepped back around the counter. "Glad to do it. Day like today, I suspect this is the last place you all want to be."

Zeke grumbled, hunched over his coffee. "Yeah."

Ruth still looked at the machine with curiosity. "Surely we won't be here for long."

Jimmy could not figure the unusual look on his great-aunt's face. He took note of the girl, who kept turning around and smiling at Ruth, and Ruth smiling back, and he kept wondering what he was missing.

The girl's game ended, and frisky as a squirrel, she walked up to Ruth, who regarded her as one would a leprechaun, with delight and a bit of wariness.

"You want to play?"

"Amy!" The woman was slightly amused, but very embarrassed. "Really, you know better than—"

"I'll show you how."

"Amy. Now I'm sure she doesn't—"

"Well." Ruth was already rousing herself to stand, motioning for the girl to reach her her cane. "I just might give it a try. Won't hurt nothing. Will it, Amy?" She smiled at the woman, who did not to know how to respond at first, but who smiled finally.

The girl clutched Ruth's other hand and Ruth rose to her crooked position, and in her crooked fashion made her way, much to Jimmy's dumbfounded disbelief, to the video game.

Zeke crossed his legs, resting his chin on his hand and making a sucking sound with his teeth. He reminded Jimmy of an annoyed old hound dog regarding puppies playing a bit too close to him. His eyes betrayed disapproval, Jimmy realized, and something more—like disdain.

"Now." The girl's voice took on a schoolmarmish tone. She stood just beneath Ruth's sagging breasts and between her arms. Ruth gripped the console of the huge black box and balanced herself there.

"This little man," said Amy, "he wants to eat all these little dots here. But these fellows here, they want to eat him. Understand? But if he gets a hold of one of these here blue pills here and eats it, he'll get big and strong and then he can beat them folk up and send them back to jail where they belong." She looked up at Ruth. "Think you got it?"

"Well, we'll see."

"Okay, I'll do the first game for you. Now watch." She dropped a quarter in the machine, and a merry music bounced out of it. Jimmy walked over, hoping not to get Ruth's notice.

"Oh, look a there," Ruth squealed in a voice Jimmy had never heard before. "Uh-oh, he's gone get him. Watch out. Watch out! Oops. Now you's dead, ain't you?"

"Yeah, but I got five men. Your turn."

Ruth grasped the lever and began to play as she had seen the girl. In less than a minute her game was over, but the glee—that's what Jimmy decided it was—in her face was like a revelation. He looked over at Zeke, who was eying it all with suspicion.

After the girl's game, Ruth played again, faring a little better, and cheering loudly. When the quarter was up she asked Jimmy to reach into her pocketbook and get another. They wound up playing five games, Ruth yelling at the end, declaring that the video game was a treat indeed.

"See, Miss. You'll be a great player someday."

Ruth laughed and touched her head. "Thank you, Amy. If I get as good as you I'll be a mighty good player, yessiree."

"And what's your name?"

"I'm Ruth." They shook hands.

The girl went over to her mother, who gave her a banana and sent her on an errand. Ruth, who Jimmy fathomed had to be monumentally exhausted, walked toward Zeke, who glared at her sternly. His perturbation was unchanged, if anything more intense. She threw her head back again and laughed the hearty laugh of a woman who has gained the right to laugh and cares not who hears or how they might judge it. Wordless, she turned, slower now, but bold as ever, and walked out toward the garage and the falling rain.

When she had gotten outside the door, Zeke made a tisking sound with his mouth. "That's one curious old woman."

"Any more curious than you?"

"Don't vex me, boy."

"Let me ask you a question, Uncle Zeke. Did you and Grandma raise me to behave the way you've behaved today?"

"The way I've 'behaved' today? And how have I 'behaved' today, sir?"

"Spiteful. Selfish. Small. Compassionless."

"You talk about compassion a lot, young fellow. Know what it means, do you?"

"Yes, I believe I do."

"And do you know what all forgiveness entails?"

"Well, the Bible says—"

"No. We ain't talking about the Bible, James Malachai Greene. I'm talking about you. What *you* know. What *you* understand. Do you understand what forgiveness is?"

"You got to lay something down."

"You got to lay something down, and you got to leave it there, don't you?" Zeke sighed and peered into the rain. "It takes right smart of a man to forgive, and I'll tell you, boy. I don't know if this old man is man enough. Strong enough, to walk to way I ought. That surprise you?"

"Yes, sir."

"You suppose to be *my* preacher." He chuckled to himself. "And you been telling me how shamed you been of me?" Zeke raised his eyebrow toward him, staring. He ran his hand over his face. "One day. One day you'll understand. One day you'll know."

Not understanding what had just been said, baffled as to how his chastising had suddenly turned into his chastisement, he groped for a sly rejoinder.

"But this is today, Uncle."

Zeke looked at him and shook his head. "Yeah, it is, ain't it." Zeke stood and walked to the garage.

She stood at the wide door before the water that fell like a curtain between her and the world. Jimmy stood in the arch of the inside door, listening. Zeke walked out to her. She had to have heard him, his feet shuffling so, but she did not turn around.

"Raining hard, ain't it?"

"Oh, yeah. But I bet it'll turn into snow soon."

"Snow?"

"Yeah."

"You might be right."

They stood there. Silent. Jimmy expected quiet, soft concili-
atory words. Then he realized he had already heard them, as
pure and as honest as the rain.

By the time he pulled the Oldsmobile into Ruth's drive, it was
dark. Six o'clock. When they had dropped Zeke off they had
parted as family, not as warring factions. And as Jimmy saw his
great-aunt to bed, watching her familiar slow steps, slower now
from a day so full of activity; as he waited for her to disrobe
and change into her nightclothes; and as he helped her to bed,
he considered the myriad ways things could have been different.
Today. Yesterday. Tomorrow. If Anne had not died. If Horace
had not died. If his grandmother had not died. All so soon ago.

Seemingly, Ruth closed her eyes as soon as her head touched
the goose-stuffed pillow, and said dreamily: Snowing now, I bet.

He turned off the lights in the house, closing and locking
doors behind him. On the way to the car a fat snowflake pelted
him on his face and mingled there with a fresh and hot tear.

April 30, 1984
4:45 am

But really, Mr. Cross—might I call you Horace?

Of course.

Horace—I am Veronica. But really, Horace, people can be so crass. You understand what I mean, don't you? Just unforgivable. I'm afraid people have lost manners and politeness. They abide by no rules. Beasts is what they have become. Beasts. Don't you agree?

Yes. Yes. Why, of course.

Picture a buffalo standing in the middle of a stage. Picture it wearing a white dress, simple, almost plain, not too many frills, but decidedly expensive. Picture it wearing gold spectacles and a yellow hat with green and white flowers. Picture it drinking tea, its lionlike, snakelike tail switching from one side of its wide haunches to another, lazily. Horace's foot throbbed.

I remember when I was a little girl . . . why, everyone seemed to have the most superb manners. My Cousin Charles, I remember, had the most graceful . . .

Horace had barrelled into Crosstown with tires screaming and pistons drumming, a cackling demon in his head who punctuated each curve with the word, Faster. Though the men back at the school had been left many, many miles back and could never catch up with him, let alone know where he was headed.

. . . a party for my Aunt Clara and everyone came dressed so elegantly. Oh, it was quite a spectacle. One of my most pleasant memories. Why, people just don't turn out that way nowadays. Such a pity, isn't it?

Why, yes, ma' am. It is.

Of course you're really too young to remember, but there was a time. Ooooo . . .

Without the demon telling him, he had hurtled into the empty parking lot of the Crosstown theater. He turned the car off and stepped out, looking at the low building that sloped down into the woods. He clutched the gun tightly. The lights were on at the box office, illuminating a brightly colored poster that read:

RIDE THE FREEDOM STAR
A Musical
The saga of an
American Family.
Their trials through the
Revolution,
through the
Civil War
through the trials and hardship
through birth and death

through the tumults and tribulations of love
This is their story
The American Story
June 24–August 15

On the poster was a rendering of all the generations of the family, the settlers, the revolutionaries, the rebels, the businessmen, the planters, the statesmen, their arms all raised high bearing the tools of their trade—guns, swords, hoes. The United States flag ballooned dramatically from the left, the Stars and Bars to the right. The men were hearty and robust like comic book characters, their chests barrelled and near to bursting through their shirts; the women were either voluptuous or petite, big-boned and buxom or frail and feminine. They all had shiny white teeth and wide smiles. Off to the right of the group stood three black people. A man, shirtless, horse-muscled, and bronze, and a woman, her head beragged, both with an out-of-place grin on their faces. Standing beneath them was a young boy, his eyes much too big, the smile on his face lost somewhere in the conflagration of counterfeit glory.

He had worked here the summer before his senior year in high school, getting the job as best boy through recommendations from his English teacher, Mr. Phelps. His grandfather had been dubious: he mistrusted the number of white people Horace would be working with and the long hours. But he could not argue with the salary, which was more than Horace would have made cropping tobacco, though not a lot more. Reluctantly Ezekiel agreed. Horace had just gotten his driver's license that spring, so he could drive himself to and from work, about twenty-five minutes from home. He began working two weeks after the summer vacation had begun.

I think television has had a lot to do with it, said the bison, who did not move very much, only shifting her weight from time to time. She continued: People don't interact with people the way they used to. My sister Effi says that she knows families who watch the awful thing during supper. Imagine that!

Imagine, Horace said. He wanted to ask the buffalo how it managed to pick up its teacup.

Why, in my day . . .

The entire theater was out of doors, except for the box office and the hidden costume barn. Horace didn't even try the door this time; he merely limped over to a trash can under the high wooden wall that surrounded the amphitheater, holding onto his gun awkwardly. Rather than jump down and risk landing on his foot, he held onto the top of the fence once he was up and let his feet dangle down, finally releasing his grip and landing on his good foot. That's when the compulsion began, something calling him, again. Not the demon. Something quieter. Yet larger. Strange.

The Crosstown theater had been built by the town with a grant from the Cross Endowment and with contributions from the Southern American Oil Company and the First American Mercantile National Bank, both family-controlled companies. The last of those Crosses to live in Crosstown was Owen Oliver Cross III, who took his aged mother to Winston–Salem to live back in 1944, where he went to manage a newly acquired bank and the other family investments that had swollen after World War I, and even more after World War II, riding the tide on into the seventies and the independent oil boom. Also there had been three good marriages for his daughters. Philip Cross was the last male of the white Cross line. He had grown up in New York, Martha's Vineyard, and Winston–Salem, traveling between his divorced Yankee mother and his classically philandering father. And to his grandfather's dismay, Philip Quincy Cross was not in the least bit interested in corporate commerce or acquisitions or the art of high financing. All through Philips Exeter and Brown he had harbored the ambition of becoming a playwright.

Because of North Carolina's long tradition of outdoor theaters, he thought it a brilliant idea to found the Owen Oliver Cross Memorial Outdoor Theater and to use as its main fare a play, by him, about his illustrious family's history, a stage biography with music. The idea had its merits, except for the fact that Philip was a horrid playwright.

Ride the Freedom Star was a lavish production. No expense had been spared in costumes, fireworks, lighting, stage work, props, music—he had hired one of Broadway's near-prominent (and expensive) composers for the score. But as a piece of drama it was miserable, originally running over three hours and forty-five minutes. The director and producer battled for speeches to be cut, for entire sections to be cut, for extraneous characters to be written out, but Philip in his patron/author conviction stood firm over every comma and semicolon. Finally, they settled on a two-and-a-half-hour version with three intermissions; there were sixty characters, thirty speaking roles. There were long static passages of fathers patriotically extolling the virtues of riding off into battle; of mothers enumerating the travails of the Civil War–torn plantation system. The dialogue was clunky and dull, and many of the historical facts were just plain wrong. The director was constantly rewriting parts of the script, only to be met by the protesting Philip invoking what he saw as "literary license" and changing the script back. Though they hired fair-to-middling actors and dancers and singers, not even the most inspired performance could rise above the mishmash of ill-conceived, ill-wrought, cliche-ridden drivel, the doggerel verse and the melodramatic romanticizing of Southern American history.

Ironically, the thing that kept the crowds coming back—aside from the vigorous advertising on the state and local levels about "The new, grand, exciting, funny, glorious family history," subsidized substantially by the State Commission on Outdoor Drama, largely underwritten by the Cross endowment—was Philip's concession to his family's slave-owning past. He had tried to create a picture of domestic bliss for the house slaves and of jolly camaraderie for the field workers. Despite the interjection of a speech here or there that reflected the reality of the hard life of the slaves, the blacks were mainly there for buffoonery and hijinks that brought laughs and chuckles from the audience, for the church scenes with their raw and dynamic singing, and for the minister's sermon, which was the most passionate, hell-raising moment in the entire play.

The bison stepped closer to Horace, and said: Now I had an Aunt Zelda, who, in her eighty-fifth year, still gave tea parties every Thursday afternoon. They were quite something, those tea parties. Everyone getting together and chatting. Just chat. There was none of this horrible gossip that goes on today. Then, now that I think, I believe we were quite bad, oh yes indeed. We did do a . . . little . . . reputation damage, here and there. But of course the reputations were already . . .

The bison gave a brief tee-hee, her tail popping against her rear like a whip.

Once over the fence he had stood in the back of the amphitheater and looked down its graduated steps and over its low, backless seats like picnic table benches that sloped to a wide, elevated triangular stage with a wall on either side and a clear view to the woods behind in the middle. Looking to see what was calling him, he saw instead this buffalo, standing on the stage, whereupon she had begun her tirade, which was just beginning to annoy Horace. Why was he here? He sat on the edge of the stage, his genitals resting on the wooden floor, listening to this interminable lecture that did not interest him in the least. He wanted to ask her, Do you know why I'm here? but was not given a chance.

People just don't like to be nice anymore, she was saying. It seems to me that everyone is trying so hard to be vulgar. It's as if they were trying to outdo one another in their impropriety. Don't you think?

Uh-huh.

There it was. The feeling. As if he had forgotten to be someplace. As if something important were happening and he was key to its getting done. As if someone were dying and needed to say goodbye.

He rose. I'm sorry, he said, I have to go—

Go! But I haven't finished my—

I have to. I'm sorry.

Horace turned to walk away.

Rude. Rude. Rude. The bison stamped its foot on the stage. Well, I never!

Ignoring the beast, Horace stepped up on stage and walked past it, turned around once he reached the back. Nothing or no one was there, just an empty theater. The theater and the compulsion to move on, toward . . .

He wanted the voice to return and tell him what to do, not this vague ringing in the mind, this subtle urging.

He wandered backstage, which was no more than elevated concrete platforms that jutted back and into the woods, a little prop house, chairs, narrow trails that wound and cut through the woods around the full length of the theater. He remembered the long hours he had spent back here, first building, then moving, then fixing, then rebuilding. In June he would start at eleven in the morning and would work well into the evening after stopping for dinner at five. Just before the show went up he worked from ten in the morning until two or three into the next morning, stopping only to grab a greasy hamburger and fries. Once the show went up in early July, he was at work until twelve or one in the morning. Sometimes later.

Of the sixty actors in the cast, most were local folk who, for free, jumped at the chance to "be involved" in community work and, more importantly for them, the ego massage of being seen on stage. But the company did hire eleven professional actors for the lead roles, five from New York, three from Los Angeles, one from Washington, one from Chicago, and one from Miami. They were young, ambitious men and women who were waiting for that elusive "break" of which they all spoke with a familiar awe and loathing, as if it did indeed exist but was a fickle thing, awarded more often to the unworthy and the lazy than to the talented and the hardworking. They were hyperbolic, animated, bawdy, and energetic. They looked at summer stock as a necessary evil, something to fill out their resume, "paying their dues." A way to keep working. Crosstown paid no more than most regional theaters—which was not much—despite its abundant funding; so, compounding the bruised egos, the frustrations, the fatigue, and the isolation from city lights of these hungry people was their gruff indignation, causing them to look askance and aloof at sleepy, backward Crosstown.

The men were mostly gay, which haunted and taunted Horace, for to him they were physically beautiful. With tall, lean, almost animal bodies, or stocky, strong and solid frames, or faces that carried such charm as to be cherubic—clearly here lay danger. But how could he avoid it? The lead, Edward Gordon, was an aristocratic Georgian who had gone to New York to make it big—though after six years, he was still awaiting that auspicious day. He had classically English bone structure, blond hair, blue eyes, strong teeth . . . so flawless he was almost boring. There were the stock jet-black-haired, green/blue/brown-eyed hunks, including Antonio Santangelo, who was part Italian, part Puerto Rican. He was a born and bred product of Brooklyn, sly and sarcastic. The shadow of his beard was almost blue.

But the man who had changed Horace's mind—or, more accurately, convinced him that his mind had lied to his heart—was the only professional black male actor. Everett Church Harrington IV, a singer/actor/dancer with light brown eyes and skin of caramel. The first day Horace saw him, he was gripped by anger.

Horace had been crouched on the steps of the aisle leading down to the stage. He was trying to untangle a huge length of Christmas lights used in the opening musical show. Everett came down the steps, his nose stuck in a script, oblivious to the tangle of wires underneath his feet, and when Horace looked up he was immediately jealous—uncannily, unfathomably, without explanation, doubt, reason, or relief, full of a red, stinking, unmitigated envy. And lust. So he did not even think to tell the man about the wires beneath his feet—and part of him would have loved to have planned it. When Everett's feet became inextricably tangled in the muddle, he came tumbling, graceless and beautiful, down the steps, down right into Horace's arms, who caught him successfully, but who also lost his balance, sending them both down a few more steps to a painful halt.

"Jesus." Everett was annoyed and looked at Horace as if he were the wire around his feet. "Why the hell didn't you say something?"

Was it a sinking feeling? Like falling unexpectedly into a river? Was it a dangerous feeling? Like playing on a railroad track? The eyes. The eyes. "Something?"

"Do you speak English?" Everett pushed away from Horace angrily and began taking the wires from his feet.

"Look, I'm sorry. I didn't . . ."

Everett was having trouble with the cord around his left foot. It was pulled taut and twisted about a bench. "What the fuck!"

"Here, let me help you." Bemused by his own mixed feelings, Horace spoke haltingly, finally stepping toward the stranger.

"No." He rolled his eyes at Horace, jerking his foot from the mass. "I think I can manage it." He stood looking for the script, which was scattered about the floor. "Shit." He began to pick up the pages.

"I'll help." But Horace did not move, suddenly affronted by this man's gruffness and the hateful way he went about picking up the script. Looking at him, seeing the shape of his behind, firm and round, as he bent over, the well-made, thick neck, the hands as they picked up the paper, even . . .

"No. I have it. Just be careful in the future."

"But I—"

"Yeah, yeah. Save it. Really."

"You know, you're not very nice, are you?" Horace stunned himself with his frankness.

Everett looked at Horace and narrowed his eyes. He lifted his top lip, just a wee bit. The effect was of sustained, unshakable superiority. "No, I'm not." He turned and walked away, returning to his script. Horace stood and watched him leave the theater, transfixed, not so much by his beauty as by his own reaction to it.

What did ECH IV become to Horace's mind? Where did he lodge in his brain? An obsession? Perhaps an irrational fixation? Or a figment of emotional displacement? But one thing was beyond doubt. Horace hated him. Despised, loathed, abhorred him. His father was a law professor, a descendant of Boston freedmen with Beacon Hill addresses; his mother was of old Washington, D.C., stock and position, a member of the Church Terrell clan. Everett had gone to the right schools. Everett wore the right clothes. Everett talked the right talk. Everett had the right friends. Everett read the right books. Everett saw the right movies. Everett could do no wrong. Beautiful. Sophisticated. Right. Everett became like a thorn in his eye. Everett. Everyone loved Everett. And so did Horace. Or did he really?

Horace found himself in front of the costume barn. A lock hung down on the high, wide metal door to the prefabricated aluminum block of a building. For some reason, not from the demon's order, Horace wanted to go inside. He went around the side to a window. He pushed it and it slid free; he clambered over, landing on his sprained ankle and emitting a yelp. The racks and racks of costumes caused a strange configuration of shadows, and the musky scent of the warehouse, with its high ceiling, was of dust and rotting cloth, cotton and wool. Suddenly he felt a presence. It was as if he knew someone was in the building with him. He could see a glowing light coming from the other end of the barn, stronger than the moonlight, but not too bright. He walked as stealthily as possible toward the end, hiding in the costumes.

The closer he got to the light, the more he felt there was indeed someone there. He heard something and stopped stock still. Should he go on? Now it was curiosity that pulled him along.

He pulled back a coat, clutching the gun, and saw someone sitting in front of a mirrored dresser, putting on makeup. He was a black man, dressed in a sun-bright costume, orange and green and blue and red, like a harlequin's. As Horace looked into the mirror, the face appeared more and more familiar, though it was becoming obscured by milky white greasepaint.

He realized. Saw clearly. It was him. Horace. Sitting before the mirror, applying makeup. Of all the things he had seen this night, all the memories he had confronted, all the ghouls and ghosts and specters, this shook him the most. Stunned, confused, bewildered, he could only stare at his reflection, seeing him and him and him.

As if on cue from his thoughts, the Horace at the table turned to the Horace standing there in the moldering clothing. He looked at Horace for a moment, still and calm, as if he had been expecting him and knew he would be late, and then motioned for Horace to step closer, closer.

Who are you? Horace asked. The image said nothing. Slowly Horace moved toward the image, and when he was standing just behind him, the specter turned again to the mirror and resumed its task.

What are you doing? But the reflection of himself continued to cover his entire face with white goo, deftly, expertly, with fingers, Horace's fingers, that seemed accustomed to this odd activity. As if it were normal.

Soon the entire face was obscured, though Horace could recognize the face, the nose folks said to be just like his great-grandfather's, the lips rumored to be like his grandmother's, his father's determined chin, his maternal grandmother's sad eyes . . . but all was white now, finished in a white like porcelain, smooth and thick. The phantom picked up a brush, dipped it in what appeared black ink, and, with an uncanny grace, painted his lips a midnight black. He looked at Horace's reflection in the mirror and ran his tongue over his top lip, but the ink did not smear. He just stared at Horace, expressionless, giving no indication as to why he was doing what he was doing or what he would do next.

The double stood up. He was exactly the same height as Horace, the same build. In his sparkling color, he turned to look at both their reflections in the mirror: Horace in his brown nakedness, covered with dirt and ash and grass in his hair, a gun in his hand, and the other Horace, white-faced, dressed as a clown.

Motioning toward the chair, the doppelgänger bade Horace sit, not saying a word. Nervously, Horace sat, wondering why he did not simply leave. He was becoming more and more uncomfortable, more and more frightened. Something awaited him. Something grave.

With an ominous movement, and with delicacy, the image picked up a tube of the same white greasepaint he had used and handed it to Horace, who eyed it with caution. He had no intention of taking it. He wanted only to leave and forget what he had seen.

No, he said.

But the spirit stood there, holding the tube for Horace.

I won't.

They looked at one another, their eyes, the same eyes, trying to peer past the will of the other. Horace decided he would leave, and he moved to stand, but his reflection put his hand firmly on Horace's shoulder and pushed the tube into Horace's face.

I don't want it. Leave me alone.

Grabbing Horace's hand, the image put the tube in his hand and forced him to make a mark on his face. He turned Horace's head to look in the mirror. But he did not see himself there,

nor the perverted image of himself. Instead the mirror began
to shift images, warping them, causing them to bow and bend,
and when it settled he saw himself and Antonio Santangelo, in
a room, on a blanket, naked, engaged in sex, almost violently,
their mouths touching, their tongues probing one another, their
hands grasping, clutching . . .

Had it not been for the presence of Everett Church Harrington in the cast, Horace told himself, he would have never
fallen into sin with Antonio. But whether that was the truth
or merely a hope, he did what he did, having sex with Antonio and eventually with two other members of the cast, all the
while thinking that this would get him closer and closer to the
person who gave his dreams cinnamon and ginger starch, and
his heart a new exercise.

He justified his sinful promiscuity by the fact that the entire
theater was a hotbed of fleshly affairs. The director slept with
Edward, the leading lady slept with the costume designer, the
producer's wife slept with the head dancer, the second lead slept
with the electrician, two married actors often shared their bed
with another—male or female. These and other bits of juicy
gossip were well known among the cast and crew, and they created a general atmosphere of overactive hormones, the motto
being: What else is there to do in *Crosstown*? So Horace thought,
I'm just a simple country boy. How can I resist such freedom?
Especially when it's so irresistible?

Looking now at the figures of him and Antonio, the dark
walnut skin against the golden amber, he remembered how
Antonio had seduced him, telling Horace that he looked a
lot like the lover he had left in New York, named Andre, and

that he thought about Andre every night, and how he missed the things he and Andre would do together, going to the park, to movies, to plays, to dinner . . . He thought Horace might help to assuage his . . . loneliness. Horace was in fact eager to help out.

In the mirror the lovemaking reached a fevered pitch, and they ended in a fit of predatory growls and purrs and exhalations that made Horace, watching it now, embarrassed. Yet a voyeuristic side in him was transfixed. Antonio rolled over, sweat covering his tanned brow, his coarse black hair considerably mussed, faced the ceiling, and sighed.

At least three times a week they would meet in the wee hours of the morning after the rehearsal was over, when they were both exhausted. Yet they managed, in the backseat of Antonio's 1978 blue Datsun or Horace's grandfather's car, parking in some wooded area Horace knew or in some empty parking lot behind an abandoned factory or warehouse. Then one day they passed by that house.

Antonio, in his bullish, unthinking way, pulled over saying he wanted to explore. It was a large house, though not a mansion; it sat off from a dirt road, desolate, reminding Horace of the haunted houses of his childhood fears. He told Antonio that he had no intention of ever going into such a house, and certainly not that house, and especially not at one o'clock in the morning in the middle of the summer. Antonio looked at him, his eyes glittering with the reflected light of the headlights, and said mockingly: "Ooooh, is my wittle Horace scared? Do he tink de big, bad putty wolve in dat house?"

"No, he tink de big, bad putty snake is in dat house."

Antonio put his hand on the inside of Horace's thigh. "I'll protect you."

"You and what elephant gun?"

"Pussy."

"Fool."

Finally shame convinced Horace to go in. The door was open, hanging off its hinges. Once inside, surrounded by the overpowering smell of dust, decay, rotting wood, motes rising from their movement in the flashlight's beam, they looked along the grey floors and peeling walls, seeing no furniture, no sign of a family ever having lived there. Horace sensed no ghosts. They explored upstairs, Horace clinging to Antonio, constantly attesting to the lunacy of their actions while Antonio made crude jokes about the way Puerto Ricans attract snakes. They came to a room over which Antonio began to wax affectionate —not so much over the room as over its large octagonal window with delicate wooden ribbing that he was sure dated back to antebellum craftsmen. They got a blanket from the car, and for several nights this became their place, quiet but for the sounds of rats in the rafters and down the halls, the hoots of owls and the munching of termites, in this dilapidated shell of a house. Here Horace was shown pleasure Gideon himself could not have dreamed of, understanding the truth behind the lure of the flesh, not just its power, but its promise fulfilled. They went further and further, exploring, touching . . . ecstasy? Was that the word? he thought.

Afterwards, most nights, they would lie there, exhausted, sweating in the July heat, listening to the small claws clattering on the roof and the unexplained groans coming from the downstairs rooms, and Horace would ponder why he felt unfinished. In the back of his mind was Everett, standing there in all his pure, stalwart, untaintable beauty.

Horace liked Antonio. Physically. They were not tender, they were animal; they were not loving, they were lustful; they were not lovers, they were sex partners. He did not *love* Antonio. Now that he had tasted the forbidden fruit, he was filled with regret. Now he wished he had something more than sweat and orgasms.

In the mirror Horace saw himself playing with the actor's hair. "So what do you think of this play?"

"It's shit. What do you think I think of this play? What do you think of this play?"

"Well, it's more than a little inaccurate, to tell the truth. I didn't have a great-great-great-grandfather named Ebenezer."

"Damn, you know, I never put two and two together. That's *your* fucking family, too, isn't it?"

"Sort of."

"Shit. Well, how does it feel? I bet it makes you mad as hell."

"Yeah. Kind of. But . . . I don't know. It's funny. I'm kind of proud, too. You know. Not about the slavery stuff, but to know where we've gotten, you know?" He rubbed the back of his neck, rising and walking over to the window. "You know, I often think of how I'm going to make my family proud of me."

"Don't you think they're already proud?"

"No, I mean really proud. I'm the next generation."

"How?"

"I got my plans."

"Look out world. Superfag is on the move."

Horace turned, trying to be stern. "Don't call me that."

"What?"

"You know."

"Faggot?"

Antonio got up and walked over to Horace, enfolding him from behind, nestling his chin in his head. "What's the matter? Don't like to be called what you are?"

Horace struggled and broke away. "What I *am* is brilliant."

Antonio rolled his eyes and fell onto the blanket.

"No, I'm serious. I'm going to major in physics in college and . . . who knows . . . well, Edwin Land did it, David Packard did it, Ray Dolby and Percy Julian did it—Horace Thomas Cross will do it, too."

"Do what?"

"Create . . . create . . ."

"God, you're sexy when you're talking bullshit."

"Bullshit?"

"Yeah. Bullshit. Come here. I want you."

"Well, you can't have me."

"I said, 'Come here.'"

"No."

"Come here, *boy!*"

Unsuccessfully suppressing a smile, Horace slowly walked over to Antonio. He sat down and quickly snaked his leg around the man's body in a wrestling hold. "Don't call me boy, punk."

"Why?"

"Cause I ain't one."

With three deft moves Antonio flipped Horace, pinning him down. He bit Horace's bottom lip and said through clenched teeth, "Oh, yeah? Well, you're going to be treated like one."

"Stop! Damn it!"

"Naw. I think I'll rope you up. You'll like that, won't you, *boy*?"

"I'm warning you, Tonto."

Suddenly the mirror Horace sat before warped as one in a carnival would, and the image shattered with an explosive force. Horace covered his eyes to shield them, but after a second or two he felt not glass, but hands. He opened his eyes to find the mirror intact, reflecting his naked body, and his silent, clownish image behind him, beckoning him to stand. Horace stepped over to a costume rack, and the harlequin pointed toward an oversized navy-blue coat with an inverness, which Everett himself had worn in the final act of the play. He had portrayed an educated, crusading, reconstructionist minister from the North who, along with the carpetbaggers, had been sent to make sure the slaves got their due. The ghost motioned Horace to put it on. It was a little large, but it fit well enough, the silk lining cool against his flesh. Horace looked up and saw the brightly costumed figure climbing out the window. Horace ran out of the barn after him, his bare feet slapping on the cold concrete floor, wearing the huge overcoat.

The lodging for the actors was provided by the theater. It had once been a school. Abandoned for five years, it was now renovated to appear an old Southern mansion with its gothic heights and columns and corners. The kitchen was equipped with a table long enough to seat the entire cast and crew. The auditorium smelled of old polish and older wood, the hall was long and gloomy. Most of the actors hated it, but usually they were too tired to complain actively or even to notice.

He could see the specter waiting for him at the top of the path leading from the costume barn toward the building. As Horace followed he remembered that long, hard-work-filled summer, the ribald situations he found himself in. Most stingingly he remembered Everett Church Harrington IV, whom in some ways he had endued with a more than human status, thinking him more beautiful than he actually was, more virtuous than he could ever be, blinding himself to his obvious faults. It had been the longing, he told himself, the damned, almost vengeful longing that made him do the things he did, and as he walked up the path this night of ghosts and harmful spirits, the clown-Horace moved toward the building, implicitly asking Horace to follow. As he did he thought more and more of opening night, and once again he heard music; but this time he cursed it, the damned, loud, ubiquitous music. Why did it cut into him like arrows? Why did it stir him to consider his considerings? His failings? His desires? Old pop songs. The Clash. The Beatles. Aretha Franklin. Billie Holiday. And he began to cry and feel naked, though he now wore a coat, and he finally sat on the steps of the old building, sobbing.

Opening night. The party after the show. Just the day before Horace had decided he must confront Everett. He had been told Everett was gay, so that was not the problem. But how would he approach him? What would he say? How would he say it? He didn't want to come off as a country hick, suddenly enamored by the slick and pretty city boy. He didn't want to seem small before him. He hated him too much.

I'm in love with you.

Excuse me?

I'm in love. With you.

You are? You don't even know me.

I don't have to.

Oh, really. I see. And what do you want me to do about it?

I . . . I . . . I don't know.

You don't know. You don't know? Listen, little boy, let me tell you something. Now I don't know where you got the balls to do something as stupid as to ask me over here and then tell me something as asinine as that. Do you know what kind of trouble I could get you into? I . . . look . . . Really. Look. I'm attached. I've got a lover. Okay? It's not possible. See?

I don't care.

You don't . . . you don't care? Well, that's too bad, you know. I care.

Look. I'm sorry I told you. I don't know what I was thinking about. Really. Forget it. Okay?

Fine by me. Take it easy.

The music played on and on. It seemed to live a life of its own, almost supernatural to Horace now in his despair. Drums, horns, rhythms. He suddenly wished he could become a single note of music, reverberate against the walls, and evaporate into the ears, into the ceiling, into the night. The energy he had gathered had gone, leaving him empty and numb.

Why was he crying? Surely not because one actor who was stuck up about the fact that his skin was lighter than tobacco didn't want to hug and snuggle or tell him Horace was the cranberry of his eye? No. And that was why he was weeping.

Because he understood. He had understood even that night in a backward, unconscious way. That is why he had done what he had done, and with such wild, unkempt fury.

> *Jeremiah was a bullfrog*
> *He was a good friend of mine*
> *I never understood a single word he said*
> *But I helped him drink his wine*
> *And you know he had some mighty fine wine*

That night of out-and-out debauchery Horace took advantage of every can of beer, bottle of wine, glass of whiskey . . . and they all laughed and danced and drank.

> *If I were the king of the world*
> *I tell you what I'll do*
> *I'd throw away the cars and the bombs and the wars*
> *And make sweet love to you*

At one point, through his alcohol-clouded brain, he decided to confront Everett once more, to ask him to reconsider—what? Perhaps Horace could take advantage of Everett's drunken state. He kept an eye on Everett, noticed him with the blue-eyed Georgian, Edward. They were getting closer and closer physically there in the corner, as the other cast members boogied about. Horace waited for the right moment to walk over and talk to Everett. Antonio came up to him, telling him that he and a few others were going over to the graveyard. The graveyard?

Why? Just to go, man. (wink) Just to go. Come on. I'll come along later.

Horace never got a chance to talk to Everett because he left the party with Edward, giggling drunkenly but staring into those Georgian eyes with clear intent. Horace rose unsteadily to follow them. What did he plan to do? Beat up the six-foot-two Edward? What would he say?

Sitting on the steps, Horace got cold for the first time and was glad he had finally put on a coat. Looking up, he saw the figure again, and knew that he was being led toward something.

Why? He asked, not really expecting an answer anymore. Being reminded of stories he loved as a child. Being reminded of their fateful endings. Across the highway from the theater was an old cemetery, bordered by high maple trees, the graves cutting far back into another wood.

That night. The night. He watched as the two men left the auditorium and went out into the hall. He went down both ends of the hall, looking, casually, for any sign of them, Perhaps they had gone outside for a breath of air. In the back of his mind he knew where they had gone. Was he going to sit down with them and discuss the political situation? He went to Everett's room. The door was open; it was empty. He walked back down the long hallway, down the stairs toward the other actor's room, feeling silly, impotent, defeated. Edward's door was closed. He stood motionless for a moment, swaying from the alcohol. Laughter came drifting through the door. It was Everett's voice. Horace leaned against the door and thought of space ships and running and fresh-baked bread and comic books and new shoes that don't hurt and Thanksgiving turkey and Christmas presents and the sound of waves crashing against the piers at the beach and asked himself why he was here, and wondered what had compelled him to lean against the door, and he felt tired, weary, but he turned just the same and went back to join the party.

The house was jumping. People were ranting and raving and running up and down the stairs, hanging out windows, throwing water, throwing up; some kissed and touched and nearly fornicated in the open, some danced barefoot swinging bottles of drink to the music—the loud ever-present music—their heads thrown back in almost religious exaltation, the music pounding, pounding through it all like the tom-tom drums of the warriors just after the pillage and the plunder have ceased, and the warriors, happy and drunk, thank their gods that they, unlike their fellows, lived to make love to their wives and to rock their children on their knees. Antonio stumbled over to Horace once again, saying the group was about to go to the graveyard. Do you want to come along? Why not?

Standing here, now, far into the cemetery, over the very spot he had originally been with the seven actors, men and women, he was both disquieted and fascinated with that night, and dissected it in his mind as a true scientist—clinical, clean, objective. The pot. The pills. The literal orgy. The strange inevitability of it, for, in a way—like witches in a coven under a full moon, like wild wolves tearing hungrily at one another's flesh, like hogs wallowing in their own excrement and sin and lonely inarticulateness—they were left to this for expression, this for comfort, this for attention, this for love. But as he did what he did, he did not feel the thrill he expected would accompany such things. It was not the otherworldly event he knew it should be, nor was it satisfying. The moon did not change color or phase, lightning did not flash, the earth did not quake, the sun did not rise They were left only tired and stoned and dirty and smelly and empty.

This memory lodged itself in his soul like an unmelting, unmeltable sliver of ice.

Within the cemetery he suddenly felt colder, much colder, wanting to ask the apparition only a few feet in front of him where they were going, why the voice had abandoned him, where the other spirits were, why he was here within this parody of a parody. So many questions. But he did not ask, and the spirit moved on, through the tombstones, across the now dew-covered grass, beneath the solemn and silent oaks and maples and syca-mores that had stood here, had grown here, for decades upon decades.

Horace thought of life beneath the ground. He did not wish to die, but the things he had witnessed and remembered this night caused him only more confusion and an ache that led him to wonder: *Where will it end? Will it end?* He thought of his family, of what they wanted of him; of his friends and what they offered him; and of himself . . . what did he, Horace, truly want? Suddenly life beneath the ground had a certain appeal it had never had before. It was becoming attractive in a macabre way. No more, no more ghosts, no more sin, no more, no more.

The graveyard stretched for scores of yards in all directions, but up and beyond sat a high fenced-off mound, the original graveyard holding the graves of the first Scots-Irish Crosses, the Englishmen who died here in the early 1700s, the babies who succumbed to croup and cholera and influenza and mere colds, the women who died in childbirth, the men who died much too young.

Convincing himself he knew the outcome of this story, he fully expected to see his own grave. Though he did not understand the point of this transparent charade, he was convinced that would be the best end. But as he looked around he saw nothing amiss. Only the chipped and eroded stones, greyer in thin moonlight, the shapes askew from the plane of the uneven earth.

Then, near the end of the graveyard-within-a-graveyard, beneath a diseased long-leaf pine, he saw what he had led himself to see, the reason, the logic, the point. It was round and square. It was hard and soft, black and white, cold and hot, smooth and rough, young and old. It had depth and was shallow, was bright and dull, took light and gave light, was generous and greedy. Holy and profane. Ignorant and wise. Horace saw it and it saw Horace, like the moon, like the sea, like the mountain—so large he could not miss it, so small he could barely see it. The most simple, the most complex, the most wrong, the most right. Horace saw. *Your sons and your daughters shall prophesy,* said the prophet Joel, *your old men shall dream dreams, your young men shall see visions.*

But what will they see?

People. The sons of the sons of the sun and the earth. Dark and bold and alive and free. Men and women hunted by their own kind on the shores of a great land where the sun burns hot and the ground bears up bountifully, fully, *It's gonna rain, it's gonna rain,* and they are shackled up and loaded onto ships like barrels of syrup and made to sit there crouched in chains, to defecate and urinate and choke on their own vomit, in the heat, in the stench of days and weeks and months, and they will bring forth children who will die, who should die, rather than be born into this wicked world, *You better get ready and bear this in mind,* and they cry to the heavens and the heavens only answer in storms, storms that take them to a new land, a land of fields and streams, a land of torture, *God showed Noah the rainbow sign,* but the chains are not cut, no, and they are given new names, hateful names, and they are examined like cattle, like hogs, like chickens, and sent to the fields, to the mills, to the bowels of the cities, and they toil and sweat and sing songs of sorrow, *Said it won't be water, but fire next time,* but the gods have new names and sit high and look low, but never reach down.

What will they see?

Wars. Wars and rumors of wars, bloody and full of woe. Wars. Of men who raise up arms against their own brothers and die like so many insects, men who, out of greed, power lust, envy, honor, jumbled and misplaced, seek to rule, *Come by here, my Lord, Come by here,* while the sons of oppression are freed only to be bound up again and again and again, with invisible chains and ropes and painful snares, and they are hunted and murdered and burned like torches that light up a thousand thousand nights, nights full of screams, nights full of horror, nights full of sorrow, *Kumbaya, my Lord, Kumbaya, Kumbaya, my Lord, Kumbaya,* and they will sing to the gods to come and they will speak with tongues like as fire, *Someones crying, Lord, Come by here, O Lord, Come by here,* but there is no Pentacost, no Ascension, no Passover, they bear offerings, but they never seem good enough for these fickle new gods.

Lord, what will they see?

Hard times, brother, can you spare a dime? Men stand in the streets seeking jobs, women try to feed children who don't understand, no jobs, nowhere, *My house burned down, ain't got nowhere to go,* wars come, men breathe hateful fumes and try to straddle the earth, try to unleash God's own sun, but only release the devil and the suns of hell, but the sons of the sons of oppression sing, *My house burned down, and I can't live there no more,* sing the songs of sorrow sung by their fathers, sung by their mothers, long out of the land of milk and honey. But the rain won't come down? Where? Where is the rain?

O what will they see?

Women and children big-eyed and big-bellied, no food, no where, over there, over here, Lord, Lord, Lord, work, toil, endless, uphill, women who slave in the homes of the ill-willed, men slaves of the factories, slaves of the fields, and men slaves of themselves, *It's gonna rain, it's gonna rain,* they all are put out, put out like rats, no food to eat, put out like hateful dogs, no clothes to wear, put out like mean cats, put out from their jobs, their hope. How? How will they feed their children? How? How will they see tomorrow? *God showed Noah the rainbow sign,* and the children of the children of oppression, my Lord, cut themselves off and crucify themselves? Who will be the savior? Where is the rain? *Won't be water, but fire next time.* The people try to sing, but find they have no voice. Did the gods turn their heads in shame?

Horace saw clearly through a glass darkly and understood where he fit. Understood what was asked of him.

Horace shook his head. No. He turned away. No. He turned his heart away. No.

This had been Horace's redemption, and Horace said no.

He turned to leave, shaking and on the verge of tears, not looking for the harlequin. Dispirited, dejected, he did not care to see it.

If it were only so simple, a voice cried.

I'll do as I please, Horace said as he turned to see himself again, but this time as naked as his image.

His reflection stood there, his hand extended. I'm your way, he said.

Give me a break.

I'm serious. And you know it. I'm what you need.

You? Me, you mean.

Exactly.

Bullshit.

You can follow the demon if you want. It's your choice.

Horace looked at his hand. His hand. Never had he felt such self-loathing, and by and by, his depression became anger as he glared at the spirit.

Stop whining, Horace, it said. Stand firm and be—

Shut up! Don't lecture me! I can't—

You mean you won't—

It's not possible!

That's not what you mean, son. You mean—

Leave me alone, God damn it!

In such a rage he could barely see, Horace raised his gun and fired. The report was not as loud as he had expected. But there on the ground he lay, himself, a gory red gash through his chest. His face caught in a grimace, moaning and speaking incoherently. Why? Why. You didn't have to. You shouldn't have. Oh,

God. Please. No. No. He looked at his hand, covered in blood, and Horace looked up at Horace, his eyes full of horror, but in recognition too, as if to say: You meant it, didn't you? You actually hate me?

Horace ran. Ignoring the pain in his foot. The gun held tight. He kept telling himself: I shot no one. Only a ghost. Not even a ghost. It wasn't real. But the tears that burned his face were true, as was the gut-wrenching feeling in his belly. Not like this. Not like this. As the wind whistled in his ears he heard a voice, his voice, softly say: You can run, but you cannot hide.

So, this is it, said the demon.

The Buick stalled just outside Tims Creek town limits. The sun was rising and Horace felt a particular anxiety, a strong urge to be someplace, but he could not remember where or why. The car had run out of gas, and perhaps the ramming it had taken earlier had damaged it. Horace stepped out, regarded it disappointedly, and walked away, leaving the door open.

I have something to show you, said the demon.

They marched along the side of the road; morning traffic was slowly beginning, a head or two craned to look at him. What did they see? A black boy no more than sixteen. Look at him, Helen. Look at his hair. Caked with some kind of mud or something. And wonder what he's doing with that old, heavy overcoat on for. And look! He ain't got on shoe the first nor—Helen—pants! Why, he's naked but for that coat! Look at him.

He crossed the bridge over the tributary of the Chinquapin River, pausing to look at the water in the violet morning air, wondering if mermaids and river nymphs, winged toads and

talking alligators gallivanted beneath its surface, cool and dim.
Once across the river, the voice told him to walk into the woods,
and he did. The nettles and bristles and twigs sometimes cut
his bare feet, but he walked on, replacing the magical noise that
had bantered in his mind last night with questions, conun-
drums, puzzlements, a maelstrom of doubts and worries. His
mood shifted wildly: at one moment he found himself laughing, remembering the most frivolous of jokes from high school,
laughing with more glee than he had then; the next moment he
wept heavily, remembering some small sadness, tiny, some small
hurt that never truly mattered, but that had not healed, and he
wailed like a lost kitten, forlorn. He was overcome with a deep
sense of futility, of uselessness and failure, deep and personal.
And there was a feeling of weariness, deep and old, the way he
was sure an octogenarian widower would feel, and he wished
for the voice to give him answers, to provide a hope, or at least
to give him some release.

The fall season after his summer of debauch had actually
been fun, and he remembered the months of September through
November as a rare reprieve from the anxiety. He had found
his group.

There had been five of them. Four white boys and Horace.
Five boys who did not fit into the archaic, close-knit, rural ways
of York County. They were from elsewhere. Nolan's mother had
been a doctor in San Francisco, but when she divorced a year
before she moved her two children here, back home, and set up
her gynecology practice. Ian was an Army brat whose father,
a retired colonel, had decided to return home. Jay's father had
been a plant manager for Du Pont in Delaware and Atlanta

and was now overseeing a new plant in York. Ted's father had been a New York lawyer before he decided to return to North Carolina, set up practice, and run for the House as soon as he could. All were bright boys—malcontents, quick to set themselves apart from the tedious banality of East York Senior High School. They had traveled, been to better schools—Horace was just smart and black.

Did he consider why he was so easily accepted into this group of illustrious outcasts? Consider that they might be condescending in their innocent way, accepting him merely as a reaction to the traditional racial bias of the area? That by showing their lack of prejudice and befriending a black as their peer, they could somehow show their superiority?

A token? But they were close, tight, doing as much as they could together. Movies. Ball games. Trips to the beach. Playing tennis. Late-night bull sessions at all-night pizza parlors and burger joints where they debated politics and economy and arctic thaw and nuclear winter. Together they read Hesse and Kerouac and Hemingway and Camus and Beckett and comic books. They spoke of travels and volunteering for foreign wars and political ambitions and winning Nobel Prizes. They smoked and drank and drove too fast the cars their mothers and fathers bought while listening to Bruce Springsteen and Pink Floyd, fully expecting the world owed them everything for nothing, and even more in return for a little effort. And Horace, enchanted by their singular, infectious freedom, identified with their sense of entitlement, believing the world owed him what it owed them. Believing wholeheartedly he would receive it in the end.

He ignored the criticisms of his friends, the labels that were being placed on him. Oreo. Greyboy. He refused to notice how other blacks stopped talking to him, stopped dishing the dirt, and pretended not to pay attention when he walked into their midst at school, and they all huddled and looked away, a few glaring at him with contempt.

Even when John Anthony approached him he decided not to understand.

What's up, man?

Not much.

Not much? You sure been hanging tight with them fellows of yours. What's up?

Like I said. Not much.

I mean, you know, we ain't good enough for you these days?

J.A., man, what are you talking about? I—

Look, I call them like I see them. Okay? And what I see with you ain't too cool. Comprende?

No.

Well, hey man. What can I say? It's your bag. Know what I mean? See you at the races.

Yeah.

Then came November, and Jay decided to pierce his ear along with Nolan, who convinced Ted and Ian. Horace agreed to come along. They would be branded as Musketeers, Caballeros, Brothers-in-Arms.

You in with us, Horace-dude?

Yeah.

Way to do, dude.

He suspected his family might object to his action. But he had no idea they would pronounce treason and declare war. From top to bottom, uniformly, they condemned him. It was not the piercing of his ear, it was what it represented, they said. He was commanded to remove that stud from his ear, not to contemplate replacing it, and by no means to consider "hanging out," as you calls it, with them no-account white boys. I don't care who their daddies are. Leave them be. I didn't raise you to run the road with a bunch of fools, drinking and carrying on, not with black ones, and my God, not with white ones . . . I don't want to hear it. Look at that, to think that a grandson of mine would do a damn fool thing like that. Them white boys done took a hold of your mind. Well, no more. Do you understand me? No more. You go to school. You come home. You do your school work. Curfew, young man . . . I don't care if you "just pierced your ear." By Jesus, you'd "just kill somebody" if one of them white boys asked you to. Wouldn't you? Wouldn't you? It shames me right much, boy. Shames me to see you come to this. We come this far for this. I'm glad your grandmother ain't around to see it. Shamed.

What does a young man replace the world with, when the world is denied him? True, the world was never his, but if the promise of the world, free of charge, is suddenly plopped in his lap and then revoked? If the rights and freedoms of patricians are handed to him and then snatched away? If he is given a taste of a shining city of no limits, and then told to go back to the woods?

Horace had no alternative but to retreat into a world of guilt and confusion, not understanding the reasons for his exile.

So he wrote his autobiography, without stopping, one long suspended effort, words upon words flowing out of him, expressing his grief. But he never read what he had written, hoping rather to exorcise his confusion. So strong was his belief in words—perhaps they would lead him out of this strange world in which he had suddenly found himself. In the end, after reams and reams of paper and thousands of lines of scribble, he had found no answers. In frustration he burned it.

He reread his favorite books, the classics that had brought him joy and an answer, but neither Ahab nor Gatsby nor Holden Caulfield nor Hamlet nor Bilbo held the key to the door. He turned to his comic books; perhaps there he could discern the way out—among the friends he had made years ago when he first learned to read. So he escaped with Clark Kent, slipping into phone booths and emerging powerful and all-knowing; he followed Bruce Wayne, and he too need only change his clothes and put on a cloak to mask him and give him honor and nobility.

His loneliness led him into careless and loveless liaisons with men who cared only for his youth, and though he pretended not to care, he worried more and more for his soul, and his increasing confusion took on a harsher guilt and self-loathing.

Word came to him that Gideon had taken his place in the group. Gideon had won this scholarship, and Gideon is being courted by that university, and Gideon has won thus-and-such award. And Horace's grades mysteriously slipped. Why, Horace? Why? All you do is sit at home and read. You were such a good student, such a promise. All through school your grades were excellent . . . how could you make a D-plus in History? a C in trig? you failed Spanish?—Horace? What can we do? Why are you doing this?

He sat and read and in his reading sought a way out. And while reading the Bible one day it suddenly came upon him. Sorcery. Had not the prophets battled magicians in the courts of kings and pharaohs? Didn't Saul die in the tent of the witch of Endor? Had not Jesus spoken of such things as demons and conjurers and men who walk in the way of magic? Why would witchcraft not work for him? He rushed after the hope like a man into quicksand after a will-o'-the-wisp. He had one hope, one faith, one reason, and would warp and distort and realign endlessly to fit his purpose.

He stepped through the trees into the sunlight, now yellow and sparkling off the dewy grass, and at the opposite end of the lawn, for he was behind the Tims Creek Elementary School, was Jimmy. But Horace did not know it was Jimmy. Horace was no longer there.

"It is time," he said.

Old Gods, New Demons

Subjunctive (səb jungk´ tiv), Gram.-adj.
1. (in English and certain other languages)
noting or pertaining to a mood or mode of
the verb that may be used for subjective,
doubtful, hypothetical, or grammatically
subordinate statements or questions, as the
mood of be *in* "If this be treason."

Horace Thomas Cross
Confessions

I remember the first time I saw Granddaddy kill a chicken. I remember it, dirty-white and squawking, and Granddaddy putting it down on a stump. I remember him telling me to hold it still. I remember the way the chicken made a high-pitched kind of purring in the back of her throat and scratched at me in an annoyed sort of way, and Granddaddy telling me to step back and bringing down the axe on the hen's neck. I remember seeing the blood, beet-juice red, and I remember the chicken hopping clean over the top of the magnolia tree, flapping its wings, and then hitting the ground hard, the blood not squirting but flowing from its neck, and it jumping up again, this time not to the top of the tree, but almost halfway, and then up less high and less high until it couldn't jump no more. It just flopped about, and then it just twitched. I remember looking at the head sitting there on the stump by itself and thinking that it looked kind of funny, like something off Saturday-morning cartoons, a filmy kind of eyelid half-closed and a long orange tongue slung out of its orange beak. I remember sometimes when Granddaddy would kill a chicken it didn't jump but it would run and run fast, in a kind of womanish strut, as if somebody had told it some bad news and it was trying to run away and not hear it, all the while running with no head and blood just a streaming red over its dirty white feathers.

I remember Grandmamma didn't chop the heads off. She would take a chicken in each hand by the neck and swing them around and around like small sacks and then let them loose, and they would flounce about, flapping their wings, their heads drooped down like balloons half full of water, turned around, beating against the chickens' breasts, beating a rhythm. I remember a time a chicken jumped up into a old chinaberry tree and Grandmamma had to knock it down with a broom. I remember Grandmamma let me wring a chicken's neck one time and it pecked me.

I remember my Grandmamma and my Great-Aunt Jonnie Mae and my Aunt Rachel and Aunt Ruthester and Aunt Rebecca tending great big pots of boiling water, and they would dip the dead birds into the scalding water and turn them over a few times. I remember the stink of the wet, hot chicken and the smell of the feathers that fell in the fire. I remember them hauling the birds out with sticks and yanking the feathers out. They would come out easier after being scalded. I remember Grandmamma letting me pluck a chicken. The feel of the wet feathers. The feel of the hot and cooling bird. The feel of the pinfeathers, stiff close up on the skin that was pale pink and white and beige.

I remember music. Aretha Franklin. Diana Ross. Al Green. Bruce Springsteen. Pink Floyd. The Jackson Five. Elton John. Roberta Flack. Smokey Robinson. Fleetwood Mac. Marvin Gaye. I remember *What's Going On, What a Fool Believes, It's Over Now, Freebird, The Wall.* I remember television. I remember *I Dream of Jeannie, Bewitched, Gilligan's Island, The Brady Bunch, The Wonderful World of Disney, Julia, The Flip Wilson Show, The Andy Griffith Show, American Bandstand, The Flintstones.* I remember watching the news and asking my grandfather where Peking was and him telling me overseas. I remember watching a movie with my Great-Aunt Jonnie Mae and her turning off the set when the people got into bed together. I remember my first G.I. Joe and wondering if he could feel pins when I stuck him. I remember getting a toy robot for Christmas and it being broken before New Year's. I remember show-and-tell in kindergarten and bringing my first record player and listening to Simon and Garfunkel's "Mrs. Robinson." I remember blowing bubbles.

I remember finally playing sports in high school and enjoying it. I remember sweat and breathlessness and a burning chest. I remember playing volleyball and soccer and basketball and tennis. I remember winning and feeling good and sorry for Terry Garner cause he never won; I remember losing and the coach telling me that I had to lean forward more when I ran the 220 and swing my arms more. I remember tripping one day and skinning my knee so bad that it hurt for two weeks and left a big scar.

I remember Batman and Superman and the Human Torch and the Thing and Wonder Woman and the Black Canary and the Green Arrow and Spider-Man and the Avengers. I remember wanting to be a superhero and first trying to design a suit like Iron Man's so I could fly and then a costume like Batman's so I could look tough, and I would think I could hide it under my clothes and come to somebody's rescue, mysteriously, when something went wrong. I remember trying to build a shield like Captain America's and finding out that there was no such thing as adamantium. I remember feeling tricked. I remember wanting to be rich and white and respected like Bruce Wayne and invulnerable and handsome and noble like Clark Kent. I remember my first Avengers comic book and that the Black Panther was in it and that he was the first black superhero I had ever seen and how he was angry cause they were making him be nice to a white man from a country called Rhodesia. I remember asking my grandfather where Rhodesia was and him telling me overseas.

I remember watching men, even as a little boy. I remember feeling strange and good and nasty. I remember doing it anyway, looking, and feeling that way. I remember not being able to stop and worrying and then stopping worrying. I remember the sight of men's naked waists. I remember the abdomen that looked sculptured and the sinews' definition. Solid. The way the dark hair would crawl from the pants and up the stomach toward the chest. I remember looking at arms, firm arms, with large biceps like ripe fruit. I remember the thrill of large, thick bare feet, clean and full and warm and powerful with round plump toes like grapes. I remember thighs, the way they looked like mighty columns, steel bundles of fiber, covered with hair like down. I remember the way my neck would prickle and my breath would come shallow.

I remember the first picture I saw of a naked man. I remember feeling ashamed. It made me hard.

I remember fear. I remember dark nights at home, looking out near the woods. I remember hearing crickets, owls, frogs, howling dogs, turtledoves. I remember thinking about unexplained snapping twigs or rustling leaves. I remember sleeping with my head under the covers. I remember worrying about claws or paws or just hands reaching out from under the bed and taking me away. I remember my grandfather saying, Just say your prayers and the angel of the Lord will protect you. I remember saying back, But I can't never see it, and him saying back, But you can't see God neither, can you? and I said, No, and he said, But you believe in him anyway, don't you? and I said, Yeah, and he said, Well then, and I said, But I'm still scared.

I remember Dracula and witches and Frankenstein and the mummy and the werewolf and the Headless Horseman and Bigfoot, but mostly I remember Dracula and vampires and the fear of him coming after me late at night and grabbing me in his arms and me not being able to get away and him breathing hard against my neck with his yellow teeth shining and biting my neck and sucking away my life.

I remember *Star Trek* and rushing home every day after school to see it. I remember Captain Kirk and Mr. Spock and Bones and Lt. Uhura and Scotty. I remember the song at the beginning and the sound of the ship zipping by. I remember wanting to be like Mr. Spock and wanting to become a physicist, just like him, and maybe one day being chief science officer on a starship. Maybe even commander. And I remember asking my science teacher in high school about starships and I remember her laughing and saying that I might not live to see one, let alone live on one, and I remember being so mad that I vowed to build one one day. I remember beginning to design a matter/antimatter reactor and finding out that I needed to learn calculus, then finding out that I didn't know enough trig to study calculus yet. I remember deciding to invent teleportation instead.

I remember reading *The Hobbit* and *The Lord of the Rings* and wanting to live in a hole in the ground with a perfect round door like a porthole, painted green, with a shiny yellow brass knob in the exact middle. I wanted to smoke a pipe that was larger than me and talk to wizards and elves and travel around and slay dragons and wargs and hobgoblins and trolls. Perhaps ride on a giant eagle. I remember being disappointed to find out that J.R.R. Tolkien died before he could finish the *Silmarillion*. I remember he lived overseas.

I remember studying Einstein's theory of relativity and I remember reading on my own about time/space and Maxwell's equations and quantum dynamics and black holes and time/space warps and white dwarves and neutron stars and supernovas. I remember the equation $N = R_f n_e f_l f_e l$ and working out the equation again and again to see how many populated planets there probably were in the galaxy if-this-were-true or if-that-were-true. I remember never knowing if I was working the equations correctly.

I remember food. I remember chocolate cakes and strawberry shortcake and pork chops and barbecue and fried chicken. I remember my grandmother's pound cake, though I don't remember it too well. I remember my Great-Aunt Jonnie Mae's pecan pies and her blueberry cobblers and her carrot cake. I remember my Aunt Rachel's spaghetti with ground hamburger and onions and mushrooms and garlic and how she would let it simmer all day. I remember my Aunt Rebecca cooking chitlins, fussing about the work it took to clean them. I remember the stink they made in the house and everyone complaining and then eating their fill. I remember my Aunt Ruthester's chocolate-chip cookies and how she would make an extra batch for me. I remember them best hot, the chocolate pulling long when you broke it in half. I remember the way it made my mouth happy, dissolving almost as soon as I ate it, buttery and hot.

I remember finally touching a man, finally kissing him. I remember the surprise and shock of someone else's tongue in my mouth. I remember the taste of someone else's saliva. I remember actually feeling someone else's flesh, warm, smooth. I remember the texture of hair that was not mine, thighs that were not mine, a waist that was not mine. I remember the gamy smell of pubic hair. I remember being happy that I was taking a chance with my immortal soul, thinking that I would somehow win in the end and live still, feeling immortal in a mortal's arms. I remember then regretting that it was such a sin. I remember the feeling I got after we climaxed, feeling hollow and undone, wishing I were some kind of animal, a wolf or a bird or a dolphin, so I would not have to worry about wanting to do it again; I remember worrying how the other person felt.

I remember church and praying. I remember revival meetings and the testifying of women who began to cry before the congregation and ended their plea of hardships and sorrow and faithfulness to the Lord with the request for those who knew the word of prayer to pray much for me. I remember taking

Someone once said that if man is but a figment in God's mind then the characters in men's imagination are no less real than we are. Perhaps. No one can say for certain. But we cannot deny the possibility.

Consider the demon. Regard him with awe and loathing, for he is what men despise. Or think they despise. Themselves. That day the demon, if indeed he existed, was there all the while perched on the boy's ear whispering words for him to say. He would have made him say: Fuck you. Now it's my turn, preacher-boy. This is the new order—no order. The new day—night.

He could have put hate in the boy's mouth as easily as he put the fantasies in his head; he could have caused him to clutch the gun for lo those many hours. He could have . . . if he did indeed exist.

Perhaps he heard the man say:

"Horace. Why? Why are you doing this? Why?"

And the boy answer: "It's like the boy wants off the roller-coaster ride. He wants his money back. See. No fun. Poor Horace. He don't like life, see. Too many fucking rules. Too many unanswered questions. Too many loose ends. You see, life the way Horace wants it ain't condoned, you know what I mean? And condonation—if that's what you call it—is what he wants. So—"

"I can't believe this. You're too intelligent, Horace, to fall for this crap. It's a copout."

"Save it. He knows. They tried hard already. He ain't going for it. He made his choice, see. He chose not to play in this ball game."

"You have so much of life ahead of you, Horace. I don't understand. Why would you even think of such a thing?"

"See, he has this image of the world as it should be, and this ain't it. This ain't the world he ordered. So he thinks he'll get a new one."

"I can't believe this. This is a joke, isn't it? I—"

"Joke? I don't think so. Les you laugh at funerals."

"Horace, let's talk about this."

"Talk. Talk. Talk. Nothing to say. You keep on talking. Hear? I'm exiting. Watch."

Whether or not the malevolent spirit existed is irrelevant, in the end. For whether he caused it or not, the boy died. This is a fact. The bullet did break the skin of his forehead, pierce the cranium, slice through the cortex and cerebellum, irreparably bruising the cerebrum and medulla oblongata, and emerge from the back of the skull, all with a wet and lightning crack. This did happen. The blood did flow, mixed with grey brain matter, pieces of bone and cranial fluid. His entire body convulsed several times; it excreted urine. Defecated. The tongue hung out of the mouth and during the convulsions was clamped down upon, releasing blood to be mixed with the ropes of saliva stringing down. His heartbeat slowly decreased in pressure and intensity, soon coming to a halt; the arteries, veins, and capillaries slowly collapsed. The pupils of his eyes, now tainted in a film of pink, stopped dilating, resting like huge drops of ink surrounded by brown liquid in a pool of milk. Finally the eyes themselves rolled back, staring up, as though examining the sun through the canopy of tree limbs. In awe and respect. These are facts. Whether or not the demon was a ghost of his mind, or a spirit of the nether world, this did happen. And the man screamed, a helpless, affronted, high-pitched, terror-filled scream of disbelief, of anger, of disappointment. His screams shifted into a sobbing, moanful wail, unconsolable and primal. This is true, and has nothing whatsoever to do with the existence of dybbuks, djinns, or demons.

Most importantly, the day did not halt in its tracks: clocks did not stop. The school buses rolled. The cows mooed. The mothers scolded their children. Plows broke up soil. Trucks were unloaded and loaded up. Dishes were washed. Dogs barked. Old men fished. Beauticians gossiped. Food was eaten. And that night the sun set with the full intention of rising on the morrow.

Ifs and maybes and weres and perhapses are of no use in this case. The facts are enough, unless they too are subject to doubt.

REQUIEM FOR TOBACCO

You remember, though perhaps you don't, that once upon a time men harvested tobacco by hand. There was a time when folk were bound together in a community, as one, and helped one person this day and that day another, and another the next, to see that everyone got his tobacco crop in the barn each week, and that it was fired and cured and taken to a packhouse to be graded and eventually sent to market. But this was once upon a time.

Once, in early spring, men planted tobacco beds, strowing seeds over the ground, covering them with burlap (or later, plastic), and waiting about a month for them to germinate and grow into small tobacco plants. Then they would pull the healthiest plants up, put them into tins with water, and walk the fields, poking them in the cultivated earth in straight rows, putting a little water to them, coming to the end of a row and looking back on their work, their backs weary, their legs tired. Is it possible you have heard of these things? They seem so long ago. But it was only yesterday.

Months later, by late June, July, or August at the latest, those same plants would be small trees, taller than a man, with leaves the size of large oars, a dusty bright green. Men would come along those rows each week and crop off the bottom-most leaves, tucking them under their arms until they could carry no more, then dumping the leaves in the bed of what they called a drag, pulled once by a mule—later by a tractor—that rode along with them. These men had been working from early in the dim hours of the morning, for they had risen at four o'clock to

286

take the dried leaves from the barn. They had clambered up tier poles—sheer rafters ten rungs high, all the way up in the barn—on which the tobacco hung for a week on sticks. Fires, once fueled by wood, later by propane gas, burned underneath for weeks, slowly turning the hearty green leaves a mellow brown. Those pungent leaves were later taken to the storehouses you've heard about, where old women sat on summer evenings sorting through the tobacco, picking out the large ones, the dark ones, the pretty ones, the ruined ones, the trash. You're familiar with this, aren't you? Someone told you, once . . .

When the drag in the fields is full and can hold no more of the emerald leaves, the mule or the tractor heads slowly back to the barn, over bumpy, rocky trails, narrow and gulley-bound, under trees, past stumps. Under the shelter, women mostly will stand around a pile of tobacco the men left earlier, picking up the leaves in bunches, seeing that the stems are aligned and handing them backwards to a woman who ties three or four around a thin wooden stick in a loop-de-loop, up and around, so that fifteen or twenty bunches hang on each side of the stick like huge green hands pointing down. The stick is held on what is called a tie-horse. The sound the twine makes is a whuurr-zzzipp, whuurr- zzzipp, whuurr-zzzipp. Their conversation is legend, these women, their heads beragged, their hands caked with thick tar and dirt, their brows covered with ever-flowing sweat. Here, beneath these tin-roofed shelters around the tobacco barns, all the world's problems seem to have been solved, or at least pondered; here reputations have been made or destroyed, and old women impart good and practical wisdom to younger girls—those who listen. You've heard of these things, I'm sure? Didn't you see it in a play, or read it in a book or . . .

You've heard how the men come back at the end of the day, when the fields have been attended for that week, and how they stand about the women as they finish tying the last drag-full of tobacco leaves and look at the piles of tobacco on sticks and dread the day's ultimate task? Surely you have. For they form a chain of men and women from the high long pile that teeters slightly, and they pass the sticks off the pile, one by one, from one person to the next, through the door, inside, up, up into the belly of the barn, where they will hang, waiting for the fire that will cure them and make them valuable.

But as I say, this was once upon a time. No longer do people gather once a week to help Edgar Pickett or George Harris pick, tie, hang, and take out tobacco from the family barn. Chances are that old Edgar Pickett is dead and George Harris has leased his land and now drives a bus. Chances are that one of them sold their land to someone with more land, someone who is no one at all, but many in the name of one. The many who have replaced those brown hands and sweaty brows and aching backs with the clacking metal and durable rubber of a harvester that needs no men, that picks the leaves, stores the leaves, slaps them into small bulk barns that look like chicken coops that cure quicker, easier, cheaper. The many who are concerned with yields and overheads and tax writeoffs. The many who introduce the chemicals, the new super seeds, the superior fertilizer. The many who know nothing of the day Hiram Crum was kicked in the head by that old mule they called Lightning, or the day Mrs. Ada Mae Philips blew out Jess Stokes for telling her she was nosey, or the day Henry Perry took Lena Wilson behind the cottonwood tree and stole pleasure there. The many who have no memory.

Oh, but it was bound to happen. You realize this, don't you? This is not an evil thing. In many ways it is good. Work has become less torturous . . . for those who work. But it is good to remember that once upon a time hands, human hands, plucked ripe leaves from stalks, and hands, human hands, wrapped them with twine and sent them to the fire. And it is good to remember that people were bound by this strange activity, this activity that put food on their tables and clothes on their backs and sent their young ones to school, bound by the necessity, the responsibility, the humanity. It is good to remember, for too many forget.